From *The*

He flicked me a look. "Anything I store away in my mind is always ready and waiting when I want to take it out again. Try me on any bit of your own past history."

"How did I get one hundred on my arithmetic examination in seventh grade when it was always my worst subject?"

"You sneaked into the classroom before school and copied the questions off the blackboard, you damned little cheat," Kelly said smoothly.

I followed him down to the second floor in astounded silence and with renewed confidence in him.

The only things we brought to light on the second floor were the facts that Mabel wore a double-chin reducer at night and that Aunt Violet owned a makeup box fitted with rouge, lipstick, and powder—and then kept her face shining with soap.

The first floor took more time because it was large and sprawling and had a number of deep cupboards, but we didn't find anything.

Just before Kelly started for the cellar I began to feel sick again, and I drew back. "I'm going outside for a minute, if you don't mind," I said, holding a handkerchief to my mouth. "I need some air."

He produced a coat of some kind and threw it over my shoulders, and I went down the steps to the back lawn. The cold air made me feel better almost at once, and with my stomach in its right place again, I glanced idly around at the wintry, dead garden.

The ancient stone lion had fallen from its crumbling foundations and toppled into the lily pond!

I walked toward it, smiling at the odd accident, until I stood on the broad band of concrete that edged the little pool and looked down.

A cold blue hand floated lazily on the surface of the murky water.

Books by Constance & Gwenyth Little

The Grey Mist Murders (1938)
The Black Headed Pins (1938)
The Black Gloves (1939)
Black Corridors (1940)
The Black Paw (1941)
The Black Shrouds (1941)
The Black Thumb (1942)
The Black Rustle (1943)
The Black Honeymoon (1944)
The Great Black Kanba (1944)
The Black Eye (1945)
The Black Stocking (1946)
The Black Goatee (1947)
The Black Coat (1948)
The Black Piano (1948)
The Black Smith (1950)
The Black House (1950)
The Blackout (1951)
The Black Dream (1952)
The Black Curl (1953)
The Black Iris (1953)

The
Black Honeymoon

By CONSTANCE & GWENYTH LITTLE

With an introduction by
TOM & ENID SCHANTZ

The Rue Morgue Press
Boulder, Colorado
1998

The Rue Morgue Press
P.O. Box 4119
Boulder, CO 80306

PRINTED IN THE UNITED STATES OF AMERICA

The Littles
Creating mayhem from their beds

FOUR AND A HALF decades after their 21st and final novel, *The Black Iris*, appeared, Constance and Gwenyth Little continue to have a following of fanatical readers who haunt used bookshops looking for their more elusive titles, all but one of which, the first—*The Grey Mist Murders*—had black in the title. If these two Australian-born sisters from East Orange, New Jersey, are not better known today, it's probably because they chose not to write a series.

But if the characters in each of their books had different names, you could always recognize a Little heroine, whether she was a working woman or a spoiled little rich brat. Nothing held her back. Or kept her from speaking her mind. Which may explain why she so often fell under suspicion when a body turned up. And why she was so often able to extricate herself even as the evidence against her mounted to amazing levels.

Sometimes she had to resort to a family member for a little help. Fathers play important roles in the Little books, usually adding a touch of comic relief. The Little's own father, James F. Little, an insurance executive, was known to be a bit impulsive. Iris Heitner, a third Little sister (who wrote two mystery novels herself as Robert James in the 1950s), reports that he once announced to the family that he had grown tired of Australia and packed one and all off to England, even though he had no job prospects lined up. It's a situation you might find in a Little novel. Whether the fathers were rich, like Hammond Vickers in *The Black Gloves*, or down on their luck, as in *The Black Honeymoon*, the daughters maintained a playful, affectionate relationship with them. At times these fathers acted more like wayward uncles or interfering big brothers than a parent figure.

There was usually a romantic element in the books. Whatever the outcome of the murder investigation, the typical Little heroine always got her man—and a ring around her finger—but it was always on her terms, not his. Love might be in the air but the Little heroine is always practical. After all, a girl's gotta eat and if she can get out of housework too, so much the better. Marriage seldom meant settling down.

Settling down was something neither the Littles nor their heroines ever did for long. Whether it was with their families or just the two of them, the Little sisters liked nothing better than hopping on an ocean liner and heading for someplace new. Three times they managed to make it around the world. No wonder their heroines so often celebrated the conclusion of a successful murder investigation with the suggestion that a trip was in order.

When *The Black Honeymoon* first appeared in 1944, the world was at war and so was the Little heroine. Miriel Mason Ross was still quick with a sharp retort, still independent and still very much her own person, but she was also determined to do her bit for the war effort—and the country needed nurses. In several other Little wartime and postwar books, their women went to war, even going to far as to enlist.

Gwenyth was the sister who set out to be a writer—"Gwenny used to write ditties even when she was a child," according to Constance—and when she had a short story accepted, she decided to try her hand at a novel but couldn't make it jell. Constance, who during this period was concentrating on tournament tennis (a background that was used in *The Black Gloves*) and running a dance studio with sister Iris, looked at this effort and told her sister, "Let's try one together. I think your plots are weak."

Their first joint effort wasn't a mystery and apparently lacked any action. After their mother fell asleep reading the manuscript, the sisters decided to try their hand at something a bit more exciting. Eight months later they shipped *The Grey Mist Murders* off to the Doubleday, Doran Crime Club which published it in 1938.

If their books—call them screwball cozies, the kind of thing that Frank Capra or George S. Kaufmann might have come up with had they written mysteries—were unusual, so was their writing regimen. They gleefully admitted to writing all their books in bed. Constance (her family called her Con) thought of the plots, outlined them in great detail in large script, all from her bed, and sent them over to Gwenyth who did the rewrite and injected the humor, all from her bed. "Use a desk?" Gwenyth gasped in response to a contemporary interviewer's query. "Chairs give one backaches."

Years later Gwen confessed that their collaboration didn't always follow that plan—except for the part about writing in bed. "I couldn't really say that Constance outlines the plot and I do the writing because that is not entirely so," she told a reporter while the pair was working on their 19th book in the early 1950s. "Sometimes I fix up the plot and sometimes she does the writing but Constance usually handles the clues. She may be working on one chapter while I'm working on another. Con will send me what she's done and say, 'I don't care what you do, only don't mess up my clues.' "

The sisters did all of their writing in the morning, working about an hour and a half a day, which allowed them to finish three books over a two-year span.

During a December 1938 interview published just after *The Grey Mist Murders* came out, a photographer asked the sisters, "How can you write about a murder when you never saw one?"

"Oh, my!" recoiled Gwenyth.

"I can tell you some good murder stories," the photographer raced on enthusiastically. "Did you ever hear of the Indian girl in Newark who was so slashed up her body was almost in ribbons? Did you know ice picks don't leave noticeable wounds? Did you—"

"Oh, my!" moaned Gwenyth.

"Our murderers strangle," said Constance coldly. "We have no sliced up corpses in our books."

But as the books continued to flow from their respective beds—even after Constance moved to Boston—so did the murder methods continue to evolve. Certainly the feathers used in *The Black Honeymoon* constituted one of their more unusual methods but they employed others in the same book that might have made even Edgar Allan Poe wince, although the reader never sees the blood flow.

That photographer wasn't the only person willing to lend the Littles a hand with their books. Years later, Gwenyth lamented that their friends in East Orange "completely ignore" their prowess as writers and "suggest plots which they will gladly give us for nothing."

"And which are always impossible," added Constance.

The sisters, however, did listen to suggestions from their publisher, who sent them a drawing of two ladies viewed through a window, each with a gun in her hand pointed at the other, along with a note: "Our art department went wild over this picture and think it would make a good story for your next book."

The Littles accommodated Doubleday and the result was *The Black Iris*, their 21st and final collaboration, published in 1953. It's been incorrectly reported that the sisters stopped writing in order to care for their ill husbands, but this wasn't the case. Gwen's husband did die from cancer during this period but Con's actually outlived her. It was a different era and the demand for comic cozy mysteries evaporated about the time television aerials started popping up on rooftops. It's unfortunate. One can only imagine what mischief a Little heroine might have gotten into at Woodstock.

The Little books are, after all, wonderful portraits of what life was like if you were young and just starting out in life during the 1940s. You get a sense of what people did for entertainment back then or how they coped with conditions on the home front while the men were overseas. You get a feeling for what life was like when the war was finished and the men came back to face an incredible housing shortage when even people with money, like the young doctor in *The Black Goatee*, couldn't find a place to rent and had to resort to incredible subterfuges to put a roof over their heads.

If the Littles missed writing at all, their new-found free time at least provided them ample opportunity to travel. That, after all, was their real passion. From an early age, they took off on long jaunts whenever they could. When their mother, who believed that young ladies should have an education in case something happened and they had to support themselves, suggested school, the two sisters pointed out that travel was very educational. The family compromised on art school in England, where the sisters stayed with an English family as paying guests.

During a visit to London Gwenyth met and married Bernard H. Jones, an executive with the Prudential Insurance Company. Born in 1903, Gwen died in 1985 in Newton, New Jersey. Constance's husband, Lawrence Baker, started his career in the fashion industry in Rome before returning to the United States where he was a men's clothing designer for the Dubois Uniform Company in New York City. Born in 1899, Constance died, also in Newton, in 1980.

Neither sister had any children but they'll be remembered by readers well into the next century for their marvelous and eccentric mystery novels and for giving us a vivid portrait of a time that even now is fading into history.

Tom & Enid Schantz
Boulder, Colorado
June 1998

For more information on the Little sisters see the introduction to The Black Gloves *(Rue Morgue Press, 1998).*

The Black Honeymoon

CHAPTER ONE

THE BATHROOM DOOR was open, and I grabbed my shower cap, towel, and soap and hurried quietly down the hall. I had been sure that one of Father's paying guests would get in ahead of me and spend a leisurely hour or two bathing self and a week's supply of soiled stockings and handkerchiefs. It was against Father's rules for guests to do laundry in the bathroom, but he could hardly send his spies through locked doors, and a keyhole is useless when it is draped with a towel.

I shook bath salts into the tub and bathed in an aroma of apple blossoms, and my pleasure sharpened to a keener edge when two separate people tried the door and crept away, disappointed. I hoped they were Mrs. Mullens, who had the most expensive room and took advantage of the fact, and Mr. Forsythe, whom I had nursed once and hated ever since.

I presently hurried back to my room accompanied by a faintly persistent whiff of apple blossom and was thrown into a mild panic when I saw that it was twenty minutes to five. I began to scramble into my wedding finery—white satin scraps of underwear, new hat, new dress, and short fur jacket. And new shoes—small, dainty, high-heeled—not comparable in any way with the white boats I had to wear in the hospital.

I hurriedly packed my small suitcase and sighed happily over the new negligee and slippers. It was not an extensive trousseau by any means, but I thought it was well chosen and altogether successful—and I had bought the whole thing the previous afternoon in two hours!

I locked the suitcase and eased into my new gloves, and then I had only to get out of the house without being seen and I could relax a bit. I tiptoed to the head of the stairs, found everything quiet, and crept down. The coast seemed to be clear, so I made a dash across the front hall and out the door.

As I walked rapidly down the driveway I began to have faint pangs of remorse. It was a shame, really, to do Father out of a big, splashy wedding—he'd have enjoyed it so much. I would be draped in white satin and tulle and my three sisters in pale pink or yellow, holding chiffon muffs with flowers dribbling from them. Father would give me away—his pride divided between me and his striped trousers and cutaway coat.

But it would have taken him several days to make all the arrangements, and Ian's furlough would have been over almost as soon as the wedding. "Oh well," I thought resignedly, "Father will be disappointed, but at least he won't be broke and in debt." Which didn't do much for my conscience, because I knew that Father never minded being broke or in debt. He always made it sound as though it were a credit to him.

Ian, tall and browned and good-looking in his uniform, was waiting on the steps of the City Hall.

"Late, aren't you?" he said amiably. "I thought I was being stood up."

"Not this time. I'm young and inexperienced at this sort of thing—so here I am."

He took my suitcase and then my arm, and we mounted the steps together. "Everything's in order—all we have to do is go through the motions. 'I do'—shove the ring on—and then you'll be mine."

"Bought and paid for," I said, trying to control my lower lip, which was quivering like an aspen for no particular reason.

Ian said absently, "Yes, except I'm going to get my aunt to pay for some of it."

"Rat," I murmured, and then we entered a gloomy and distinctly shabby room, and the thing began.

It was all over, and we were out on the steps again in no time at all. My lip had stopped quivering, and I felt fine—except that where my fur jacket stopped, and from there on down, I was freezing.

I said so, and Ian took my arm companionably. "We'll get a cab, although of course a trolley would come cheaper."

The cab, when we finally caught one, was warm, and I sank back gratefully and lighted a cigarette.

"You didn't buy me any flowers," I observed after a moment's thought.

"I was too self-conscious; I thought the cops at the City Hall would laugh at me."

"Listen," I said earnestly, "don't ever give me that self-conscious excuse again. Not you. It isn't seemly."

He laughed and kissed me. "I'll tell the truth, then," he said after we had recovered my cigarette from the floor. "In a nutshell—I spent so much on the courtship that I find myself without funds for the marriage."

"That won't wash either," I declared while he snuggled my hand into his coat pocket. "You courted me for five days exactly, and you belong to one of the city's Wealthy Families. That's why I married you. Money."

"Poor Miriel." He took my hand out of his pocket and kissed it. "Did you think you were going to be able to give up nursing, honey? Wealthy families always have poor members who hang around for the crumbs. I'm one of those."

I said, "Let's go back and get the knot untied again so I can marry your uncle."

Ian laughed. In fact, he laughed so long and so heartily that I said, "It's not as funny as that."

"It is, though—only you don't know everything. I'll tell you someday."

I glanced out of the window and was diverted. "Where are we going, by the way? We're out of the hotel district."

"Yes, I know. I told you I was broke. A lieutenant's pay is scanty, and most of it has to go on the lieutenant's back—so I got my aunt's permission to spend our honeymoon in her house. She's so extremely retiring that we probably won't see her at all—and since Uncle Richard is in the hospital we can practically roam the house at will. How is the old boy, anyway?"

"Fair. I guess he'll pull out all right now, barring the relapse. He was pretty sick."

"I'm glad of that," Ian said. "I always liked him, although I can't remember that he ever gave me so much as a nickel."

"I thought he paid for your education?"

"Indirectly," Ian admitted. "Aunt Violet paid for it from what she saved of the allowance he gave her. She hasn't much use for money, living the way she does. Do you know, I don't believe she has been outside of that house for almost thirty years."

"But what's the matter with her? There must be something."

He shrugged. "The only story I've ever heard is that when she lost all her hair she became acutely sensitive about it. Although she has a fancy wig."

"It's funny," I said thoughtfully. "Your uncle Richard with all that money spends his life in that gloomy old house with his sister—never has any fun, or anything."

Ian pulled the glove off my left hand and admired the new wedding ring with his head on one side. "Aunt Violet has a worse life even than that," he said absently. "She doesn't so much as go to the movies or have anyone in for afternoon tea. Uncle Richard may be fooling everyone, at that. Maybe he sneaks out at night and drops his inhibitions for an hour or two."

I laughed scornfully. I was Uncle Richard's special nurse at the hospital on the seven-to-three stretch and I felt that I knew him well.

"Here we are," Ian said suddenly. "But don't bother to put on your party manners. When I spoke to Aunt Violet on the phone she instructed me to tell Annie that we were to have the large corner bedroom, so I assume that she doesn't intend to show."

We turned into a short driveway and pulled up in front of a large red brick house. I noticed that it was well lighted, and Ian muttered, "That's funny—there's usually only one dim light showing from wherever Aunt Violet is hiding out—and one to guide Annie in the kitchen. The illumination must be meant as a welcome home for us."

We stood at the door for some time before our ring was answered, but at last it swung back, and Sara Lang peered out at us. Sara was married to Ian's cousin, Dr. John Lang, and she was a tall, rather rangy girl with a lot of dark red curly hair, a few faint freckles, and a pair of lively yellowish-green eyes. She worked at the hospital as a volunteer nurse's aide on Thursday afternoons and Friday mornings, and I had seen her on the floor several times.

"What are you doing here?" Ian asked, staring at her.

"Hello, Ian—'lo, Miriel. Come on in, will you, before the house freezes. It's freezing, anyway—such a place to live. Maybe you could look at the furnace, Ian. Papa Benson has been fooling around with it, but all he's done is put it in a bad humor."

Dr. Benson Lang was her father-in-law, Dr. John's father, and the two of them had trod the halls of our hospital for years.

"Doc Benson here?" Ian asked, looking astounded. "Come on, Sara—what is it? Has anything happened to Aunt Violet?"

Sara shook her red curls. "As far as I know, Aunt Violet is still sulking in her room. Annie, of course, up and left as soon as she heard that we were coming. I suppose she told Aunt Violet she'd come back as soon as we all left. Mean pig."

"Never mind Annie," Ian said, fixing her with an eye. "There are other cook-generals to be had. Let's hear the whyfor of you, husband, and parents-in-law settling in here. And don't tell me that you merely wanted a little change."

Sara giggled as Dr. John Lang lounged into the hall, smoking a cigarette as usual. He gave me a cool nod and said, "We need Ian, and I'll pour some drinks."

Ian squeezed my arm and turned me in the direction of the living-room. "Go and get a drink, honey, and I'll see what I can do about the furnace. It's like a barn in here."

He disappeared into the gloomy cavern of the back hall, and Sara led me into an immense room that was cluttered with hideous old-fashioned furniture. A small fire burned under a mantel presumably upheld by two lions' heads, and Sara made straight for a chair that had been drawn close to it. I followed, pulling off my gloves, and stood with my chilled hands extended to the inadequate little blaze. Dr. John busied himself at a table where bottles, glasses, and ice were already set out. Sara made a little face at his back and murmured, "Doctors have to keep going, you know."

I grinned at her, and Dr. John handed me a glass, informed Sara that she had had enough, answered the telephone, and was into his overcoat and out of the house, all in the space of a few minutes.

Sara removed her shoes and vigorously rubbed her cold feet. "That's the way it is these days," she said with a gusty sigh. "I see him for a few minutes at a time, and then he has to rush off again. I don't know how they stand it. John just drinks to keep going, and he knows himself that that's no good."

Ian came back and said, "The furnace is all right—you people just don't understand it. Now, look here, Sara—in a few terse words, now that we are alone, what's the dirt? I want to know."

"In a few terse words, then," Sara replied equably, "our combined extravagances have finally got the best of us. Papa Benson mortgaged the house until it got so top-heavy it capsized. In other words, they foreclosed, and John and Papa Benson were too proud to move to any of the places that we could afford—they said their prestiges would suffer, or something—so Papa Benson persuaded Uncle Richard to let the family move in here. Uncle Richard didn't seem to mind at all—said there was plenty of room, and it would be good for Aunt Violet."

"But I thought the pill-slinging boys were making money hand over first these days," Ian said.

Sara slipped into her shoes again and fished around for a cigarette. "You don't know the extent of our debts—and anyway, Mabel can spend money faster than anyone can make it."

Mabel was Sara's mother-in-law, Mrs. Benson Lang, and she was on the Women's Auxiliary of the hospital. I had seen her working in the coffee shop, smartly dressed, gray-coifed, and well corseted.

She sailed into the room as Sara finished speaking and looked us over.

"How are you, Ian?" she said graciously. "And Miss Mason. How nice."

"She isn't Miss Mason any more. She's Mrs. Ian Ross."

There was a dead silence for a moment, and then Mabel gave a small gasp.

"Oh, Ian—you fool! You didn't need to go so far as to marry the girl."

CHAPTER TWO

I WENT RIGID with surprise and anger, and Ian swung around, his eyes stormy.

"Don't be an ass, Aunt Mabel. I don't know what you're talking about, but I do know that you're being damned rude."

"You don't know what I'm talking about?" Mabel cried shrilly. "When you came here on purpose to steer her away from Richard?"

Sara was laughing helplessly, and I realized that she had had a bit too much to drink.

"You're talking utter nonsense," Ian said sharply. "Aunt Violet said we were to take the corner room. I suppose it's ready for us?"

Sara stopped laughing and stood up quickly. "Darling, I'm so glad to have you in the family," she said to me. "Come on upstairs and we'll find a nice room for you. Come on, Ian." She caught each of us by an arm and urged us out of the room. On the stairs she said confidentially, "Don't let Mabel bother you—she's all in a dither. Moving, and all the rest of it. It always makes her cross when she tries to subtract her debts from her balance and then finds it has to be done the other way around."

At the top of the stairs she hesitated. "As a matter of fact, children, Papa Benson and Mabel are installed in the corner room, but you wouldn't want it, anyway. It's cold, because it catches the wind coming and going. Now, let's see—John and I have the middle front, and the next one is Aunt Violet's, and behind her, at the back, is Uncle Richard's room. But I think there are a couple of more rooms back there. Leslie settled herself up on the third floor—said she wanted a little privacy." We walked down the silent, carpeted hall, and Sara presently stopped and opened a door. "Oh—single room." She hurried on and opened the next door. "Another single room. Hmm. There's a connecting bath between those two, but—er—of course—"

"That will do very well," I said grimly. "Regular suite, isn't it? I like to read in bed, you see, and probably my husband doesn't."

Ian said, "For God's sake, Sara, isn't there something else? After all, we were told—"

I turned on him. "You go down and get the suitcases. I like these rooms, and I want to wash up a bit."

Sara chewed uncomfortably on her thumbnail, and Ian gave me a black look and departed without a word.

"Maybe you could change with us," Sara suggested uncertainly.

"No—it's all right." I slipped into the first single room and sat down on the bed. I was cold inside and out, and I hated everybody. I knew that Richard Lang had gone a bit mushy on me; it often happened with male patients, and it didn't mean a thing. They got over it when they recovered—or the older ones did, anyway. But apparently the family had got wind of it and taken fright. Perhaps he had told them he intended to marry me, and they had faced the prospect of their inheritances being diverted into my pocket. So they had taken the trouble to send for Ian to come and prevent something that would never have happened anyway.

Ian returned with your two suitcases and dropped them onto the floor.

"Pity you went to so much trouble to save your inheritance," I observed, eying him up and down. "I had no intention of marrying your uncle. I'd made up my mind to wait for love to come and sweep me off my feet, or something."

He dropped onto the bed beside me and put a firm arm across my shoulders. "Now, look, darling—you surely can't believe that I'd marry you for a cheap reason like that?"

"I don't really know," I said coldly. "I hardly know you well enough. Anyway, I suggest that you court me for another several days until I make up my mind whether to divorce you or stay married."

His hand tightened on my shoulder. "Miriel, you don't really mean that—you wouldn't do it—"

"I mean just that. I'll go home, if you prefer it—after all, I can't marry your uncle now, so you've nothing to worry about."

He removed his arm and stood up abruptly. "Or—?"

"Or I'll stay here in this room until I'm satisfied one way or the other about this nasty affair. I don't much like to go tamely home after buying a trousseau and getting married, but it's up to you."

"I'd prefer that you stay here. I suppose you'll come to the conclusion that I'm innocent when I'm on the station waiting for the train. No doubt you'll give me a nice kiss and wave good-bye."

"I might. If you leave at a reasonable hour."

He picked up his suitcase and banged through the bathroom to the other single room, and I put my head on the pillow and wept a round, wet patch into it.

Having relieved my feelings to that extent, I went into the bathroom, washed my face thoroughly, and then spent a lot of time fixing it up. There was a sharp knock on the bedroom door just as I finished, and I went to find Ian standing on the other side all wrapped up in cold formality.

"Take off the false face," I suggested, "and deliver the message."

"Aunt Violet never had anyone but Annie," he explained. "She did a lot of the work herself—it was something to do, I suppose. Anyway, Annie walked out when she heard about the incoming mob, as you know. Aunt Mabel will attend to it tomorrow, but tonight we'll have to forage. Unless you'd like to go out somewhere?"

I shook my head. "Let's forage—I'd rather. I have to telephone my family, and then I'd like to pay my respects to your aunt Violet."

When I got through to Father and broke the news he roared into the phone until I thought he'd break it. I held the receiver away from my ear until the noise seemed to have calmed down, and then I brought it back cautiously, to hear Father inviting us for dinner and a celebration on the following evening in quite a decent tone of voice. He went on to say that it was all very bad form, because I had been practically engaged to Richard Lang. After which he wished me luck, anyway, and hung up before I could ask him what the devil he meant. I sat there for a while, absently running my finger around the base of the telephone, and wondering what it was all about. Father and Richard Lang were friends, and I knew that Father had visited him at the hospital. I could only suppose that they had had their heads together, disposing of me without my knowledge or consent, and I began to see why Father had bellowed into the phone like a wounded bull. He had been all set to be rich again, and I had knocked over his house of cards.

I shrugged and made my way to the kitchen. It was a huge old room, comfortably shabby and cheerful. Ian was standing at the stove, vigorously stirring something in a pot, and Dr. Benson Lang sat at the large center table with his daughter Leslie. They had an assortment of cold odds and ends spread out before them and were busily eating. I knew Leslie slightly—she was a nurse's aide at the hospital, too, and I could always pick her out by the way her uniform drooped limply around her. Most of the aides came in with shoes brightly shining and cap and uniform starched and immaculate.

They walked briskly, too, for the most part, but I had never seen Leslie either hurrying or in any way hot or bothered. She wandered around in a pair of shell-rimmed glasses and looked as though her mind were on Einstein's theory of evolution instead of on nursing, where it should have been.

She got up from the table, kissed me, and said, "Congratulations on your marriage."

Dr. Benson shook hands with me. "Ian has done mighty well for himself," he beamed cordially. "Unfortunate you had to find the house full of people. Had we known, we could have gone to a hotel for a few days. But Richard has been so anxious to have us here, you know—he's a bit worried about Violet having been alone. It will be a weight off his mind to know that we're looking after her. And really, it's been no trouble to us—such a large house—nearer to our offices too."

"It appeared to be a satisfactory arrangement all around," Ian said amiably. "No sense in letting the house go to ruin, the way Aunt Violet seems to be doing."

"Exactly, exactly," Dr. Benson agreed, a shade too eagerly. "Mabel will have things shipshape in no time, and when Richard is able to come home the place will be cheerful for him. I've been hoping, too, that I can get Violet to come out of her shell a little—although, so far, she has refused even to see me."

"She has refused to see any of us," Leslie said flatly, "and you know perfectly well that she'll go on refusing. She dislikes Mother, and she dislikes you for marrying Mother, and she dislikes me for being Mother's daughter."

"You're exaggerating," Dr. Benson snapped. "And incidentally, I expect you to be civil to her if you run across her in the hall."

Leslie shrugged without committing herself, and after a moment Ian asked, "Has she had any dinner?"

"She's waiting until we're all bedded down for the night," Leslie explained indifferently. "Then she'll creep along to the kitchen and get herself a crust."

Ian clattered two plates of unrecognizable foodstuff on to the table and followed it with two cups of coffee.

"What is it?" I asked suspiciously.

He gave me a cool glance and held a chair for me. "No particular name. I made it up as I went along—but you'll like it."

I did, too; it was delicious, and I ate heartily. Dr. Benson presently raised his napkin and dusted off his lips with a sweeping right-to-left gesture, after which he stood up and excused himself. Leslie presently followed him, and Ian and I were left chewing self-consciously into the silence.

After a while he sat back a little and looked full at me.

"If you'd like to hear the whole story of what led up to my fool aunt Mabel's fool remark, I'll tell you," he said tentatively.

I fished around for a cigarette and murmured, "Proceed."

"You know that my mother died last summer, and I may have told you that when my leave came up I found that I preferred to avoid Boston, where she had lived. I decided to visit her relatives here and wrote to let them know. Aunt Mabel answered my letter and told me all about Uncle Richard's illness. She rambled on about how an ambitious nurse was trying to make off with him. She seemed to think I might be able to create some interference and, not to sound too self-seeking, added that it would be a better thing for Aunt Violet to be made the victim of an unscrupulous young woman who was merely out for position and wealth.

"When I arrived here I put up at a hotel and then took myself around to the hospital to have a look at this scheming piece. It was you, and I rushed you for two days to save Aunt Violet's inheritance—I owe her my education—and for three days because I couldn't help myself; I'd fallen in love with you."

I said, "How opportune," and he pushed his chair back from the table abruptly and stood up.

"See if you can find a tray. I'm going to take Aunt Violet something to eat. "

We presently went upstairs, Ian carrying the loaded tray and I following for a duty call upon the old lady. I tapped at her door, and after a moment's silence a voice called, "Who's there?"

We identified ourselves and were immediately bidden to enter. I don't know what I had been expecting, but I was faintly surprised to find that Aunt Violet appeared to be a reasonably normal elderly lady. Her gray hair was, perhaps, a little too perfectly arranged, and I remembered that it was a wig. She wore a gray crepe dress that looked as though she might have made it herself, and her complexion was bad and her cheeks hollow, but she had nice blue eyes. Unlike her brothers, she was quite short.

She said, "Come in—it's nice to see you, Ian—very. Your letters were always so pleasant; I looked forward to them. But you've been here for several days. Why didn't you come to see me before this?"

Ian put the tray on to a small table and smiled at her. "I phoned as soon as I arrived, you know, and when you didn't ask me to come up I thought perhaps you didn't want me. I decided to get in touch with the rest of the family first and contact you again later."

She turned to me and gave me a comprehensive going over with her eyes. "Is this your bride?"

"Yes—but come and eat your dinner, and we'll sit down and talk."

She established herself at the little table, and although Ian and I made polite conversation she devoted herself entirely to the food until it was gone. In fact, she wolfed it. She relinquished her fork at last, and then, as though it had suddenly occurred to her, she padded over to me and kissed me lightly on the cheek. "Welcome into the Lang family, my dear. We are pleased and proud."

"Mrs. Benson Lang is proud," I conceded, "but far from pleased."

She gave a little snort and said, "That old biddy. The woman moves herself and her entire family in here, and I can't do anything about it. It isn't fair."

"Come on out and give her a run for it," Ian suggested. "You can't fight her by staying in your room."

Her face changed, and she turned her head away. "No, no— I don't like her. I don't like any of them—so many people. I'm tired now—I think I'll go to bed."

We stood up at once, and Ian picked up the depleted tray. Just before she closed the door in our faces she asked me, "How is Richard, dear?"

"Better," I nodded.

"I'm glad. I'm lost without him—simply lost."

She closed the door then, firmly, and I turned to Ian.

"Look—I have to be up very early in the morning—have to get to the hospital."

"But didn't you get a substitute for a few days?"

I shook my head. "It's almost impossible these days—and anyway, I didn't want to put him into strange hands right now. But I've had quite a day, and I want to sleep it off."

He raised his shoulders and his eyebrows and said, "I believe the bed is made up. If you want anything, let me know. Good-night."

I went along to my room, wept a few more tears, and took a couple of aspirins because they always make me sleep.

I did sleep, too, but I woke up to darkness and stillness and to the sight of an unidentifiable figure slipping out of my room and closing the door silently behind it.

CHAPTER THREE

FOR A MOMENT I was too scared to move, and then I forced myself to get out of bed and switch on the light. I opened my door a crack and peered out, but the hall was dark and quiet and seemed to be deserted. I backed in and closed the door firmly, and a glance at my watch showed that it was three-thirty. I hesitated and then made a hasty check of my things, but I could find nothing missing. My uniform lay stiffly over a chair, ready to be put on, and my white shoes stood side by side on the floor beneath.

I could not lock the door because there was no key, and at last I wedged a straight chair under the handle and went back to bed. I fell asleep on the thought that I did not like people wandering around my room, uninvited, even if I knew them.

It was still dark and miserably cold when my alarm went off, but I found that there was plenty of hot water, and by the time I was dressed only my hands were still chilled. I slipped into the fur jacket and made a mental note to pick up my polo coat when I went home, since the uniform and jacket were a bit incongruous—to say nothing of the wear and tear on the precious fur.

I hurried down the stairs and landed in the arms of my husband, who was waiting at the bottom. He enfolded me, jacket and all, and kissed me three times.

"I'm not mad any more," he announced superfluously.

I said, "Well, that clears everything up," but he ignored my sarcasm and led me to a small breakfast room where an open fire burned cheerfully. He had fruit and coffee and scrambled eggs on the table, and when I murmured halfheartedly that I had planned to eat at the hospital he patiently begged me not to be an ass. "It's understood between us that I am a pariah and an outcast—so why go on to the point of ignoring your own creature comfort to prove it further?"

I slipped off my jacket and sat down immediately. "Thanks," I said. "It's nice of you, and I appreciate it."

"Reason along a bit," he urged cheerfully. "Had I married you simply to save Richard from your clutches, my job would be done, and I'd still be sleeping in my warm bed. But I get up in the cold and dark, light a fire—"

22

"Eat your breakfast," I interrupted. "It's really delicious."

"Right. But before I settle down to it, I'd like to make a date with you for this evening."

"It's made," I said dubiously. "Father is entertaining for us."

He said, "O God!" and dropped his fork. "I'm a soldier—fighting for my country—kicked around by the brass hats—and then I come back to a leave like this."

He drove me to the hospital, and after he had left me I found that my spirits were rising in spite of myself. I decided that Mabel was a sour plum and that her embittered remarks were not to be taken seriously.

I left the elevator at the sixth floor and walked jauntily down the corridor toward the nurses' dressing-room. Rhoda Mills, the supervisor, was at the desk, and she let out a long, low whistle as I came into view. "Holy night!" she observed in her usual stentorian tone. "Where did you get that fur coat? Don't tell me you bought it yourself?"

"I won't," I promised agreeably and passed her by.

"No kidding," she called after me, " is anything going on?"

But I pretended not to hear. Rhoda had a long nose for gossip, and I didn't want Richard Lang to know about the marriage for a few days yet. He was supposed to be kept very quiet, and apparently he had had other plans for me—if Father was to be believed.

He was awake when I went into his room, but Amy Morrison, who looked after him from eleven at night until I came on, was sitting straight up in her chair, sleeping as usual. I nudged her, and she jerked to attention and said brightly, "Hello there. Well, well, we've had a fairly good night."

"You have," Mr. Lang conceded acidly. "Mine was not very comfortable."

I saw Amy off to the elevator after receiving a sketchy report of our patient's condition, which I am convinced she made up as she went along, and then went back and washed the old gentleman's face, hands, and false teeth in preparation for his breakfast. I had to face Rhoda again when I went to the kitchen for his tray, but she seemed to have forgotten about my fur jacket and was grumbling because the breakfast trays were late. She asked me, as woman to woman, how she was expected to keep the floor going on schedule when people wouldn't co-operate.

Mr. Lang ate his breakfast and gave me a fairly comprehensive sketch of Amy Morrison's character at one and the same time. He said that youth was inclined to be selfish and unfeeling, but when a healthy young nurse flagrantly slept through her patient's insomnia, he thought it was carrying things a step too far. He said he'd tell me another thing, too, and while I waited, breathless, to hear it, he quite suddenly went off to sleep.

I took his tray back to the kitchen, where I ran into Leslie, uniformed and sleepy-looking. She said, "Hello, Miss Mills told me to collect trays, but nobody's finished eating. How's the old man?"

"All right. How come you're here on a Thursday?"

"Beanie couldn't make it. I'm taking her place."

"Had a luncheon and bridge, maybe," I suggested.

Leslie regarded me mildly through the shell-rimmed glasses and said, "Don't be sarcastic. If your father hadn't spent all his money before you grew up you'd be doing the same."

"That has nothing to do with it," I pointed out. "The fact remains that I'm on the other side of the fence, so naturally I must get bitter about it."

She said, "Listen, Miriel—I want to get some photographic supplies, and all charge accounts have been suspended for two months, so I'll have to get the money from Uncle Richard. See if —"

"No," I said firmly. "He's to be kept quiet, and he's going to be kept quiet if I have anything to do with it. If I find you in there pestering him I'll report you to Rhoda Mills. I mean it."

She turned away. "Oh, all right, but I think you're mean. You could easily get the money out of him."

The morning went by quickly enough, but just before I went down to lunch Mr. Lang sneezed twice. I knew that he was intensely allergic to feathers—he had to have a special pillow, and the upholstered armchair had been removed from his hospital room before he was brought into it—and I felt a faint flicker of uneasiness. But we had been extremely careful, and there had been no trouble, so that I presently brushed it from my mind.

I stopped to ask Rhoda to keep an eye on him, and she informed me that they were serving liver in the nurses' dining room, so I passed it up and went along to the coffee shop. I dropped down at an empty table and was looking over the menu, when Dr. Benson and Dr. John came in with their heads together in a low-voiced conversation. They saw me and hesitated, and then they both nodded, and Dr. Benson asked courteously if they might join me. I knew they didn't want to, and I didn't want them to, but I had to give a polite assent, and so they both sat down. They began at once to question me about Mr. Lang's condition, and I was getting pretty bored with it all, when Sara walked in and broke it up.

"Hello, everybody," she said gaily, "I thought I might catch someone here to pay my check."

Dr. John gave a short laugh. "Don't look at me. Maybe you can stick the new relative."

Dr. Benson puffed a bit and said fussily, "That's not particularly funny, John—and it isn't nice."

I turned to Sara and suggested that she was going to be late, since she was due to report at twelve. She glanced at the clock and replied indifferently, "I have to eat, don't I?"

The doctors Lang presently left us, and then Sara and I went into a girl-to-girl conversation, during which she told me to pay no attention to what she called her mother-in-law's drivellings.

"Mabel can't help being theatrical, and you're silly to let it upset you. I get along fine with her because I think she's funny, and I don't waste my life getting insulted and mad every time she says something rude to me. Besides, Ian's a nice guy "

"All right—don't overdo it," I said, picking up the checks and getting to my feet. "Come on, we ought to be getting upstairs."

I handed the checks to a golden-haired debutante who puckered her forehead prettily as she leaned over to add it up.

"You'll have to pay it all," Sara murmured, squinting into the mirror of her compact.

The debutante was using her fingers by this time, so I said impatiently, "It's a dollar ten," and handed over the money.

Sara followed me out into the hall. "That's fifty-five cents I owe you—you'd better write it down in a little book."

We met Leslie coming off duty at the elevator. She said, "Hello, you two," and without pausing to take breath, added "Have you any money you can lend me, Sara?"

"Don't be naive," Sara replied amiably. "Ask Miriel—she's oozing with the stuff. I saw her pocketbook."

Leslie's eyes shifted over to me "I could pay you back in about—"

"I know—two months, when the moratorium on charge accounts is lifted. And then it wouldn't be money—I'd have to charge up to the equivalent."

Leslie beamed at me. "That's a very good idea. You're sure to need something by them." But I slid hastily into the elevator, and the doors closed between us.

Sara laughed all the way up to the sixth floor. "The vultures are hovering, Miriel; you'd better watch yourself."

"I'm going to sew my purse up," I said absently.

Rhoda came out of Mr. Lang's room as we approached, and her eye lighted up with a predatory gleam as it fell on Sara. "Hello, Mrs. Lang—lots of work for you this afternoon."

She bustled Sara off, and I went in to find my patient awake. He nodded at the chair beside his bed and said, "Sit down, Miss Mason, and let's talk for a while."

"I'm waiting for your luncheon tray," I explained, "but I'll sit down until it comes. Only you must let me do the talking."

He fell silent and eyed me expectantly, and I discovered, to my mortification, that I couldn't think of a thing to say. I glanced out of the window in search of inspiration, and my mind drifted off to my fur jacket, what I would say to Ian when I saw him, and a speculation as to whether he would be waiting for me when I got off at three.

I came back with a start to the realization that Mr. Lang had been talking steadily for some time.

"—so felt that it was my duty to warn you. You know that I love you, and of course he doesn't. You must be on your guard against any such declaration from him, and it is your right to know that my money is going elsewhere. I shall not leave a penny of it to any of them."

I stared at him with my mouth hanging open, and he went on, "That surprises you—but, you see, I know my sister-in-law Mabel, and she is deplorably greedy about money. I am quite prepared to believe that she offered Ian a large sum to come here and interfere between you and me, since I know that he had planned to go to Boston to see his young lady. Mabel is stupid enough to suppose that I can't see through her schemes, but I am fully aware of everything and I have not forgotten the enormous sums I have handed over to them from time to time to keep them out of trouble with their mounting debts. But you and I will be married, my dear—your father is in complete agreement—and I'm sure I can make you very happy. You shall have everything that you want."

I got my breath back and spoke to him gently: "You mustn't talk any more, Mr. Lang—you'll exhaust yourself. In a few days, when you're stronger, we'll talk about it again."

He smiled up at me contentedly and closed his eyes. And then he sneezed. I stood up, my glance sharpening on his face, and he sneezed again. In the space of about three minutes his nose had started to run, and his eyes were almost closed up.

CHAPTER FOUR

IAN was waiting for me when I went off at three o'clock; I climbed into the car and slumped back with a sigh. He gave me a lopsided grin and said, "Don't become too accustomed to luxury, honey; this car belongs to the old man, and Aunt Violet told me to use it during what she calls our honeymoon."

He supplied me with a cigarette, and I said wearily, "I don't care who owns it, as long as it gets me back to the house. Mr. Lang has had a little trouble."

I tried to explain what had happened, and Ian listened with gradually mounting astonishment. His final comment was, "I don't understand you medical people at all. Pat a guy on the back and tell him not to worry over a simple little thing like cutting open his tummy and removing some of his insides—and rush around breathing fire from your nostrils because a fella has a touch of hay fever!"

When we arrived at the house Mrs. Benson Lang received us at the foot of the stairs. "Your father has phoned several times," she said to me, "and wants you to call him as soon as you come in. I don't know what he wants, I'm sure."

"Didn't you ask him?" I inquired, pulling off my gloves and slipping out of the fur jacket.

"Well, yes, but he refused to leave a message. I can't imagine—"

I telephoned Father, and he talked at great length, but all it amounted to was that Ian and I were expected for dinner and that I was to wear a dinner dress. When I hung up Mrs. Lang was behind me, trying a vase first on one end of a small table and then on the other, so I put her out of her misery.

"Father is having a dinner and reception for Ian and me tonight. Everybody who *is* anybody will be there."

I left her in the hall tapping at her exquisite false teeth while I climbed the stairs. As I neared the top I heard her say in a puzzled voice, "But that's impossible—we've none of us been invited. What does she mean?"

I was relieved to find that my room had been cleaned and tidied, and I slipped out of my uniform and climbed back into my wedding dress, since it was the only one I had with me. I smoked a cigarette and then decided to go along and talk to Aunt Violet. I opened the door to find Ian directly outside, bearing a loaded tray. "What's all this?" I asked, noting tea, buttered muffins, and little cakes with colored icing.

"I'm trying to get to your heart through your stomach." He urged me back into the room and began to lay the stuff out on a table. "Two nicely uniformed maids in the house now," he informed me. "Mabel has her uses, after all."

"Your Uncle Richard doesn't think so."

"She's had a high old time all her married life, and the old boy doesn't approve—especially since he had to pay for a lot of it. And I can see eye to eye with him, after what she did to me yesterday. "

"Know something?" I said suddenly. "Unless we quietly dissolve our marriage, you and the other Langs are to be cut out of the will—Mr. Lang told me. In fact, he warned me against you."

Ian sighed gustily and bit into a muffin. "In that case, the Benson Langs are due to languish in debtors' jail, and you and I must support ourselves and Aunt Violet as well."

"You're putting a pretty good face on it," I admitted critically. "But I'll bet you're burning up inside."

He swallowed the rest of the muffin, laughed heartily, and said, "Darling, if you were not sitting there watching my every move I'd get up and bite the spout off the teapot. It's not too much to say that I am appalled."

When we had finished I stood up and said, "Thanks for the tea. I'm going along to visit your aunt Violet."

"Right. I'll come with you."

We went across the hall and knocked, and the door was flung open almost immediately. Aunt Violet glared out, but her expression changed when she saw us. "Oh—it's you." She held the door wider and added, "Come in."

She asked at once about her brother's condition and was disturbed when I told her of the setback he had had.

"But Richard has always been healthy—I'm sure he'll be all right. If that were all I had to worry me—"

That wife of Benson's, she told us angrily, was making a perfect pest of herself. Forcing her way into another person's home, engaging servants without consulting anyone. "I have had to remain in my room, Ian, to keep out of her way. And in spite of the fact that she has two girls flying around from attic to cellar doing her bidding—and Richard liable for their salaries, I'll be bound—not one of them came near me with a bite of lunch. I had to go down to the kitchen at last and find some food for myself."

I tried to soothe her, and Ian urged her to come out of her room and do battle, but she merely shook her head with a vexed frown. He could not move her, but before we left we promised to see that all her meals were sent to her on time, and Ian declared that we'd take over the household management ourselves and see that Mabel kept her place.

Sara had come home and good-naturedly allowed me to wear one of her dinner dresses. I arrayed myself carefully, because I knew how much Father cared, and then Ian and I got into our borrowed car and made our way to the old has-been section of the town. It was still quite decent, but apartment houses had been busily going up as the old residences went down. Father was holding out for a price on his house and it had not been met but, as he put it, he expected the boys to come through at any time. Meanwhile, half a dozen paying guests, Father, his daughters, and one colored and temperamental maid kept the flag flying. Two of my sisters had good office jobs, and the youngest was still in school.

Ian glanced down at me as he swung the car into Father's driveway and asked casually, "Where did you get the dress?"

"I bought it from Sara," I said, "for fifty-five cents and five coffee-shop lunches."

He nodded. "It's a bargain. When you've paid the five coffee-shop lunches, add them to the fifty-five cents and give me the bill."

"Did you want to file it, or something?" I asked politely.

"I was thinking of paying it," he said mildly. "But perhaps I have delusions of grandeur."

Father came rushing down the steps of the veranda to meet us and, as usual, slipped on the ice, but he managed to save himself before he broke a leg. And, as usual, he muttered, "Next time it snows I'll shovel it off right away."

He bowed us graciously into the living-room, where he was serving cocktails, and I noticed that he had bullied the paying guests and my sisters into evening attire. The outside guests were necessarily few for dinner, but Father assured us that the rest of the gang were coming later.

At dinner he seated me between Ian and his dearest friend, Montgomery Kelly. Ian was enjoying himself and whispered to me in an aside that he apologized for groaning at the prospect of this binge. He said the old man was swell and my three sisters beautiful. I told him to take his pick because I was a bit tired of married life, anyway.

I turned to Montgomery Kelly, who had been glooming noticeably on my other side.

Kelly was a very successful private detective who had been thrown off the police force earlier in his life for a too-determined devotion to the bottle. He was already in an alcoholic mist, and as soon as he had my attention he reproached me bitterly for having gone off and married without letting him know. "You could have had me at any time, girl," he said mournfully.

"Don't be absurd. You're much too old for me."

"Old?" he echoed, opening his sea-blue eyes very wide, and added, "Old!" with a certain amount of indignation. "Good God! I'm only forty-nine."

"That's practically ancient," I said, "and you know it."

This stunned him into silence for a while, but he presently forgave me and kindly told me all about a baseball game he had seen last summer.

Not long after dinner people began to pour in, and I realized that Father would be in debt again without a doubt. Champagne flowed like water, and a caterer had been engaged to supply all kinds of fancy tidbits.

My sisters made much of Ian and called me a lemon when I asked him to take me home at one o'clock, but I stood firm.

"She has to roll out before six in the morning," Ian explained for me, and went off to get my coat.

He put the suitcase I had packed into the car, and when we were rolling down the driveway he said contentedly, "That's a good sign. Looks as though you were going to stay for a while."

I yawned into my fur shoulder, and he asked tentatively, "You haven't thawed out yet, have you?"

"Not quite." I yawned again and added, "I was nearly thawed today, until your uncle gave me a chilling talk about you."

"O God! What did *he* say?"

"Same stuff. Family scheme to keep money safe in family. But it leaves a bad taste in my mouth."

"I suppose so," he agreed gloomily. "I seem to be unlucky."

"Don't hand out the pity angle," I begged. "I liked you better the other way."

He shook his head. "That's unreasonable. Self-pity is one of the most enjoyable emotions."

The house was in darkness when we got back, and we had to feel our way through the hall and crawl up the stairs because we did not know the location of any of the light switches. Ian banged my suitcase against the banister once or twice, but otherwise we managed to reach our suite without making any noise. He kissed me good-night and murmured, "Tomorrow you thaw out—or else."

"Right, " I said. "Or else I don't."

I fell into bed without bothering to do any of the usual beauty treat-ments, but instead of going out like a light I was kept awake by a noise—curious and intermittent—which seemed to come from the room above me. It sounded as though water were being poured into something and then scraped around with a stick.

CHAPTER FIVE

I CAME to the conclusion, at last, that Leslie must be playing around with her photographic equipment—her room was up on the third floor somewhere, I knew. I reflected that it seemed such a waste—a girl who could, in periods before and after occasional moratoriums, charge what clothes she would in the city's best shops—and she elected, instead, to charge expensive photographic gadgets so that she could pour water into them late at night.

My breakfast was served to me next morning in the small room with the fire, but one of the new maids waited on me. Ian was there when I came down, and I saw, to my surprise, that Aunt Violet was seated at the table.

She poured coffee for us, and Ian applauded her decision to venture out of her room. "It's much better for you to get out; you'll feel better in every way. Suppose you let me drive you to the hospital, and you can go up and see Uncle Richard."

She looked frightened and said almost wildly, "Oh no—no. I can talk to Richard on the telephone. I couldn't go into a hospital."

"Have you heard how he is?" I asked.

"The doctor said 'fair,' but he thinks he'll be all right now. I cannot understand how he got that attack, though. The people at the hospital were told all about his failing, and they assured me they'd be most careful."

"But we have," I protested unhappily. "We've been over that room with a fine-tooth comb. I just don't understand it."

She nodded mournfully, and two tears gathered at the corners of her eyes and presently spilled over. Ian took her hand and patted it while he spoke soothingly to her. "Uncle Richard has always been tough—I'm sure he'll pull out of it."

"I don't know," she wailed, mopping at her eyes. "I don't want him to die. He's left most of the money and the house to Benson—I have only an annuity—and I'll have to stay in my room while *she* runs thing— the way she's doing now. I can't think why Richard allowed them to come."

We tried to cheer her up and, failing completely in that, at last escorted her back to her room, where we left her huddled in her chair and stuffing a damp ball of handkerchief into her bosom.

Ian drove me to the hospital and gave voice to a mood of dark bitterness.

"It's the world's prize honeymoon, and it's my own damn fault. If I'd stinted a bit on the courtship we could have gone to a hotel. But how was I to know? I supposed we'd have the entire house to ourselves—I didn't expect to see Aunt Violet, even. Listen, Miriel—let's move to a hotel tonight. Days are passing, you know."

I shook my head. "There's no sense in moving now. After all, we have a nice suite. You—you call for me at three and we'll start afresh—we'll simply ignore the people who surround us."

He bounced the car to a stop at the side door of the hospital and kissed me violently. "Till three o'clock, then, honey—and don't be late."

I felt quite gay on the way up in the elevator, and I made up my mind to pay no attention to anything that Mr. Lang might say. Ian and I would have a good time for the remainder of his leave, and the family could go to the devil.

Rhoda Mills gave me a weary greeting and said that, as far as she knew, the old man was improving. "Amy Morrison said his doctor was fussing about dust last night, and Amy vowed there wasn't a speck of dust in the entire room—so after that he practically accused one or all of us of getting the pillows mixed up and handing out a feather one. He knows perfectly well, and I practically told him so, that if anyone gave Mr. Lang a feather pillow it was Amy or you—or that blonde frill who works on him after you go."

She referred to Eva Marks, who took over from me at three o'clock until Amy came on at eleven, and I giggled.

"Nobody handed him a feather pillow," I said pacifically. "But it's part of a nurse's duty to be the goat when it becomes necessary."

"Well, but that isn't right," Rhoda protested seriously.

I found Mr. Lang asleep and Amy awake and yawning her head off. "Touch of insomnia?" I asked.

"Oh, shut up," she said crossly. "How did you get here, anyway? I've watched every bus for the last ten minutes. I'm in a hurry, see?"

I hustled her off and listened without interest to her final explanation that there was a sale of fur coats that she did not want to miss.

Mr. Lang was awake when I returned to his room and ready to deliver his morning critique on Amy Morrison.

"The girl unquestionably has but two things on her mind when she is caring for me. The first, how much money is to be made out of the job, and secondly, how can she best spend the money when it is made. I have omitted her frantic desire for sleep at all times because I believe that to be a chronic state with her whether on duty or off. I have twice spoken to the doctor and asked to have her removed, but nothing has been done."

"Well, you see, we can't leave you alone at night, and nurses are so very scarce right now. But—"

"Yes, yes, yes—I know. All that talk—I've heard it from the doctor."

I folded my lips and went on with my duties and decided privately that he was a pest and an old crank.

At about nine o'clock Sara poked her head in at the door and whispered, "How is he?"

"Sleeping," I said briefly.

She shook her head. "No—I mean how's he doing?"

"He seems better, from what I see and hear."

Sara nodded. "That's good—I'm glad." She backed out quietly, and I went to the door and enjoyed myself for a while, watching her fly hither and yon at Rhoda's behest. Rhoda, I decided, was no slouch when it came to thinking up things for the aides to do.

I went to the coffee shop for my lunch, and Sara dropped in and joined me five minutes later. She dropped into one chair, cast her cap onto another, and ran her fingers wildly through her red curls.

"Tell me one thing," she said aggrievedly. "Why in the name of misery did you take up nursing? And you can tell me another thing too—why, having taken it up, didn't you drop it like a hot potato?"

"I give up," I said, stirring my coffee with loving care. "Why?"

Sara ordered a sandwich, which I noted with relief was only twenty cents, and coffee. "Now, take my own case," she rambled on. "I thought this uniform was cute—but now that I'm in, there's really no decent way of getting out."

I laughed at her and bit into my own sandwich. "Soak your feet when you get home."

Leslie wandered in and sat down with us. She hung her crumpled little cap on the knob of her chair and reached for the menu.

"You know," she said seriously, "this volunteer work is wrong in principle. It's unsatisfactory to the worker and to the people for whom she works."

"O God!" Sara groaned. "She's up on the soapbox again."

"You could always go into nurses' training," I suggested mildly.

Leslie murmured, "I'll have a liverwurst sandwich and coffee," and added, "No, I couldn't—I know myself too well. My upbringing has made me soft and lazy—I'm no good for anything."

"Oh, horseradish!" said Sara. "Did you get your photographic supplies?"

Leslie's forehead wrinkled up, and she looked almost as though she were about to cry. "No, I didn't, and I need them so badly. I want to try an experiment and I'm absolutely stuck because no one will advance me fifty to seventy dollars. That's all I need—maybe sixty dollars or so for about two months—and not one soul—"

Sara interrupted with a calculating glance at me. "You might sell your mink coat; you never wear it, anyway."

Leslie raised her head and looked at me eagerly through her glasses, and I was lost. There was no use in my trying to resist and be sensible— I simply could not help myself. I paid for both their lunches, and Leslie told me where to find the coat so that I could look at it when I got back. I went upstairs on air. I was practically the owner of a mink coat—and all for fifty to seventy dollars!

I was a bit too cheerful to suit Mr. Lang; he complained about it. "I don't believe you realize how ill I feel," he said reproachfully.

I switched to the kind of sympathy that he liked, and he became affectionate and insisted upon my sitting on a chair beside the bed and holding his hand.

"Only I have things to do, you know," I said, wondering what they were, in case he should ask me.

"No you haven't," he said fretfully. "You can sit here for a while. I'm going to see your father this afternoon—it has been arranged."

I made a hasty mental note to warn Father about what to say and what not to say, and Mr. Lang glanced at my face.

"It's all right, my dear—we're going to talk things over and arrange your future. Older heads like ours are wise with experience, and I think you may trust us."

He thought it over for a moment while I gaped like a fish, and then he went on: "You see, we need some life in that big house, and that will be your duty, my dear—your only duty. My brother Benson is there just now with his family, but I do not intend to allow them to stay. They probably suppose that they are well entrenched for the rest of their lives, but they're vastly mistaken. I'm going to have a little talk with Benson about financial matters, and the entire family will have to turn over a new leaf. And I am troubled about Violet. I don't suppose she likes them being there—she has not written to me this week at all. You can write to her for me—I'll tell you what to say."

He stopped, frowned in a puzzled way at the ceiling, and sneezed three times. I don't believe he ever uttered another word. His eyes filled up, his sneezing became more violent, and the struggle for breath was the only thing in his world.

He died just before three o'clock.

CHAPTER SIX

IT WAS some time later, when I was hurrying down the corridor, that I ran across Leslie. She was blowing her nose and she looked at me out of woeful pink-rimmed eyes.

I stopped and put my arm around her. "You go on home, Leslie— I'll be staying here as long as it's necessary."

She gave me a look of relief and muttered, "Thanks, I think I shall. I—don't know why I'm crying. I didn't even know him very well."

I watched her as she went off toward the elevator and reflected that actually she had not known him very well—probably not as well as I had myself.

I returned to find the doctor furiously searching the room for some sign of dust or feathers. When he found nothing of the sort he began to sniff around the subject of diet. I declared hotly that the diet had been exactly as ordered—at least while I was on duty—and he presently subsided with a few mutterings.

What with one thing and another, it was after five before I walked out in a daze of fatigue and depressions more or less usual feeling with me when a patient dies.

Rather to my surprise, Ian was waiting with the car. He said soberly, "Leslie told me you'd be late. I don't know why she couldn't have stayed and helped you out."

I shook my head and sank back gratefully into the seat. "All I want is to get home and get a little sleep."

He drove rapidly and in silence back to the house, and I had visions of going straight to my room, straight to bed, and straight to sleep— only it didn't work out that way. The family—with the exception, of course, of Aunt Violet—were sitting around in the living-room sipping sherry, and they had me in their midst before I could open my mouth to protest. Dr. Benson and Dr. John questioned me closely, and Dr. John said at last, "Should have moved him from that room—must have been something there."

Sara wriggled her shoulders and made a small sound of impatience. "John dear, you ought to be starting. You know they're waiting for you."

He gave her a cool glance, with one eyebrow slightly elevated, shrugged, and left the room without another word. I tried to sneak along in his wake, but Mrs. Benson Lang rose up majestically before me. "Do sit down, my dear, and tell us all about it—we wish to hear about the end, you know."

"I'm sorry," I said desperately. "Some other time. I'm very tired."

"But you were his nurse, and I think you should make an effort and grant us that courtesy. We have been told practically nothing, and we should know. People might ask, you see."

I sighed and told them what I could as briefly as possible, and then Ian put a firm hand on my arm and turned me away from them. At the door he paused and asked over his shoulder, "Has Aunt Violet been told?"

"I had to shout it through the door," Sara said. "She wouldn't open up. And then she didn't answer me, but I guess she heard it all right."

Ian and I went on up the stairs, and I could hear them start buzzing again in the living-room behind us. Ian shook his head as though trying to rid himself of some troublesome intangible. "They don't care, of course," he said flatly. "But I don't know why they should, at that. Uncle Richard never saw much of them—nor of anybody, as far as I can make out."

"Well, your aunt Violet never wanted visitors in the house, so Mr. Lang was in the habit of going out about twice a week to visit friends and relatives. He used to come and see Father about every six weeks or so."

We reached the upper hall, and Ian led me to my room.

"Better lie down and rest. I'm going to look in on Aunt Violet— she's the one who might really feel this. I'll call you in time for dinner."

I nodded and went into my room. I slipped out of my uniform and threw it across a chair—and then stood wondering what I'd do about the laundry situation. I supposed I'd have to find a place somewhere in the shopping neighborhood, or perhaps one of Mabel's neatly uni-formed maids would do it for me. I didn't think that Father would want to continue laundering my uniforms, because the fares from his house to my new home would come to more than I paid him for the job, since he always used a taxi wherever he went. Father was all for keeping up appearances. I turned the water on in the bathtub and decided that I needn't bother about it just yet. I'd probably be resting for a day or so and, in any case, I still had a clean uniform with me. Anyway, I'd be visiting him from time to time and could take the laundry along with me, perhaps. It seemed a shame to cut off any of Father's income—he needed it so—and besides, he made a good job of the uniforms. A little too much starch, possibly, but they looked very smart, even if the noise disturbed my patients.

I wallowed in a deep, warm bath and then put on my underwear and my fancy new negligee and slippers and stretched out on the bed with a cigarette.

Ian presently knocked on the door, wandered in, and asked for a cigarette too. His eyes had a rather absent expression, but as I supplied him they sharpened into focus, and he said in a voice of mild surprise, "Why, you're beautiful."

"Am I not, indeed!" I murmured. "How is Aunt Violet?"

He frowned and sat down on the chair over which I had thrown my uniform.

"She's gone a bit haywire. She cries and declares she'll never get over her grief, and in the next breath she storms about Uncle Richard's will. Says it's not fair that she should be thrown out of her home."

"They might let her stay here," I said thoughtfully. "If I know that bunch, they'll be heading for a bigger, finer, and more modern house— something a bit beyond what they can afford. "

He grinned and after a moment's silence said, "I don't believe she has anything to worry about. But at that, he might have left her the roof over her head, since it's all she seems to care about."

"How do you know he hasn't?"

"Well, I'm not certain, of course," Ian admitted. "But John told me the details of the will, and he seemed to be pretty sure of it—in fact, I gathered that Uncle Richard had told him. The house and most of the money goes to Uncle Benson. Leslie, John, and I get a tidy sum each, and Aunt Violet an annuity that she can't touch. Mabel's supposedly left out in the cold, but she can have her fun showing Uncle Benson how to spend his share."

I laughed a little and sobered up again. "The poor old soul—nobody really cares about him, do they? Except Aunt Violet."

"And she's more annoyed than grieved. But you can't blame them entirely, Miriel. If he'd sprayed some money around when we most needed it . . . . You see, my grandfather left all the money to Richard, as the eldest son, but he was supposed to look after the others. When I graduated from high school my mother wrote to him and asked for an education for me out of the money—some of which she considered was rightfully hers. But he refused and gave as an excuse that he did not believe in college for young men. So, as you know, Aunt Violet paid for it out of her allowance. She and my mother and Uncle Benson all had to ask the old boy for money that they felt was due to them—and he rarely gave. It didn't make for affection and love, exactly."

"No-o." I squashed my cigarette in the ashtray and folded my arms behind my head. "And there at the end he wanted to marry me—probably so that he could divert some of the money away from you all."

"He wanted to marry you because you're Miriel," Ian said. "I'm glad of one thing, though—that he never knew of our marriage. Not that the money matters, except that it means you can stop working."

"No, I can't. I'll be working my head off for the duration. Do you want me to be a slacker, or something?"

"May I kiss you today?" he asked formally.

I said, "Yes, I think so. I can't think of any reason why you shouldn't."

He got up off the chair, and my uniform fell crackling to the floor behind him. He replaced it carefully, but the fancy handkerchief which I wear in the blouse pocket—purely for its looks—slipped out, and he had to stoop over again. He made some comment, which he purposely blurred, but as he straightened up again I could tell instantly that something had happened. He stood quite still with the handkerchief in his hand, and the line of his jaw was rigid. He was silent for so long that I asked him in a puzzled voice what he thought he was doing.

He dropped the handkerchief then and turned to face me. He started to say something, appeared to change his mind, and with a muttered excuse walked through the bathroom and into his own room, where I presently heard him pacing the floor.

I got off the bed slowly with my mind in a whirl. What on earth had I done to him? I knew I had not showed much concern over his uncle's death, but neither had he. Had I been too callous? I frowned and shook my head. Ian had really been more callous about his uncle than I had about my patient.

Then what was it? I walked over to the uniform and stood staring at it. It was still quite fresh, although it was due to be laundered. I usually wore one for two days but never longer than that.

And then I saw it. On the floor, just beneath the pocket from which the handkerchief had fallen, lay a small scattering of feathers—and some of them still clung to the handkerchief itself.

CHAPTER SEVEN

I DROPPED slowly to my knees and gathered some of the feathers up into my hand. Through a haze of fear and bewilderment I realized that they might have come from a pillow—the sort of pillow that sent Mr. Lang off into a frenzy of sneezing and struggling for breath.

I stumbled to my feet again and frantically brushed the feathers from the palm of my hand as though they were burning me. I went and sat on the bed and found that I was trembling and on the verge of tears.

Someone had put those feathers into my pocket two nights ago. I clearly remembered preparing my things for the following morning, and I had had to pull the pocket open, because it was glued with starch, before I could tuck the handkerchief into it. Certainly there were no feathers in it then. But somebody had come into my room during the early hours of the morning, and whoever it was had put feathers into my pocket. And Mr. Lang had died of it.

I began to pace the room restlessly. Obviously Ian thought that I had done it myself—and why shouldn't he? Everything pointed to the fact that I had taken steps to safeguard his inheritance for my own ends.

I wheeled around and marched straight through the bathroom, determined to have it out with him at once, but when I stepped into his room I discovered that he was not there.

I hesitated, and my eye fell on a telephone that stood on the bedside table. Montgomery Kelly slid into my mind, and I walked over and lifted the receiver. He had always been a nuisance to me before, but he was going to help me now—if there were any help for me. He was not at his office, but I located him on the second call at his favorite tavern. I did not give him the story but merely told him I had to see him that night, and I would appreciate it if he would keep himself as sober as possible. He agreed at once and offered to pick me up at eight-thirty or so, and I told him to make it eight-thirty and not bother about the or so, because it was very important and I was in a bad jam. He showed enough curiosity to convince me that he would keep himself reasonably sober, and I hung up with a little breath of relief.

I went back to my room and put on a dress, and Leslie presently came to my door to tell me that dinner was ready. We went down together, and she delivered a message from Ian to the effect that he had

had an unexpected and urgent call and would not be back for dinner. Aunt Violet was not at the table, either, but Sara explained that her meals were being sent to her room as requested.

Mabel Lang was in a happy, exalted mood and was having a little difficulty in keeping her face molded to lines of sober mourning. Sara and Leslie seemed bored and indifferent, and the two doctors were discussing Richard Lang's demise—Benson gravely, and John with puzzled impatience.

I extended an ear for a moment, and Dr. Benson was saying: "Pneumonia left the heart muscle weakened to the point of acute degenerative myocarditis, with a resultant progressive dilation of the heart chamber, so that the violent allergic reaction which produced violent coughing and an accompanying edema of the larynx—"

"Daddy, would you mind saying that again in English?" Leslie interrupted peevishly.

They ignored her completely, and Dr. John muttered, "But how do you account for the allergic condition? Damn it, I looked over that room myself."

I nearly told them about the feathers, but a last-minute sense of caution urged me to wait until I had seen Kelly.

Mabel, who had been chasing her salad around the plate while she was lost in what might have been a happy shopper's dream, suddenly lowered the corners of her mouth and looked up.

"Benson! How many times must I ask you and John *not* to bring these unpleasant details to the table? Poor Richard's gone, and it seems to me almost indecent to go snooping around trying to find out just what happened. You can't bring him back, so please let his memory rest. I want him to have a *good* funeral. He was a *good* man, even though I don't think he cared much for me."

Just before the meal ended she got out her claws and tentatively scratched at me. "You are very good-natured, my dear. I'm afraid there would have been tears and trouble, if Benson had left me alone for dinner only two days after we were married."

"Oh, that's all right," I said amiably. "We common girls don't expect much."

I escaped to my room, where I put on my old coat and hat, and then went quietly down the stairs again. They had all shifted into the living-room, and I could hear Mabel and the two doctors more or less talking in chorus. There was no sound from the girls, and I supposed that they were probably stretched out on a couple of couches, sleeping.

I slipped out without being seen and walked to the end of the driveway in order to stop Kelly before he turned in, but it was wasted effort.

He swooped past me with a flourish, stopped the car at the door with a screech of brakes, and ran lightly up the steps to the porch. I caught up with him just in time to stop him from ringing the bell.

"Didn't you see me waiting for you out there?" I asked crossly.

He swept his hat from his head and said, "My dear—such a charming surprise. You never allowed me to take you out before, but now that you're married . . . Well, I have ceased to resent your marriage."

"Shut up, Kelly," I said, scrambling into the car. "And hurry, will you?"

He closed the door on me and flew around the front of the car tripping over the bumper and righting himself again en route. He sent the car hurtling down the driveway and out into the street, and I closed my eyes and grimly hoped for the best, as I had learned to do when riding with him.

He slowed down a little after a while and asked politely, "Where are we going?"

"O God! I don't care. Somewhere where we can talk—and I don't want too much smell of saloon, either."

"My dear child," said Kelly, "I have a little finesse where women are concerned, I hope."

"Me too," I sighed.

He took me to a fancy hotel bar with little red tables and black and silver running berserk around the walls, and it was a good half-hour before I could get down to business. He had to decide first on a suitable drink for me—after having brushed aside my usual manhattan with a sneer. I don't know what he ordered for me, in the end, but I do know that it had a nasty smell. He started himself off with plain Scotch.

"Have you realized," I asked idly, "that you can't have a second drink until I do? It wouldn't be finesse at all."

"Don't you worry your pretty head," he said, patting my hand. "You are the daughter of one of my best friends, and I will protect you with my life."

"Maybe you're not kidding," I murmured. "But what I need now is advice. I don't know what's going on in that morgue of a house, but it's—evil."

I told him my story, and he looked amused at first. He made a few facetious remarks and suggested that I was working too hard. In the end, however, he became more serious and asked me who was doing my laundry.

I was stumped for the moment. I couldn't tell him that Father did it, because I knew that Father would be terribly mortified if it ever got about. After a certain amount of hesitation I said that my youngest sister Diz laundered my uniforms for a price. Diz would be mortified, too, of course, but she was young and adjustable.

"Well, that's it, my dear," Kelly said, as one explaining things to a child. "She put the feathers in your pocket for a joke—probably thought you'd sneeze when you used your handkerchief. It went bad, as jokes sometimes do—although, as a matter of fact, I doubt that a few feathers could kill anyone."

"Don't go sticking your nose into my department," I said sharply. "I say the feathers *did* cause his death, and my husband thinks I did it on purpose so that we'd get the money. In any case, I know that Diz didn't put them there, because I opened the pocket and put the handkerchief in it myself, and there were no feathers at that time. I know, too, that someone came into my room that night—and it seems almost certain that whoever it was put the feathers there and knew just what he or she was doing."

Kelly pulled himself together and started to concentrate.

"The whole thing is really too odd," he observed after a lot of thought.

"Odd or not," I said impatiently, "I want to know what I ought to do. Shall I go to the police?"

Kelly closed his eyes for a moment in a pained sort of way. "God, no. I never could abide the police."

"Prejudice," I suggested.

He brushed the police aside and started to question me, and there is no doubt that he covered the ground pretty thoroughly. I told him what I knew about the Lang family and did not omit Mabel's remark when Ian had introduced me as his wife. In fact, the only dirty linen that was not aired was Father's undercover job as washwoman.

Kelly considered it all with narrowed eyes and the fingers of one hand tapping the table.

"I'd like to know where the feathers came from," he said presently. "If the old gent was so sissy about them, he'd hardly have any in the house."

It was a point that had not occurred to me, and I said slowly, "No, from what I knew of him, I'd say he would not have allowed anything of that sort in the house—under any circumstances. He was inclined to take his ills seriously, you know, and I'll bet that even his sister Violet and the maid Annie had to sleep on horse-hair pillows."

Kelly lost his finesse at that point. He laughed gaily, and carelessly ordered another drink—although mine still stood before me practically untouched.

"These are deep waters," he said, "and fishy—very fishy. But your

ass of a husband has no right to suspect you of anything. If he doesn't
know you better than that—"

"He doesn't know me at all," I said flatly, "and I don't know him.
We met about a week ago. We're merely in love."

"My dear," murmured Kelly, "do you think under those circumstances that you should have married him?"

"That isn't the point right now."

"Well, no," Kelly admitted. "But we cannot overlook the possibility
that he married you so that his uncle could not. You may be quite right,
of course—he may be in love with you. But we'll have to look into it."

I dropped my eyes to the nasty-smelling drink and miserably fingered the base of the glass. I took a sip after a while, and the evil stuff
took my mind off my troubles for a while.

Kelly patted my arm. "Don't worry, child—you have me to see to
everything now." He leaned back in his chair and added thoughtfully,
"I'll have to get into the house somehow. Perhaps I could pay a visit as
your uncle, or something."

I shook my head. "It would look phony, and I haven't enough standing there for house guests. Maybe you could get in as a butler or houseman."

I thought of Kelly as a butler and relaxed enough to laugh heartily
at the picture. When I came out of it I was astonished to find that he was
paying the bill.

"Are we going?" I asked.

"Yes, my dear. That was a good suggestion, and I'll have to work on
it. It won't be easy for a man of my culture to buttle, but I've always
wanted a job where I could step out of character. Things are slow just
now, anyway."

I stood up, and he held my coat. "Do you mean to tell me—?" I
began.

"Quiet!" said Kelly. "You're not to mention it to anyone—not one
soul. And most particularly not to that dumb goat of a husband."

I opened my mouth to protest and said instead, "How am I to get
you the job?"

Kelly stopped in his tracks. "*You don't get me the job.* That's most important—understand? I'll get it myself. I have ways. And remember,
when you see me at the house, you don't know me. And don't put in a
good word for me."

There was a light in his eye as we went out to the car, and I knew
that the thing interested him. I thought idly that that might be why he
was so successful—because he was genuinely interested in his business.

He dropped me a block away from the house and explained that we were not to be seen together at any time, or his work would be ruined before he could start it.

The temperature was dropping, and I ran the entire block and up the driveway to the house. Fortunately, since I had no key, the front door was open, but I had to stop in the hall because I had a stitch in my side. I dropped on to a small couch, and the pain presently subsided. I took a long breath and saw that my hand was resting on a cushion—a fluffy, ornate thing that was leaking feathers at one corner.

CHAPTER EIGHT

I PICKED at some of the feathers that had spilled from the torn corner and studied them. They seemed to be the same as the ones that had been in my pocket, and I felt a gloomy conviction that the pillow had been ripped open deliberately and a handful of feathers scooped out. Innocent-looking little things to send a man to his death, too.

The couch was shabby and old and dull, and I wondered how it and the fancy pillows had got together. I glanced around the hall and noticed a delicate pigeon-blood cloisonne vase on an embarrassed-looking old table, and a crystal ashtray snooting the utilitarian telephone stand that supported it—and I understood.

Mabel Lang had dotted the house with her smaller treasures, the sort of things that she would not put into storage with the furniture. Hence the feather pillows.

I heard a sound and looked up quickly. Ian was standing against one of the heavy faded drapes that hung in the archway leading to the living-room. He was watching me with a peculiar, detached expression.

"Hello," I said carelessly.

He made no reply, but his eyes dropped to the torn cushion.

I got to my feet, feeling suddenly exasperated. "I know what you're thinking, and you can go ahead and wallow in it, as far as I'm concerned. But I intend to find out who put those feathers in my pocket if it's the last thing I ever do."

I walked to the stairs and started up, but he called after me. "There's a message for you. It's urgent."

I turned around and asked, "Where?"

He was fumbling in his pockets, and I noticed that he swayed a little.

"Drunk, aren't you?"

He said heartily, "Yes, I'm drunk, and I hope I stay drunk. It feels better." He pulled a crumpled piece of paper from his pocket and handed it to me.

I smoothed it out, glanced over it, and groaned aloud. Dr. John wanted me for some patient as soon as I could get to the hospital—emergency appendix. "1 can't go," I said despairingly. "I've had no sleep. I'll have to phone."

46

"He told me to drive you over," Ian said in an expressionless voice. "Said he knew you'd help him out. It's a very important appendix that wouldn't understand about the shortage of nurses. They're short at the hospital too. Something happened there. John said just for tonight."

"O God!" I moaned. "Get the car out, then, and I'll be right down."

I changed as quickly as I could and came down to find Ian and the car waiting at the door.

"What time was he operating?" I asked as we drove away.

Ian shrugged. "He left for the hospital at about nine, and it's almost twelve now. You can figure it better than I can. " He was silent for a moment and then added, "I suppose you've been out with some former boy friend all evening."

"Which reminds me, I'd better send a circular notice to my boy friends to inform them that they're no longer former."

He said something under his breath and swung the car in to an all-night diner. "We'll get something to eat—you're probably hungry."

"I can get something at the hospital," I protested. " I should be there when my patient comes down from the operating room."

Ian got out of the car, slammed his door, and came and opened mine. "Come on," he said grimly. "They can all go to hell—including the appendix. If they're afraid he might swallow his tongue, John can sit around and hold it until you get there. Anyway, Leslie's over there, and she can run around and trip over his feet if the doctors needs some one to bow to them."

"Leslie!" I repeated, staring. "But the aides are never on after ten o'clock at night."

We climbed on to stools in front of the counter and ordered coffee and hamburgers. Ian shook his head as though to clear it and said indifferently, "Leslie was John's bright idea. Two of the nurses on that floor are ill, drunk, or dead—I didn't quite catch which—and John with a rich appendix to impress. So he yelled for the two girls to come and do the bottle washing, but Sara very thoughtfully produced a sore throat. She wouldn't have minded going on at all, she said, but she refused to risk infecting people who were already stretched on their backs with other ailments. Leslie cursed all the way from the attic to the front door, but she went. John said he knew you'd go, too, as soon as you heard the circumstances."

I enjoyed the hamburger and coffee, and it took the taste of Kelly's nasty drink out of my mouth. Ian did not eat much, but he drank black coffee and smoked, mostly in silence.

On the way back to the car I said suddenly, "This is a miserable leave for you. For heaven's sake go out and find a fancy blonde and have a good time. I'll get this mess straightened out after you go back, and we can call the whole thing off. But you might as well have a good time now and forget about it."

"Certainly not," he said indignantly. "That wouldn't help at all. Kindly allow me to enjoy my misery in my own way."

"As you wish," I murmured, and we drove in silence to the hospital, where we parted with a couple of short and snappy good-byes.

I found Leslie wandering around the floor like a lost soul, and she hailed me with acute relief.

"My God! I'm glad to see you. That Miss Evans shows up every once in a while and gives me a lot of instruction in Chinese or something—but otherwise I think I'm in charge of the floor."

"Holy Moses!" I said. "Where's my patient?"

"I don't know—take your pick. But I think it's selfish of you to take just one and leave the rest to me."

I discovered that my patient had not yet come down from the operating room, and Leslie had made an ether bed for him, so I went around with her and looked in on the other patients. The night supervisor appeared once, smiled all over her homely map when she saw me, and never showed up again.

The patients all seemed to be sleeping peacefully, so Leslie and I went back to the desk and sat down. Leslie was both sleepy and cross. "I don't believe the chairman of our chapter would approve of this," she said seriously. "Nothing was said about our working all night except in the event of an air raid, or something."

"This is the something," I told her, and after a quick glance up and down the hall I pulled out a cigarette and lighted up.

"That's against the rules," Leslie snapped.

"For you, yes, but I'm what they call a special. That means special privileges, like smoking, chewing gum, or spitting."

"Very funny," said Leslie. "Give me one too."

"They're in my pocket," I said doubtfully, "but I've had long practice, and I know how to do it. You're only going to get caught."

"So I'll be reprimanded or asked to resign. And when I'm lying in my nice warm bed of a morning, instead of getting up at the crack of dawn, my heart will break for sure."

I noticed, though, that she looked quickly up and down the corridor after each puff.

"What are you doing in the attic nights?" I asked presently.

"What do you mean? I sleep there, of course. Anyway, it isn't an attic. There's only one storeroom at the end. The rest is finished off into regular rooms."

"Well, but I heard you one night," I insisted. "You seemed to be pouring water into something and then scraping it around. I thought you were working on one of your photographic experiments."

"How could I, when no one would give me the money for the supplies I need? I told you that. I haven't touched my photography for a week." She thought for a moment and added, "As a matter of fact, I've heard some noises myself, but I think it's squirrels or maybe even rats. But things like that don't bother me—I like it up there. You know, away from everyone else—all by myself."

"Don't the two maids have a room up there?"

She shook her head. "There's a servants' wing right off the kitchen— two rooms and a bath."

My appendix came down just then, and I had to go. Dr. John was in a pretty good mood, for him, and before he left he murmured a word or two into my ear about the patient's social and financial background. He tried to be casual and off-hand, but he and I both knew that Benjamin K. Oppenheimer's was the most eligible appendix in town and a big catch for any young doctor.

I watched over Benjamin like a mother. Leslie crept in once and after looking at him critically for a moment asked me if I was quite sure he wasn't dead.

I remained quite alert until Benjamin had reacted. But after he had called me "Daisy" a couple of times, heaved once or twice into the basin, and then retired within himself to contemplate the infinite, I was suddenly so sleepy that it was a physical effort to keep my eyelids propped open.

I washed my face with cold water, shook my head violently, and went to the door. Leslie wandered over, and I could see that she was having the same trouble, so I told her to go down to the dining-room and get some supper. "And bring me up whatever you can snitch," I called after her as she went off.

The corridor seemed very long and dim and quiet after she had gone. Too quiet. I shivered a little and turned back into the room, reflecting that I always had hated night duty.

I started to think about the feathers again, although I did not want to, but I could not put the thing out of my mind. I wondered how anyone could know how deadly those few feathers would be. Dr. Benson and Dr. John . . . But surely any one of the others would simply be guessing. My thoughts congealed into an agony of listening as the sound of footsteps cut sharply into the blank silence of the floor. Not the brisk, muffled tread of nurses' shoes or the hesitating, apologetic tap of a visitor.

I flew to the door and looked out, and for a moment I thought I was seeing a ghost.

A little old lady was walking up the corridor toward me. She was dressed in the spirit of the gay nineties and was peering through her glasses at the row of closed doors with blinking, troubled eyes.

CHAPTER NINE

JUST as I identified the apparition as Aunt Violet, she came to a halt, moved her lips as though talking to herself, and suddenly disappeared into the room that had been occupied by Richard Lang.

I took a quick look at Benjamin, placed the emesis basin beside his uneasy head, and flew down the hall. Aunt Violet was standing just inside the door, staring at the empty bed. Apparently she had not been able to find the switch, since the room was dark, except for the dim path of light that seeped in from the hall. I snapped on the overhead bulb and asked briskly. "Is there anything I can do for you, Miss Lang?"

She jumped and turned her startled old eyes toward me, and I saw her face was wet with tears.

I put my arm around her and tried to be soothing, but she pushed me away.

"Where is he?" she whispered. "What have they done with him? I should have come before—I ought to have come to see him right along. And now, when I do get here, he's gone."

I put her into the armchair and took her hat off and fetched her a glass of water. When she seemed calmer I explained that Richard had been taken to a funeral home and that she might see him there.

She began to get excited all over again. "I can't go to the funeral—you know I can't do that. All those people—I don't like them. But I want to see him again. I—I want to say good-bye."

"Then get Ian to drive you to the home any time before the funeral. You'll be able to see him quietly by yourself."

She nodded, with her eyes fixed earnestly on my face. "Yes— yes, I can do that. I'll tell Ian. But where are his things? Richard's things? They should be given to me before that woman gets her hands on them."

"They've been sent home already; you'll find them there. I don't think Mrs. Lang would touch them. But, look, you should go back now—you ought to be in bed and asleep. How did you get over here?"

"I came in a taxicab. I phoned up on the telephone, you know." Her eyes strayed to the empty bed and filled up again. "I should have done it before. It was not difficult, and he would have liked it, if I'd come to see him. I wrote him letters, but he was lonely, and I could have come here and talked to him." Two tears spilled over on to the

51

soft wrinkled cheeks, and she whispered, "I came too late."

I glanced out into the corridor, and with Benjamin on my mind, I said urgently, "Miss Lang, Leslie will be back at any minute. Will you sit quietly here until she comes? And I'll send her in to talk to you."

She got to her feet at once with a look of alarm. "No, no—I can't see her. I don't like them—any of them. I'll go now. I told that taxicab to wait for me."

I took her to the elevator, but I could not leave the floor, and I hoped uneasily that she'd get home again without mishap. There seemed to be no doubt that her wits were woolly, to say the least, and in that outlandish costume she looked fit for the wagon.

I looked in on Benjamin, answered another patient's light, and then returned to Benjamin and a determined fight against my growing desire for sleep. I mentally reviewed Aunt Violet's costume and decided that it had a certain dramatic quality. Long gray coat, narrow waisted and with leg-of-mutton sleeves, and a gray hat worn high on the head and anchored by a gray chiffon veil. There had been a rose somewhere under the brim too—a deep red rose. I wondered a little how Aunt Violet had looked in the outfit when it was first assembled.

It was just after Leslie came back that poor Benjamin began to heave again, and from then on she and I were going full steam ahead.

We staggered out the side door of the hospital together at seven-thirty, and for the first time—when I needed them most— Ian and the car were not waiting. However, Leslie hailed a cab, and I was too tired and depressed to argue, although I knew I'd have to pay for it. We collapsed on to the leather seat, and between yawns I told her about Aunt Violet's visit.

"Oh, she makes me sick," Leslie said disgustedly. "I guess she was fond of Richard, all right—she just practically never saw anyone else— yet she never would visit him in the hospital while he was still alive and could appreciate it. You know, when she was a girl she was quite gay and popular, and then she had this bout of typhoid and lost all her hair and had to wear a wig. So she simply crawled into a hole and gave up the ghost. Ridiculous, isn't it? I don't believe she's so much as left the house between then and tonight."

"I don't think that could have been the only reason," I said thoughtfully. "Maybe she was crossed in love, as well. I think that always sent them into a tailspin in those days."

Leslie giggled sleepily. "Maybe she was—I don't know. I'll have to ask Daddy."

It was still pitch-dark when she opened the front door with her key, and we crept across the hall and upstairs.

"What in hell's wrong with you," I whispered, "that you like to sleep in an attic?"

"I like to be up high," she muttered defensively. "Nothing pathological in that, is there?"

I said, "For Pete's sake, no, but it's so lonely and spooky up there."

"Well, that's just it. I like privacy."

She said good-night and went her way, and I slipped into my room. I ached from head to foot, and my head felt blurred and dizzy. I dragged my clothes off, fell into bed, and went out like a light.

I was nagged back to consciousness by a persistent tapping on my door, and I was still half asleep when I yelled crossly, "What is it?"

"Breakfast, miss," said a cultured voice, and in walked Montgomery Kelly, disguised as a butler. It was well done too. He wore a small toupee where his hair had thinned in the front; he was draped in a stiffly starched white coat, and he had shaved off his moustache.

He placed a breakfast tray on my lap, and I said admiringly, "If I didn't know you so well, I wouldn't know you at all."

"You forget that this is my business," Kelly said with a certain amount of dignity. "I've only a minute, because what that woman down there expects me to accomplish in one morning is beyond belief."

I yawned and looked down at the tray apathetically. "Who told you to interrupt my badly needed rest with this mess of pottage?"

Kelly laughed. "I knew you'd be sore, but the old hag down there had it all figured out—and who was I to argue? Especially as I wanted to talk to you, anyway. She figured you'd worked all night, so she stretched a point and lets you sleep late—till ten-thirty." He paused to laugh again. "Anyway, you can get back to sleep again as soon as I go."

I yawned again and asked, "How on earth did you get the job so promptly?"

"In my business these things are easily arranged," Kelly said rather pompously. "The other maid now has a very good job elsewhere, and nobody is the wiser, except you—and you'll keep your mouth shut."

"Or else."

Kelly gestured impatiently. "Now, I believe the feathers came from a cushion down in the hall. I have some with me, and I want to match them up with those that were in your pocket."

I nodded toward the bureau. "Top right drawer. They are the same, I know."

He opened the drawer and studied the two little heaps of feathers for some time.

"Same kind," he murmured at last. "But how in hell could that stuff make anybody sneeze?"

"Search me," I said indifferently.

"Well, we haven't proved that those feathers came from the cushion downstairs, but we have proved that they could have. Now, the cushions were brought here by Mrs. Benson Lang as decorations. It seemed she stated that she knew her brother-in-law was allergic to feathers, but she intended to break him of the weakness for his own good. In fact, she came right out into the open as an avowed faith healer. Wife and mother of doctors! How do you like that?"

I leaned back on my pillows and laughed till I was weak.

"That doesn't help us," Kelly said reprovingly after waiting a reasonable time for me to recover.

"I'm asking you—did you know that she is a faith healer?"

I wiped my eyes and pulled myself together. "No," I said meekly, "I had no idea of it."

"Hell, she's very much in earnest about it, and it's possible that she put the feathers in your pocket so that she could confront her brother-in-law afterward and tell him he'd been practically sniffing feathers and hadn't turned a hair because he didn't know it. Except that he did turn a hair—only she wouldn't know there was any connection between his death and the feathers."

"So what about it?" I asked, feeling dizzy.

"So if you can find out that she was the one who put the feathers in your pocket the rest is up to you. In other words you can go ahead, then, and prove to that drip that you're innocent."

"My husband," I interpreted, and made a face. "What do I care what he thinks? I'll divorce him and marry you—if you keep the toupee on and the moustache off."

Unexpectedly Kelly became quite serious. "That's no basis for marriage," he said austerely. "The outer shell of a man doesn't mean anything—it's the inner spirit that counts."

"Not with me," I told him perversely. "You can take the inner spirit— I'll have the outer shell."

The voice of Mabel Lang was suddenly raised in the hall outside: "Kelly! Where are you?"

"Kelly!" I whispered. "Didn't you disguise your name?"

"Can you think of anything more completely anonymous than the name of Kelly?" he asked witheringly. "Get some sleep, my dear, and clear your head. I think old Rain-in-the-Face wants to discuss the funeral arrangements with me. It's going to be a grand affair."

He went through the bathroom and out Ian's bedroom door, and I heard him contact Mabel in the hall.

I finished my breakfast, put the tray outside the door and climbed back into bed. I was desperately tired, but I had always found it difficult to sleep through the day, and for a while I lay there with my eyes wide open.

I was just getting comfortably drowsy when something that looked like a small shovel fell past my window, apparently from the floor above.

CHAPTER TEN

I was wide awake again, and the question as to why people should be throwing shovels out of the attic window finally nagged me to the point where I got out of bed and went over to have a look. I raised the window and stuck my head out, and there was the shovel, lying on the grass beneath. It appeared to be part of a set of poker tongs and stand that is apt to ornament the side of a fireplace. I twisted my head around and looked up, but I could not see any window because there was a slight overhang to the roof. I decided that Kelly probably was trying out some mysterious experiment of his own and gave it up with a shrug. I went back to bed and must have gone to sleep while I was still climbing in.

The room was somber with twilight when I woke up, and Ian was standing with his back to me, looking out of the window. I stretched and yawned, and he turned around abruptly.

"Hello," I said sleepily.

He glanced down at his wristwatch. "It's almost six. If you want to put on the feed bag with the rest of them you'll have to dress now, because the new butler says he can't serve the oats any later than six-thirty."

I thought of Kelly being quietly obstinate about finishing his work early, and I began to laugh helplessly. Ian ignored my mirth and said flatly, "You're wanted at the hospital again tonight."

I yawned twice and folded my arms behind my head. "All right. Might as well be there as here."

He picked up my comb from the bureau and, after staring at it blindly for a moment, suddenly tensed his hands and deliberately broke it in two.

"Give me the brush," I said coldly, "and I'll break that."

He flung the two halves back on to the bureau and approached the bed.

"Get up and get dressed, Miriel, and after dinner we'll go to some bar and talk. When I've had something to drink I'll be able to loosen up and really discuss this thing."

"There's nothing to discuss. Someone came into this room and put feathers into the pocket of my uniform, and they were there for two days without my knowing it."

56

"You keep your handkerchief in that pocket," he said quietly.

"Not the one I use. That's a fancy handkerchief that is pinned to the pocket and it's only for show. I never remove it until the uniform is sent to the laundry."

He stared at me in silence for a while and then said rather violently, "All right—what do I care? Get dressed, and we'll go out and celebrate."

I frowned at him. "What do you think you're going to celebrate? Have you forgotten that your uncle's funeral is tomorrow?"

He looked away from me and muttered, "Never mind the celebration, then—we'll go out and have a few drinks. Only get dressed now, will you? I'm going across to see Aunt Violet. She can't seem to stop crying, and she won't see anybody but me."

"You're mistaken," I said, watching his averted face. "She I saw me last night—and the taxi driver as well."

His head jerked around sharply. "What are you talking about? I've told you she hasn't been outside this house for about thirty years."

"More like forty," I said musingly, "judging from the costume she wore."

"I don't know what to make of you," he snapped. "Either you're an accomplished liar—"

"Kindly get out," I interrupted. "I want to dress. We can talk this over tonight—if I decide to go with you, that is."

He turned on his heel and walked out without another word and I heard him cross over to Aunt Violet's room.

I went into the bathroom and turned the water on in the tub, feeling thoroughly exasperated, because all the time I couldn't really blame him. He knew very little about me beyond the fact that his family had suspected me of trying to edge in on the financial grab bag by marrying his uncle. And all I knew about him was that he had married me in a hurry. Mabel thought he had done it to secure all their inheritances, and although it seemed farfetched to me, it was still a possibility. It could be that he had thought it the only way to make sure of me, since he was bound to return to camp at the end of his leave. I bathed and dressed and then remembered the shovel again and went over to the window to look for it. It was still there, and I wondered why the person who dropped it had not gone down to retrieve it. I puzzled for a while and then decided to tell Kelly and see what he made of it.

I set off down the front stairs in search of him and found him almost immediately in the lower hall by the door. Father was with him, and they stood about two feet apart, staring at each other.

I broke it up. "Why are you looking at the butler, Father? And, Kelly—that will be all."

"Butler!" said Father in a strangled voice. "What does he think he's doing?"

Kelly spoke *sotto voce*. "Shut up, you big fool."

"Take his hat and coat," I said impatiently. "And, Father, come along with me and don't talk so much. I'll explain when I get a chance, but in the meantime keep your mouth shut."

Father followed me, but he never could keep his mouth shut. He opened the right-hand corner and said out of it, "He must be insane! He's had that moustache for twenty years. And why should he lower himself into the disguise racket? Look here, Miriel—" He stopped short and fixed me with a cold eye. "What's going on here?"

"For heaven's sake, be quiet!" I whispered frantically.

I pushed him into the living-room, intending to get him a drink and have a quiet chat with him, since I wanted to settle the laundry question, among other things. But it was just before the dinner hour and, to my dismay, the Lang family was draped all over the room.

I stopped and backed up a step or two, but Father, who was all front and no substance, swept forward with the situation well in hand.

"My dear Mrs. Lang, forgive my intrusion at this difficult time, and allow me to extend my heartfelt sympathy to you and your family in your great loss. Richard was my very dear friend, and his passing has been a deep sorrow to me."

Mabel wrinkled her forehead in a puzzled effort to place him and I stepped into the breach and introduced them. She showed interest at once, and I wondered if it was because Father had had a reception for everybody who was anybody and yet had not invited her.

He went like a breeze. In ten minutes Mabel had invited him to dinner and he had accepted. For a while I wondered uneasily how I'd get a chance to talk to him alone, since it seemed that he must have come in order to tell me something, but it presently occurred to me that probably I had nothing to do with his visit, beyond my service as a sort of connecting link. He wanted to get in among the Benson Langs because they were wealthy and social—even if they never had any cash on them. I relaxed after I had it figured to that point, and presently Kelly invited us all in to eat.

I was seated between Father and Sara, while the gloomy faces of Ian, Leslie, and John were lined up opposite. Dr. Benson lapped soup in a sorrowful fashion at the head of the table and Mabel at the foot gave her attention to Father. In fact they seemed to be having such a pleasant time that Sara nudged me after a while and asked in a low voice if I didn't have an uncle for her.

Father deliberately needled Kelly. Several times he criticized the service in a low-voiced aside. Once I heard him murmur "The serving spoon should lie in this direction, Kelly. It's just these little things that go to make the difference between a good and a poor butler."

Kelly finally had the satisfaction of telling Father to shut his goddamned mouth or he would, personally, sew it up with needle and thread. He delivered this dark threat under cover of a loud harangue from Leslie.

Leslie did not want to go on night duty at the hospital again, and John roused himself out of a sort of supercilious torpor to argue with her. He had two patients on that floor and he wanted their tempers kept sweet.

"What about Miriel?" Leslie said crossly. "She'll be there."

"Miriel is specialing Mr. Oppenheimer," John explained patiently. "But she can always help you out when you get stuck. It's only for to-night—they'll be all right by tomorrow. Good lord, I thought that was the object in training you girls—to help out in emergencies."

"I don't mind helping out in a real emergency," Leslie muttered, turning sulky. "But I don't see why I should be imposed on."

"Why, Les, the chapter will probably pin a medal on you," Sara said, comfortably secure in her real or manufactured sore throat. "I'd go in a minute if I could."

"Don't you start," Leslie howled. "Just because you thought of having an infected throat before I did!"

"Oh, come on, Leslie," I urged pacifically. "There isn't so much to do at night, and I'd like your company."

She gave in at that and agreed to come, but she finished the meal up in gloomy silence.

After dinner Ian waylaid me in the hall and said briefly "Come on, let's go out."

I nodded. "But I have to speak to Father first about a small matter."

I went into the living-room where Father was holding forth to Mabel, who was the only one showing any interest in him. I waited around impatiently, but it was impossible to break in until at last Mabel excused herself for a moment. She said she had to speak to Kelly before he left.

I leaned over and murmured into Father's ear, "What about my uniforms?"

He said, "Shh—yes—wrap them up."

"Is there anything else on your mind? I'm leaving now."

"Er—yes. I came to see Miss Violet Lang. She's inquiring about a room because she intends to move out of here."

CHAPTER ELEVEN

ASTONISHMENT held me dumb for a moment, and then I said, "Pull yourself together, Father. You're making it up as you go along."

He got red in the face with indignation, which was usual on the rare occasions when he was able to prove what he said. He pulled a letter out of his pocket and thrust it at me in silent fury.

It was signed "Violet Lang," all right, and inquired in a genteel way about a room with a southerly exposure. The writer wanted all meals served in her room and accommodation for her maid Annie. It was dated on the previous day, and I supposed Aunt Violet had written it soon after hearing of Richard's death. Heroics, I thought. Wants to get out of the house that does not belong to her and in which she no longer feels welcome.

I stuffed the letter into my pocket and glanced at Father. "Don't tell anyone about this—I'll attend to it. I'm sure she won't be moving right away, but I'll let you know if she intends to come."

"I'd rather see her myself," Father said stiffly.

"She won't see you. But don't worry, I'll take care of it. I'll give your hotel the right sort of a boost."

We had been talking barely above a whisper, and at this point I gave a quick glance around the room and was embarrassed to find that we were fixed in a combined stare from the family. Dr. John had a faint, amused smile on his face, while Dr. Benson was more or less looking through us. Sara was frankly trying to listen, but Leslie looked on indifferently with a peevish frown between her brows. Ian was standing near the door, studying the ice in his highball. Mabel came swishing back in a temper and saved my face.

"That man Kelly absolutely refuses to work before ten in the morning. He talks rubbish about it being beneath his dignity to serve breakfast, and he actually said that breakfast didn't need serving."

"We could always go without breakfast," Sara suggested brightly.

"Fire him," said John in a bored voice.

"I can't—how can I? I should never get anyone else. I'm unusually lucky as it is."

I slipped out into the hall, and Ian put down his glass and came after me.

"Are you coming?" he demanded impatiently.

"All in good time. I have to see Aunt Violet first."

"Oh, for God's sake, can't she wait?" he asked with restrained violence.

I said, "No, but you can," and went up the stairs in a temper. I stubbed my toe on a chair at the top, and I detoured into my own room because I was almost crying with anger and exasperation. I swore until I was faint, called myself a fool, and then wallowed for a while in self-pity because of my broken honeymoon. I felt better after that, so I blew my nose, combed my hair, and went across to Aunt Violet's room.

Leslie was there and rapped on the door as I came up.

"Family wants me to have a talk with her," she explained briefly. "Said to tell her we'll move out and she can stay."

"Did she say anything about moving out?" I asked curiously.

"No," Leslie whispered, "but one side or the other will have to go— the way she sticks in her room here."

Aunt Violet opened the door, saw Leslie, and closed it again.

Leslie shrugged. "She won't see any of them, but they thought she might let me in."

"I think she'll see me," I said tentatively. "I'll tell her for you."

"Good," Leslie said, looking relieved. "Go ahead."

She retired to the head of the stairs, and I knocked and called, "May I see you for a moment?"

Aunt Violet opened the door a crack and motioned me in. I squeezed through, and she said, "Sit down, dear. I don't want those others bothering me here; they keep coming, but I lock my door against them. They keep trying to get in."

She seemed frightened, and I looked at her in some surprise. "Why don't you talk to them?" I asked mildly. "They just want to get things settled."

"No," said Aunt Violet. "No—I don't want them in here. I don't know what they might do. I've made up my mind to leave, but I wish Annie were here; she'd help me." Her voice died away; and her scared eyes clung to my face.

"You needn't go," I said quickly. "They told me to tell you that they're prepared to move out again and leave the house for you. I'm sure they're willing to go immediately, so that you can stay. This has been your home for so long."

"No." She shook her head, and her eyes strayed to the window. "The house is left to Benson. Richard always said it must go to Benson. It has been in the family for so long, you see. I'll go. I'm going soon— as soon as I—"

Her voice trailed off again and, watching her, I thought suddenly that it might do her good to move.

"Father is downstairs," I told her, "and he received your letter. If you want to move over there he has a nice room for you and he can accommodate Annie when she comes. Your meals will be served in your room as long as you want it that way."

"Oh, thank you, my dear—I'm glad." Her hands fluttered excitedly, and she added, "I'll go tomorrow, as soon as I have packed. I'll just pack up what I need and go."

"Well—but the funeral is tomorrow, you now," I reminded her

"I'm not going to the funeral," she cried shrilly. "I can't—you know I can't see all those people; it would be dreadful. I shall leave when they're all out of the house. Richard would understand, I know. He always understood. When they've all left I'll go. I shall get a taxicab, as I did the other night, on the telephone, you know. Tell your father, dear—say that I shall be there tomorrow."

I nodded. "All right, I'll tell him tomorrow afternoon."

"That's right. I think it will be better, living there. Richard always said your father was a very fine person."

I left her then, although I believe she would have liked me to stay, but I supposed that Ian was still flattening the oriental in the front hall.

I went back to my room, wrapped up my soiled uniforms, primped a little, and then made my way downstairs. Ian gave me a baleful glare, but I told him to wait a minute or two longer and passed on to the living-room.

Father still had the floor, and his audience was still Mabel. I gave him the package, interrupting him in a story which I knew to be ninety percent fabrication, and said, "This is a little present to take home to the girls. I'm going now, but I might see you tomorrow. Have a room ready for tomorrow afternoon. She'll be along then, and perhaps I'll bring her myself."

"Eh?" said Father, blinking at me "Oh yes—yes, yes, yes—that will be splendid. Good-night, dear—behave yourself."

Mabel, pulled violently in opposite directions by curiosity and her refined upbringing, stuttered, "Er, what—er, who?" but I turned away and left the room. Sara, Leslie, and Dr. Benson languidly escorted me to the door with their eyes—John had disappeared.

In the hall Ian put a determined hand on my arm and grimly marched me out to where the car stood in the driveway. He slammed the door on me with a vigor that must have relieved his feelings somewhat and then swung behind the wheel and shot the car out of the driveway and along the street.

"Where are we going?" I asked equably.

"Just a place. It's quiet—Kelly told me about it. We won't be seen and we can talk without people listening all over the place. "

It turned out to be the same place to which Kelly had taken me the night before. Kelly was there, too, with his toupee off and his moustache back on again, but he turned away quickly as we passed, and I gathered that I was not to know him. Ian and I settled down at a table in a far corner, and almost at once Kelly unobtrusively shifted over to within hearing distance.

Ian ordered drinks for us and then folded his arms on the table in front of him and said, "Look, Miriel—I've been thinking. You say someone came into your room and put those feathers in your pocket."

I nodded. "Someone certainly came into my room, and I'm quite convinced that that's when it was done—since I did not put them there myself, and I know the laundry didn't, because the pocket was glued together with starch."

"It was done deliberately, then," he said slowly, "by someone who wanted to harm Uncle Richard. Who would know that the feathers would be so deadly?"

"Oh well, anybody could know it, I suppose," I replied uncertainly. "Dr. Benson knew about the condition of his heart so I suppose he'd have a pretty good idea. But people pick up all sorts of information these days—magazines and books. Only, even the doctors could not have been sure that he'd die like that."

"You sound pretty muddled to me," Ian said, shaking his head. "Anyway, I don't like any part of it, and I suggest that we take the whole thing straight to the police."

"Oh well—I—" Speech became impossible while Kelly cleared his throat thunderously. I tried again: "I thought of the police, of course, but it seemed as though their natural procedure would be to hang it on me."

Ian ran a troubled hand over his hair and said, "But not if you went to them of your own accord."

"Well, perhaps not," I agreed uncertainly.

Kelly cleared his throat again.

"What about that will?" I asked presently. "The way he was talking to me sounded as though he were cutting the family out entirely."

"It was only talk," Ian said soberly. "He opened up a bit to that afternoon nurse, and she handed it on to me. Seems he was leaving an annuity for Aunt Violet, but the rest of us were to be cut out—he said we had enough. I know now, of course, that he'd made up his mind to marry you as soon as he was well again, and of course the money was to be left to you. But he died before he could change the will. It's a nasty mess, Miriel, and we ought to get to the bottom of it or we'll never be at peace again." He was silent for a moment, and then he suddenly raised his head and looked at me. "When it's all cleared up I thought perhaps you'd come down and live near the camp—promise me you will."

"But I can't give up nursing now," I protested.

"Don't have to—there's a hospital there. Promise, Miriel?"

I took a swallow from my glass to compose myself and said, "Don't rush me. As you say, this mess must be cleared up first. And, Ian, I want to handle it myself. I—I'm working on it, and I'd rather you wouldn't interfere."

"How are you working on it? What are you doing?"

It was quite natural that he'd want to know, of course. He had a right to know, and he'd pound away at me until he found out.

I sighed, half turned in my seat, and indicated Kelly.

"There it is—private detective working day and night—and he never fails."

I don't think that Kelly had ever been in such a rage in his life before. His eyes bulged; his face turned dusky red, and his moustache fell off.

"I resign!" he sputtered. "I'm leaving the case right now. But before I go, you might be interested to learn that your wet smack of a husband and dear old Mabel had quite a lengthy discussion today about how you spent last night prowling in the back garden."

CHAPTER TWELVE

I CAUGHT KELLY by the tail of his coat and forced him down into the seat beside me.

"You're not going to walk out on me now," I hissed at him. "I've no one else to turn to, and I'm all alone in this thing. Even my husband, here, suspects me."

"Then why did you tell him about me, you damned little fool?" Kelly raged.

"For heaven's sake," I said wearily, "keep your shirt on. I won't tell anyone else—you know I won't—but Ian is all upset and confused by this business, and he wants it cleared up too. Perhaps he can help you. Please, Kelly, don't go off and leave it in my lap. Remember, you and Father were boys together."

Kelly said sulkily that he couldn't help it if his childhood pals were a bit questionable.

"Well, stick around for my sake, then. Now, about this talk of my prowling in the garden—I wasn't; I mean, I couldn't—I was on duty at the hospital. Ian knows that, so his talk with Mabel must be some sort of hogwash that he can clear up right now."

Kelly still looked angry, but he relaxed into his chair and stopped trying to get away. He turned a cold, fishy eye of inquiry upon Ian.

"It was while you were upstairs, changing, last night," Ian said to me. "Mabel went to the back window in the dining room to see if it was locked, and I wandered in there while I was waiting for you. Mabel called to me and indicated a figure out on the back lawn. It seemed to be standing at the lily pond, beside that old stone lion, and it was wearing some long, pale thing that could have been a negligee."

"You mean mine? My new one?" I asked, astounded.

"Well, Mabel says it was. She declares she knows all the negligees and wrappers in the house—including Aunt Violet's."

"Didn't you investigate this odd apparition, young man?" Kelly asked, sneering smoothly. "Or perhaps you take in your stride young women standing by lily ponds in the dead of winter, attired only in negligees."

"Of course I investigated," said Ian impatiently. "But I'm still not very familiar with the house, and I went out the front way and walked around to the back. When I got there the figure was just disappearing into the back door, and as I started to chase it I slipped on the ice and fell."

"Clumsy," commented Kelly, still sneering.

"I can't help that. Anyway, when I got in someone was going up the back stairs, and shortly after that Miriel came down."

"It sounds like pure nightmare to me," I said, shaking my head. "Why would anyone want to wear my negligee for a trip to the back yard? It's sheer, even for summer, and besides, it—it trails."

Kelly gave me a piercing look. "Are you quite sure you were not out at the lily pond on some business of your own last night?"

"Stop smoldering over your wrongs and talk sense," I said shortly. "Even if I had had some undercover business at the lily pond, why should I wear a sheer negligee to go out and attend to it?"

"Why would anyone else?" Kelly asked darkly. "Anyway if it wasn't you, that leaves Miss Violet and Sara."

Ian shook his head in a troubled fashion. "It doesn't follow. The figure was so vague that it could even have been a man."

"What about the maids?" I suggested.

Kelly compressed his lips. "They left at nine."

We were silent for a while, and then I said thoughtfully, "So many confusing things. There's that shovel, too—lying all day under my window. You see, it must have fallen—"

"What's that?" Kelly barked. "Do try and be coherent, Mirry. What are you talking about?"

I told him the story of the shovel, but his only reaction was to reprimand me severely for not having told him sooner.

We left after we had finished the current drinks, and Kelly was still with us when we reached the car. Ian made several pointed remarks about it being only a two-seater, until Kelly said irritably, "So it's only a two-seater—so Mirry will have to sit on my lap—and that's perfectly all right with me."

Ian observed stiffly that that would not be necessary, as he supposed the three of us could crowd into the seat.

On the way back I asked Ian why he had not told me of the figure in the garden the night before, and he said slowly, "To tell you the truth, I never thought it was you—I was convinced that it was Aunt Violet. She seems a bit batty to me, anyway."

I nodded. "I think that's probably the explanation. She turned up at the hospital later on too."

Kelly groaned loud and long and tore at his hair. "How do you expect me ever to solve this thing when you won't *tell* me anything?" he asked with extreme bitterness.

I apologized hastily. "But I have such confidence in you, Montgomery, that I somehow feel you know all these things as soon as I do—or even sooner."

He was appeased and said, "Well, of course, but you must tell me things, anyway—it cuts corners. Now, let's hear about this visit to the hospital."

I explained all, and he seemed a bit disappointed. "Just wanted to get the old man's things before the others grabbed," he said flatly. "She got them, anyway. They came to the house this morning, and Mabel showed no interest in them at all. Told me to take them straight up to the old dame. I was Mabel's sole interest this morning, anyway. She was busy running me ragged."

The three of us were silent for a while, and then I said suddenly, "Ian, did you take Aunt Violet around to the funeral home? She wanted to see her brother privately, for the last time, because she says she can't face the funeral."

"No," he said in some surprise. "I saw her this afternoon, but she didn't mention anything of the sort." He slowed the car down and turned his head. "Where do you want to be dropped off, Kelly?"

"I don't," said Kelly gloomily. "I have to go back and look for that shovel."

"I'll have to go back too—I've only just time to change and get to the hospital."

Ian headed the car toward the ugly mass of red brick that we called home, and presently we rolled into the driveway and stopped at the front.

Kelly slipped away immediately, heading for the back of the house, and Ian and I mounted the steps to the porch and let ourselves in.

In the hall I hesitated and then stepped quietly toward the living-room, where the voices of Mabel and Father chorused amiably together. I took a cautious look and saw that Sara, Dr. Benson, and Dr. John were sitting with glazed eyes. I backed away again, piously hoping that Father would not overdo it.

"Go and change," Ian said behind me. "We'll have time to snatch a sandwich before I drop you—only hurry."

I hurried, with my spirits rising to the thought that perhaps my hasty marriage would turn out well after all. I could go and live near his camp—away from all these frightening things. At least we could be alone occasionally, and I believed that we could be perfectly happy if we were only left alone.

We drove off in the car again, and Ian let out a breath of relief. "I was afraid that fellow Kelly would show up and climb in with us. Where did you get hold of him, anyway? I wish you'd waited and spoken to me; I'd have found someone better."

"No, you wouldn't. Kelly may have his little foibles, but he never fails—and I mean really never fails. He's told us about case after case, and in all of them—"

Ian gave me an oblique glance and a faint smile. "Don't be naive, dear, please. What of the cases he never told you about?"

"Well," I said, stuck, "you probably have something there. But still, he's a big, going concern in town and he's only working on this personally because he's an old friend—and maybe a little because it happens to interest him."

"He hasn't found out who put the feathers in your pocket, though."

"No, but give him time," I said defensively. "He hasn't started yet. And anyway, what else can I do?"

Ian shrugged. "I don't know, but I don't particularly like it."

He pulled up at a diner, and we went in and ordered sandwiches and coffee.

"Did you look at your negligee?" Ian asked after a while.

I swore softly and muttered, "I knew I'd forgotten something! I meant to look at it, but I was in such a hurry!"

"Never mind, let's forget it—and all the other troubles—and enjoy ourselves for a change."

We tried to be gay, but it was not very successful. The thing shadowed us, no matter how we tried to get away from it, and we drove to the hospital finally in a depressed silence. Ian kissed me good-by, and I went in with despairing feeling that we would never know the truth about those feathers, and the doubt about me that lay in Ian's mind would always be there.

Leslie was already on the floor when I came up and obviously in a bad humor.

"I don't like this work," she said disgustedly, "and furthermore, I'm no good at it."

"Haven't you ever read about the serve-humanity glow that goes along with it? "I asked, hauling out Benjamin K. Oppenheimer's chart.

"That I don't get," said Leslie, "on account of I don't like humanity and never did."

"You and Schopenhauer," I murmured, noting, among the fascinating details of Benjamin's day, the brief notation, "Wife visited." I made a silent bet with myself that Mrs. Oppenheimer's name was not Daisy.

Leslie went off to answer a light, and I betook myself to serve humanity in the ponderous shape of Benjamin K. He was asleep and snoring, so I sat under the shaded light and gave free reign to my yawns. Time passed, and presently Leslie stuck her head in at the door and made a frantic little sign to me.

"What's the matter?"

"It's Mrs. Johnson. She wanted an alcohol rub."

"So?"

"So I did. She hasn't any talcum powder, and I said I'd get some from the utility room."

"And?"

"Those little sprinkling cans all look alike in that closet," Leslie said, suddenly peevish. "I took one of them and sprinkled her back, and it's—it's scouring powder. I told her to stay on her side and I'd go and get her a clean drawsheet."

I said, "You come along with me and learn a little finesse. "

I made my way up the corridor, with Leslie trailing me, and found Mrs. Johnson still lying on her side—her plump back liberally coated with gray scouring powder. I bade her a cheery good evening, picked up a towel, and began to flip the stuff off. She twisted her head around at once and asked suspiciously, "What are you doing, Nurse?"

"I'm removing the talcum powder, Mrs. Johnson. I'm sure you wouldn't care for it. It's all right, of course, but we *never* use it on patients in private rooms; it's kept for the semiprivate patients."

She ate out of my hand without further ado. She said amiably, "It did seem a trifle gritty, but you needn't have bothered. I'll have Mr. Johnson bring me some powder tomorrow."

Leslie silently changed the drawsheet while Mrs. Johnson and I chatted about the price of rice in China, or some such thing, after which we tucked her up, put out her light, and left her to reflect upon the excellent nursing care she was getting.

Benjamin was awake when I got back, and my experienced eye told me that he was about ripe to tell me the story of his life. And as a matter of fact, he did start on it, but much to my relief he fell asleep again while he was still in his early childhood.

I wandered to the door and looked out. Leslie was ambling along the corridor, clutching a bedpan with a rumpled cover, and I watched her disappear into the utility room. Later on I went to the kitchen for a drink of water, and I tried to find her to ask her how things were going, but she seemed to have disappeared. When several hours had gone by with no sign of her, I was forced to the conclusion that she had left the floor and was not coming back.

CHAPTER THIRTEEN

RHODA MILLS came on early with a disgruntled student in tow and had a few harsh words to say about Leslie, but I didn't have much time to listen. Benjamin had awakened at an ungodly hour of the morning and had brought to the surface of consciousness a few wisps of fear about what he might have said when he was coming out of ether. He asked me in a carefully offhand way whether he had done any foolish babbling. Talked of flowers, perhaps? Or something silly of that sort?

For his peace of mind I kept Daisy under my hat and assured him that he hadn't said anything, and he went back to sleep looking much relieved and no doubt feeling that he'd been very clever.

I sat down and found myself wondering a little about Leslie. She had been tired, I knew, and cross, but it did not seem like her to leave without bothering to report off to anyone. I felt almost certain that she'd have come in and told me, at least, and I felt uneasy about her.

I was glad to hand Benjamin over to his day nurse, but as I was preparing to leave the floor Rhoda came sidling up and murmured, "Think you're foxy, don't you? But I know where you're living and why. Pity you couldn't answer a civil question when it was put to you. Maybe you couldn't, though, because maybe the part about your being married to the lieutenant is all birdseed—maybe—"

"Think the worst," I said blithely. "It's more fun."

Ian was not waiting for me, and I went out into the bitter morning feeling very sorry for myself. Neither Leslie nor Sara was with me to force me into a taxi, and my natural thrift urged me to walk a block to a trolley car. At the other end I had to walk two blocks, and then I was obliged to ring at the bell because I had no key. The neatly garbed maid opened up for me, and I asked her where Kelly was. She explained that he would not be on duty until later, so I asked her to fix me some breakfast and went on upstairs.

Everything was very quiet. I went into my room and then tiptoed through the bathroom and peered in at Ian. He was sleeping peacefully, and I had to control a desire to throw a cold wet sponge at him. Last night he had seemed to have recovered from his chilly suspicions and had warmed up considerably—and now, this morning, he couldn't even get out of bed so that he might have breakfast with me.

70

I flung off my clothes and jerked into my negligee—and then I took it off again and had a careful look at it. Somebody had used it all right. The sleeves at the back were half pulled from their seams, and the bottom was badly soiled with dried mud. I flung the thing on to the floor in a fury, pulled my nightgown over my head, and climbed into bed.

The neat maid brought a neat breakfast, and when she had settled the tray on my lap I asked her to take the negligee and send it out to be cleaned and repaired. She went off, and I ate my breakfast, put the tray outside the door, and settled down to sleep.

I had just gone into a comfortable doze when Kelly opened the door and pounded into the room.

"Why don't you knock?" I snarled.

"I did, but I got no answer. Here—why did you send this to be cleaned without first showing it to me? It just so happened that I spotted it before the cleaner called. Now, I'm telling you, you'll have to be more careful, you can't expect me to crack the case in a hurry if you work against me at every turn."

"All right," I moaned, "I'll be careful. Go away and let me sleep, will you?"

"Why?" he asked coldly. "I haven't had any yet."

"Please!"

He hung the negligee far back in the closet and warned me not to disturb it for any reason. He turned to go then, but as he put his hand on the doorknob I said suddenly, "You might ask Leslie why she left the hospital last night. She simply walked off some time before four o'clock, and I haven't seen her since. Perhaps there's some sort of a clue in it."

He came back into the room, but I closed my eyes determinedly, and after a moment or two I heard him leave.

I was not destined for much sleep that day, though. At one o'clock I was awakened by Mabel, who was in tears.

"It's Leslie," she said, wringing her hands. "She has never come back, and we have looked everywhere—phoned everywhere. You *must* know something; she was with you."

I struggled to a sitting position and looked at her through a blur of sleep. "But I don't know a thing. As far as I can make out, she left the hospital some time before four o'clock. I looked all over the floor for her because I thought she might have fallen asleep somewhere, but she was not there."

Mabel left with a cologne-dampened handkerchief held to her temple, and almost immediately Sara came in. Her reddish hair was attractively mussed, and her eyes were serious and concerned.

"She couldn't have come home, Miriel. Her bed hasn't been disturbed, and her coat is not here."

"But where on earth would she go?" I puzzled.

"Papa Benson has called the police—he's nearly frantic. They don't know a thing at the hospital. Said it was highly irregular for an aide to disappear without reporting off. I blame John, though; he made her go. But didn't she say *anything* to you last night? I mean anything that might give you an idea about what was in her mind? I've phoned the men she was friendly with—two elderly ones—the rest are in the Army. But I can't see Leslie eloping; it's not the way she'd do things. O God! What *could* have happened to her?"

She left after a while, and I gave up trying to sleep, and went in to take a bath. When I came back to my room I found Ian sitting in the armchair. I had no negligee and felt a bit undraped in my nightgown, so I climbed back into bed again.

"I'm going to get dressed," I said, "and see whether I can help them about Leslie."

His head was lowered on to his chest, and he was absently snapping a rubber band with his fingers. He glanced up at me from under his brows and said slowly, "There's more to that feathers business than first appeared. We should have taken it to the police at once."

I nodded miserably, and he added, "I'll have to tell them about it now."

"Yes. But what about Kelly? Have you spoken to him?"

"No."

"Call him in," I suggested, "and let's talk it over now."

He gave the rubber band a last snap, threw it away impatiently, and stood up. "All right—but I haven't your faith in that clown."

It took a few minutes to get hold of Kelly, but he came at last and gratefully threw himself into the armchair.

"You'd think with the worry that woman has today she'd forget about housework. But no—the chandelier must be cleaned. Good God! I didn't think people ever cleaned chandeliers. 'Every particle of glass, mind you—and don't break any of the prisms.' Well, I've broken three already." He settled his toupee and went on, "Well, what's troubling you? The disappearance of that girl? Don't give it another thought. I've observed her, and she's the type that muddles ideas around in her head and then tries to see them through. She's probably out seeing an idea through and has forgotten to phone. Forget it—the police will dig her up in an hour or so."

"I hope you're right," I said, feeling relief against my own obscure doubt. "But Ian is worried, and he thinks we ought to go to the police with the information about those feathers,"

Kelly rose from his chair and went into a rage that was the more violent because he had to keep it from being heard beyond my door. "Just as I'm beginning to get somewhere!" he exploded in a hissing whisper. "Just when no one knows about those feathers but the three of us and the person who put them there! Can't you see the advantage of that, you little fathead? I'll get it cleared up tonight if you'll only let me. Give me until tonight, and this Leslie will probably have turned up by them. I'll throw the whole thing over if you don't."

"At what time tonight?" Ian asked quietly.

"Three A.M. I could make it sooner, but that ass of a woman relieves her anxiety by thinking up things for me to do."

Ian nodded. "O.K.—3 A.M. After that we'll take the whole story to the police."

"How about lunch?" I asked, feeling that if I couldn't sleep I might as well eat. "All over, I suppose."

Kelly nodded. "But get dressed, my dear, and come on down. I'll fix something for you."

"Don't bother," Ian said shortly. "I'll take her out."

Kelly raised his eyebrows up into his toupee. "You might let the lady decide."

"I won't decide," I declared in sudden exasperation. "Right now I'd sooner be a chattel. Go on outside while I dress and figure it out for yourselves."

They retired together, and I threw on some underwear and went to the closet for my dress.

I had the dress over my arm and was closing the door before I saw Leslie's coat. It was the one she had worn the night before, and it hung inconspicuously among my own things.

CHAPTER FOURTEEN

IT WAS a woolen plaid sports coat, expensive material but inconspicuous in line and color, and I knew that Leslie always wore it to the hospital. It needed pressing and had an air of having been kicked around a bit, which was more or less typical of most of her clothes.

I quickly searched through the closet, but there was nothing else belonging to Leslie there, and I stood at last, staring at the coat and wondering what it all meant. Perhaps, I thought, she had worn another coat last night. But why should she suddenly change a habit of some months' standing? And even more inexplicable, why leave the coat hanging in my closet? Surely she could not have supposed that I'd want to buy it instead of the mink.

I turned away and finished dressing in a hurry while my mind raced to try to cope with this newest development. When I opened my door I found Ian standing directly outside, and he grinned cheerfully at me.

"Hello—I'm to take you to lunch. Getting to be something, you know, when I have to brush the other fellows away on my honeymoon."

"Poor Kelly," I said. "An old man like that! Where is he, anyway?"

"He's in the kitchen where he belongs, drinking the cooking sherry."

We went downstairs, and I told Ian to wait for a minute or two. I went along to the kitchen, where Mabel, Kelly, and the cook were all talking at once, but I caught Kelly's eye and beckoned frantically. He pushed Mabel aside and came toward me, and Mabel, of course, turned around to see where he was going, so that I had to duck behind the door. I quietly cursed him for a fool, and when he stuck his head around the door I whispered quickly and rather breathlessly, "Leslie's coat— the one she probably wore last night—is hanging in my closet. Only you and I know."

I ran after that. I knew that Kelly was a bit confused, but I decided that if he couldn't figure it out he wasn't much of a detective.

Ian took me to a rather nice place for lunch—probably because he'd already had his—and it was a pleasant interval. It had to be brief, though, because of the impending funeral service.

"Aunt Violet isn't going, is she?" I asked. "I think she planned on moving this afternoon."

"She changed her mind and decided to attend the service. Said it

74

would look bad if she didn't, and anyway, she felt she owed it to Richard. I promised I'd take her."

"Do I need to go?" I asked doubtfully. "I don't want to, but if you think I should—"

He put warm strong fingers over my hand and gave it a little squeeze. "You stay at home and try to get some rest. There's no need for you to go."

He took me home and up to my room and begged me to try to get some sleep. I dutifully stretched out on the bed, but after he had gone I knew that I could not sleep—my mind was far too active.

I had not told him about Leslie's coat because I was afraid that he'd rush straight off to the police, and somehow I had confidence in Kelly. I got up after a while and looked in the closet. Leslie's coat had disappeared, and I felt satisfied that Kelly had it under his wing. My own polo coat had disappeared, too, and I puzzled over that until I realized that Kelly did not know which coat was which and so had taken them both. I had worn my fur jacket to lunch, and the polo coat was much the same type as Leslie's woolen plaid. Mine was not as good as hers, of course, but it was in better condition—sprucer. I heard the family preparing to leave for the funeral service, and I wandered along to the top of the stairs and watched them go.

Mabel was fretting a bit hysterically about Leslie, and John and Dr. Benson were talking to her in low, consolatory voices. Sara walked quietly and circumspectly behind them, and a few yards behind her Aunt Violet clung to Ian's arm and surveyed the world through a long black veil that draped a large black hat. She wore a black Persian coat that belonged to Sara, and I decided that Ian must have borrowed it for her, since her outdoor raiment probably consisted solely of the gray outfit. I imagined that she didn't know the black Persian belonged to Sara or she would not have worn it.

Kelly gravely ushered them out and as soon as he had closed the door behind them turned around and bounded up the stairs.

"That coat!" he said breathlessly. "How did it get into your closet?"

"How do I know? I told you about it as soon as I saw it myself."

He considered for a moment and then said briskly, "I put them in the coat closet in the hall downstairs. Which is yours—quickly?"

I told him, and he flew off and presently returned with my coat over his arm. He hung it in my closet and told me, "The police were here while you were out to lunch. The boys know me, of course, and I had a devil of a time keeping out of their way, I can tell you. They'll be back, and they're bound to spot me, and I'll have to tell all." He gloomed for a moment and then became businesslike again.

"They looked around for that girl's clothes but failed to notice that the coat she'd been wearing was hanging in the hall closet. Quite typical, I assure you. It's all written down in their greasy little black books that the girl and her clothes are still together as far as is known—so that they are searching for her on the outside. Myself. I'm going to look for her on the inside. Those bunglers have given me this much of a head start—that they checked on the rest of her clothes and there's nothing missing—so we know she didn't come home, change her clothes, and go off again."

"You mean she's somewhere here? In the house?" I whispered, horrified.

He gave me a paternal and comforting pat on the back. "Yes, I think so. But keep a stiff upper lip, my dear. You'll have to face it. There's dirty work going on, and the guy that's doing it is trying to pin it on you. Feathers in your pocket—the negligee—the coat hanging in your closet."

I digested this for a frightened moment and then asked unsteadily, "Where are you going to start looking?"

"At the top. We'll work down."

"But haven't the police been through the house?"

"They've been through in their own way," Kelly said contemptuously. "But that's not my way."

We went up to the third floor and started with Leslie's room. It looked like her clothes, somehow—droopy and more like a boy's room than a girl's. The photographic things were piled up untidily, and a few books were scattered about.

Kelly searched quickly and expertly, and I realized with a sick feeling at the pit of my stomach that he was not looking for anything small, that he was, in fact, looking for Leslie herself.

There were two other rooms on that floor, all apparently long unused. There were odd bits of furniture in them, thick with dust, and I noticed some really beautiful pieces among the rubbish. Kelly made quick work of the two rooms and then, unexpectedly, became sentimental in the semi-dark hall and tried to kiss me.

I brushed him off and said furiously, "I can understand why you were thrown off the police force. You just can't keep your mind on your work."

"Don't be absurd," he said aggrieved. "This seemed the time and the place, and I thought you'd enjoy it. Anyone can see you're not getting along with that wet smack you married."

"What do you mean, 'wet smack'?" I demanded, but Kelly stalked away into the unfinished part of the attic, and I followed because I was too scared to stay alone.

It was very large and dark and thickly coated with dust, and there were two small dirty windows. One, I realized, was directly over my room, and I supposed the shovel had been dropped from it; the other was opposite, at the front of the house. At the side the roof sloped down to meet a brick wall which held the chimneys, and there were no windows.

I stood with my cold hands clenched in my pockets, watching Kelly search, and every time he opened a trunk I held my breath. But he finished at last and straightened up, vigorously dusting off the knees of his trousers, and I drew a long breath of relief. I hated and feared that dark, gloomy place, even though he had found nothing there.

Before we left I walked to a spot that I thought was directly above my room and asked Kelly if there was anything close by that could make a noise like water being poured. He glanced around and then shook his head. "I don't put much stock in that, though. You were probably dreaming, or else it was raining."

I said, "Oh yes, certainly. I'm a silly, hysterical girl, and you're a great detective."

He clicked his tongue at me and started to walk away, and then he stopped. "Well, yes," he said slowly, "you're right. You're not the sort to imagine things. You heard water being poured into something. I'll have to find out about that." He glanced around at the place and murmured, "Nothing here that suggests itself. But I'll keep that."

"Where?" I asked. "In your mind?"

He flicked me a look. "Anything I store away in my mind is always ready and waiting when I want to take it out again. Try me on any bit of your own past history."

"How did I get one hundred on my arithmetic examination in seventh grade when it was always my worst subject?"

"You sneaked into the classroom before school and copied the questions off the blackboard, you damned little cheat," Kelly said smoothly.

I followed him down to the second floor in astounded silence and with renewed confidence in him.

The only things we brought to light on the second floor were the facts that Mabel wore a double-chin reducer at night and that Aunt Violet owned a makeup box fitted with rouge, lipstick, and powder—and then kept her face shining with soap.

The first floor took more time because it was large and sprawling and had a number of deep cupboards, but we didn't find anything.

Just before Kelly started for the cellar I began to feel sick again, and I drew back. "I'm going outside for a minute, if you don't mind," I said, holding a handkerchief to my mouth. "I need some air."

He produced a coat of some kind and threw it over my shoulders, and I went down the steps to the back lawn. The cold air made me feel better almost at once, and with my stomach in its right place again, I glanced idly around at the wintry, dead garden.

The ancient stone lion had fallen from its crumbling foundations and toppled into the lily pond!

I walked toward it, smiling at the odd accident, until I stood on the broad band of concrete that edged the little pool and looked down.

A cold blue hand floated lazily on the surface of the murky water.

CHAPTER FIFTEEN

I MUST have screamed, because the next thing I knew Kelly was with me and had dealt me a stinging slap on the cheek. He hissed, "What is it? Are you trying to rouse the whole neighborhood?"

I pointed downward, and Kelly got down on his knees and dragged me with him. As close as that we could see parts of her body lying on the floor of the pool and pinioned by the great stone lion.

I started to go to pieces, but Kelly slapped me again and said that we must get her out at once, in case she was still living. I pitched in and helped then, and after a long, grim struggle we shifted the lion far enough to release the body. But Leslie was dead and had been dead for some time—one glance was enough to tell me that. Kelly examined her while I stared rigidly in another direction, and at last he straightened up and said soberly, "Head's been beaten in. Go and phone the police, Miriel, quickly. I don't want to move her any farther until they've seen her." He shook his head and added, "I know one guy who's due to be fired. I heard Briggs tell him to go out back and have a look at the garden; he went out back, all right, but he sprinted to the corner for a package of cigarettes instead of looking at the garden."

I glanced down again, in spite of myself, and saw that Leslie still wore her uniform and seemed to have an old sweater on over it. Her glasses, broken and crushed, still clung to her face.

Tears began to slip over my cheeks, and Kelly said gently, "Go and get the police, Miriel—and hurry. There'll be hell to pay about their having missed this, and it looks as though you and I might be in for a spot of trouble. Don't make it any worse than it is."

I went slowly into the house and made the call, and then I just sat there at the telephone table with my head resting on my hands. Leslie must have left the hospital by herself, I thought, unless someone came up and enticed her while I was busy with Benjamin. But why would she leave without reporting off? And why go home, exchange her coat for a sweater, and then walk out to the lily pond—and to her death?

I was still sitting there when the police turned up, headed by Briggs, who looked far from happy. I led them through the house and out to the back, where I delivered them into the hands of Kelly. Briggs was purple in the face, and he tried to suggest that Kelly had brought Leslie's body from somewhere else and only recently dumped it into the pool. Kelly merely looked at him with a contempt too fine for words, and Briggs presently dropped it and asked him how long he had been in service with the Langs.

Kelly was so obviously delighted at not having been recognized that I was afraid it would show. He slid back into his butler's disguise and stayed there. To Briggs's question he answered readily that it had been for only a few days and then astonished me by adding that he had been in his last place for fifteen years. He had left, he said, over a difference of opinion with the colored cook—and gave my father's name as his ex-employer. At the same time, he flicked me a quick, blank glance, and I faded from the scene immediately and made for the house.

I went straight to the telephone and called Father, but as I had expected, my hurried message merely confused him, and he started to shout and argue. I told him to put one of my sisters on, and Diz came to the phone and got the whole thing straight at the first telling. She promised to convince Father that he had employed a butler for the last fifteen years, but I had no sooner hung up than I thought better of it. Who was Kelly, after all, to get us into trouble with the police? I phoned back and got Diz again. "Change that," I said briefly. "Tell Father just to say that he's known Kelly for the last fifteen years."

I heard footsteps pounding into the kitchen, so I replaced the phone in a hurry and slid into the living-room.

Briggs, Kelly, and a policeman presently came in, and Briggs started to question me. The policeman retired to the hall, where he seemed to be doing some telephoning, and Kelly tried to ease out after him but was peremptorily motioned back.

"How did you happen to discover Miss Lang's body in the pool?" Briggs asked me.

I opened my mouth and had, perforce, to close it again when Kelly said smoothly, "Mrs. Ross came through the kitchen, saying she needed some fresh air, and went on out to the back. After a minute or so I heard her scream and ran out to her."

Briggs coldly suggested that I answer the question myself, so I gave him the same story, word for word. It didn't seem to interest him, and he turned to Kelly and wanted to know where the cook was.

Kelly said it was her afternoon off.

"You're not telling me she sashayed off for the afternoon when they had a funeral going on?" Briggs said, astounded.

Kelly looked over his head and observed that evidently he'd never employed a cook.

An ambulance that had been standing at the front door slid smoothly off down the drive, and I broke down completely. Briggs allowed me to go, and I stumbled up to my room, took a couple of aspirins, and fell into bed. I had hoped to get some sleep, but of course it did not work. I lay stretched out, tense and alert, until I heard the family come in downstairs. Mabel's scream was prompt and full-bodied and was followed by a certain amount of subdued activity, during which I could imagine Dr. Benson and John giving first aid. Once the screaming was under control I could hear talking—throbbing and interminable.

I twisted restlessly on my bed and reflected bitterly that there would not be a great deal of grief for Leslie's passing. Dr. Benson had devoted himself to his position in life and to Mabel, who graced it; Mabel quite obviously loved John more than anyone else, and John loved himself. Sara had for some time been bestowing the greater part of her affections on a Dr. Harris Colton-Smith, but I was one of the only five people who knew it. At that, I thought that Sara would grieve more than any of them. Aunt Violet, of course, I counted out of the picture.

Ian came upstairs after a while and into my room. He sat on the side of the bed without saying anything and took my hand in both of his. It was as though he were trying to reassure me, but he found no words, and I could sense his doubt and confusion. I knew he was trying hard to believe in me, but I disliked the effort and I pulled my hand away.

"How did Aunt Violet take it?" I asked abruptly.

He stood up and moved away to the window, where he stared out without seeing anything, I'm sure, but his own troubled thoughts. "I don't know," he answered me. "She's been shrouded in a long black veil all the afternoon, and I couldn't see. After Briggs told us she simply galloped up the stairs without a word."

I was silent for a moment, and then I opened my mouth to tell him about Leslie's coat, thought better of it, and cleared my throat instead.

Ian glanced at me, left the window, and came to a halt in the middle of the room.

"Listen," he said desperately, "I've got to know—had Leslie heard about those feathers?"

I averted my eyes and fixed them on the wallpaper. So he suspected me of murdering Leslie as well as his uncle!

When I could speak quite steadily I said, "As far as I know, she knew nothing whatever about it." He came a step closer, and I added coolly, "If you don't mind, I'd like to try to sleep now." He hesitated and then turned and went through to his own room.

I buried my head in the pillow and cried for some time, after which I felt distinctly better. I determined fiercely to put Ian out of my life and my mind and to shed no more tears over him—after all, I hardly knew him. Nor was it helping anyone to lie there and cry over Leslie.

I made up my mind to go down and see what I could do to help, and I got up and went to work on my hair and face. Later I would go home and then see if the marriage could be annulled. I would have liked to go home then and there to the cheerful company of my sisters, the complaints of the paying guests, and the colorful personality of my father.

I went along to see Mabel and found her lying on the bed, moaning. It was clear to me that she was far more shocked than grieved—and the moans were false.

I tried to back out quietly, but she hung on and wailed, "Don't leave me. Oh, I can't stand it—my poor baby. What could have happened to her?"

I asked her if she'd have coffee and something to eat, and she declared violently that she could not touch a thing. But she wanted to be persuaded, so I went on persuading until she gave in. I told her I'd bring a tray immediately and slid out.

In the lower hall I glanced into the living-room and saw that Sara, Dr. Benson, and John were having a session with Briggs. Dr. Benson looked desperately tired and John sullen, while Sara was walking restlessly about, twisting a mangled scrap of handkerchief through her fingers. They did not see me, and I went quietly through to the back hall and on into the kitchen

I found Kelly staring helplessly into the interior of the ice chest. He said, "God! I'm glad to see you. It doesn't suit me to be fired yet—I want to stay on tonight—I must. I'll finish the thing before morning if I'm left alone. But I'm supposed to lay out a cold supper—or maybe it's called a cold collation in a neighborhood like this—and I'm stuck."

I brushed him aside impatiently and said, "I have no time for a man who's helpless in the kitchen."

"Be fair, please," Kelly said austerely. "The places in which I've lived, such as your father's flop- and hash-house, do not encourage the guests to help in the kitchen. It might spoil their illusions."

I was murmuring, "Let's see—five of us, I guess salad, the cold chicken, coffee." I gave Kelly a few directions and got him started and then fixed some thin little sandwiches and a pot of coffee for Mabel. I picked up the tray, answered Kelly's mute appeal with a promise to return, and went on upstairs.

Mabel had washed and powdered her face and tidied her hair. She had given up moaning and was lying quietly on the bed, staring at the ceiling. I arranged a couple of pillows behind her and poured the coffee, and after she had told me twice that she could not touch a thing she fell to with a certain amount of vim. I left her so that she could eat without embarrassment and went back to the kitchen.

Kelly, with beads of sweat on his forehead, was trying to make the salad look less like a bowl of garbage by arranging a weird pattern of little radishes all over the top. I gave him a few more directions and started to fix a tray for Aunt Violet.

"If you're going to tote trays for the whole blasted gang," Kelly said irritably, "why in hell am I running myself ragged over this muck? Who's going to eat it?"

I told him to keep his toupee on, shouldered Aunt Violet's tray, and went on upstairs again.

She did not answer my first knock, and when I tapped again she quavered, "Who is it?"

I explained and then had to wait before she opened the door, because she had to unlock it first. She made a sufficient opening for me and the tray and then hastily closed the door and locked it again. She was trembling and obviously frightened, and after a glance at the tray she asked if I had prepared it myself.

I reassured her, and she gave a jerky little sigh.

"Then it's all right, child, and I can eat it. But I don't trust them any more. I knew it would come and now, you see, it has."

I placed the tray and helped her into a chair in front of it. "You can move to my father's place," I said soothingly, "and then you won't be so troubled."

But she shook her head and twisted her veined old hands together.

"I can't go—not now. I knew it would happen—I knew. And I'm frightened because I know that I shall be next."

CHAPTER SIXTEEN

"YOU'RE TIRED and upset," I said, feeling rather inadequate. "Leslie's death was probably some sort of ghastly accident."

"Oh no—no, no. That policeman came up here—forced his way in and talked to me. He said somebody hit her over the head and pushed her into the lily pond." She began to wring her hands again, and tears slid over the soft, wrinkled cheeks. "She was a nice little girl, and she used to come over here and play out there at the lily pond. She had braids and a bang and some kind of a brace on her teeth. I'd send Annie out to her with cookies. And now they've killed her."

"Eat your supper, Aunt Violet," I said, trying to swallow a lump in my throat. "It's getting cold, and you need it."

She looked vaguely at the tray, mopped at her eyes with a handkerchief that smelled of lavender, and at last began slowly to eat.

I lighted a cigarette which I badly needed and hoped that she would not object, but she merely glanced at me without appearing to see me and went on eating. After a lengthy silence I said tentatively, "Who do you mean when you say 'they' have killed her?"

"I don't know—I don't know. But one of them, I'm sure. I know it—I feel it. Ever since they came I've felt it—something evil—something going on amongst them. And Richard, too—he would not have died. They hounded him. I don't like them."

She was excited and almost hysterical, and I soothed her as best I could. I realized that she apparently had no reasonable foundation for her fear and her vague accusation outside of a thorough dislike for the entire family.

When she was more or less calm again I said firmly, "This fear that they're coming after you is quite ridiculous, you know. You must put it out of your mind and not think of it again."

She shook her head and said with a sort of quiet dignity, "It's not ridiculous, child. Richard left me an annuity which is in some sort of trust fund. I don't understand such matters, but I know that the principal will be tied up until I die, and then they are to divide it. That means that I shall be next. They bothered Richard, and in his weakened condition he could not stand it. And then Leslie—right in their midst—one of them—"

84

"But don't you see," I said patiently, "they'd have no reason to do away with Leslie. As you say, she was one of them."

But Aunt Violet was not to be convinced. She shook her head from side to side and whispered, "She must have known something that was dangerous to them."

"Which one do you accuse?" I asked, making another effort to pin her down. "Or is it all of them?"

But it was no use. She looked away and murmured faintly, "I don't know—I don't know them. It's just a feeling I have and I can't be wrong. It's something evil."

She cried a little after that and said she thought she'd rest; she was tired, and the funeral had been too much for her.

I stood up, and she took a letter from the bureau and asked me to mail it.

"I'm telling Annie that she must come back," she said, her pale eyes sparkling a little. "She's been sulking long enough."

I took the letter and the tray and heard her lock the door after I had gone out.

Ian was standing in the lower hall as I came down the stairs, and he watched me take every step. I reached the bottom in safety and turned on him irritably. "You can make a person trip, doing a thing like that."

"I thought you were going to try to sleep," he said, grinning faintly. He attempted to take the tray, but I gave him the letter instead and told him to go out and mail it.

He departed without further comment, banging his cap on to the side of his head and shutting the front door none too gently behind him.

I went on to the kitchen, grimly reminding myself that I was putting him out of my life forever. I was able to relieve my feelings a little by calling Kelly all kinds of a silly fool when I found him trying to make little balls out of the butter.

He seemed disappointed and gave up the idea reluctantly. "I found these wooden patty-cake things in the drawer there, and why would they buy them if they don't want their butter served fancy?"

I said, " Kelly, get the food on to the table and pick up those bits of butter lying all around you—we can use it for cooking. Butter's scarce."

I helped him to get the meal on to the table because I was afraid, if I left him alone, he'd find some other fool thing to do.

When we had finished I went along to the living-room and found that Briggs had just gone and had left Sara, Dr.. Benson, and John sitting in silence, apparently studying the texture of the carpet.

"Come on," I said, suddenly conscious of the lump in my throat again. "Kelly has some food for us."

They got up as though they were glad to have something definite to do. Ian came in the front door as we left the living room, tossed his cap on to the hall table, and joined us in the dining-room. He said directly, "John, have you found out yet whether she was drowned?"

"She was not drowned," John replied, and spoke as though he resented the question. Without lifting his eyes from his plate he added, "Dad spoke to Emerson on the phone. She was hit on the head—vicious attack. The lion apparently was toppled over on to her to keep her hidden. The thing has been crumbling at the foundation for years, so I suppose it wasn't difficult to push over. Probably pure chance it landed squarely in the pool."

"I've thought until my head's all queer," Sara said desperately. "But there just isn't any reason for anyone to have killed her."

"Money, " John said shortly.

Sara stared at him. "What do you mean?"

"Simply that Leslie's share of Uncle Richard's pile now reverts to her family."

Ian looked up and asked, "Are you sure of that? I've been wondering about that will. He might have changed it."

"No." John stirred his coffee as though he disliked the spoon, the coffee, and the cup that held it. "Bolton talked to us at the funeral— said the will was unchanged. He had some idea of reading it tonight, but I told him that Leslie was missing and he'd better postpone it." He drank the coffee off, stared at the wall for a moment, and said harshly, "The poor kid. Oh, what the hell, anyway!"

There was a blank silence for a moment, and then John got up and left the room. Sara gave me a watery little smile, caught her lower lip between her teeth, and followed hastily.

I glanced at Dr. Benson, who took his watch from his waistcoat pocket and regarded it fixedly for at least a minute. He replaced it very carefully, said vaguely to no one in particular, "I have a patient," and walked out of the room with his shoulders sagging tiredly. I continued to eat while Ian sat and smoked with his head slightly bent.

Kelly presently came in with a bowl of canned peaches and a layer cake. When he saw that Ian and I were alone he deposited the bowl and cake platter on the table and sat down with us.

"Didn't eat much, did they?" he commented.

"Who'd want to?" Ian muttered without raising his head.

I put my fork on to my plate with a slight clatter and began to fumble for a cigarette.

"Don't let him put you off your food," Kelly said irritably. "You're a nurse, aren't you? You've seen plenty—and you barely knew the girl. You'd be in a pretty mess if you lived on cigarettes and coffee for a day or so after every death you saw! Have some sense and finish your meal—and let old Drip-puss there look after his own intake."

Ian stirred and said with a flash of annoyance, "I didn't mean that."

"Then why did you say it?" Kelly snapped.

"I wish you'd shut up," I said wearily. "Kelly, for God's sake how are you getting on with the ghastly thing?"

He cut himself a slice of cake and sat back comfortably. "House-work," he said, waving it around so that the crumbs fell on the floor, "is a revelation to me. Work—steady, grinding, endless. You never finish, and what you have just done, with the sweat running off your brow, is ready and waiting to be done all over again tomorrow. Ah well"—he brushed crumbs from his trousers and got down to business—"I'm go-ing to clean this thing up tonight, and you two can help me by clearing this mess away and washing the dishes. I can get to work without any delay then. Those bright school children from the police department are looking for the weapon—not a rock from the pool—something sharper." He stopped to laugh scornfully and choked over the last mor-sel of his cake. When he got his breath back he added, "I know what it is, of course, but I don't know where it is yet. However, I shall find it."

"What is it?" I asked.

"One of the pokers from that set of fire-irons in the living room. It's a fairly elaborate outfit, so of course the school children didn't no-tice that a poker was missing. It takes me. That shovel, by the way, was back in its place—plus a powdering of whitish dust on the business end. Now, that means someone has been digging with it in the pile of sand out in the back yard."

"Sand?" I murmured helplessly. "What sand?"

"You should learn to observe," Kelly said severely. "There is a pile of sand not far from the lily pond. It has been there since last summer, when it was ordered by Mr. Richard Lang—but for what purpose no one seems to have the slightest idea. It has attracted the neighborhood kids like flies, of course, and they've spread it around a bit. But philan-thropy was not Mr. Lang's purpose, because he seems to have chased the kids with blood in his eye every time he caught them there."

"I don't see why the kids in this neighborhood would bother with an odd pile of sand," I protested. "All they have to do is express a de-sire, and sand would be delivered to their yards in a painted box with an awning over the top."

"Kids don't want sand in a box," Kelly explained. "They like to have it in a pile so that they can spew it around and make a mess."

Ian spoke into our conference with a touch of malice. "Aren't you getting a little away from the point? For instance, where is the poker?"

"I've told you that I don't know," said Kelly haughtily. "But I shall find it tonight. Only Briggs will be back soon, and he'll be bound to interfere, so if you will—?"

I put out my cigarette and stood up. "All right, I'll do the skivvy work. Go and find the poker, and you might look in my room first. It's almost bound to be there."

Kelly nodded. "I intend to look there first. In fact, I've looked there already, but it had not yet been delivered. I think I may hide there for a while and perhaps trap the person who comes to plant it."

I picked up an armload of dishes and glanced at the clock. "You'd better hurry, then."

"The amateur shows up in you so frequently," Kelly deplored. "The house will have to quiet down a bit before anything is done."

"How can you be sure that you haven't warned me away from planting the poker?" Ian asked suddenly.

Kelly gave him a patronizing glance. "You're definitely out of it. To a trained mind like my own it is obvious that your only interest—which coincides with mine—is to get Miriel cleared." He got up, yawned, adjusted his toupee, and left the room.

I felt a warm glow filtering in around my bitterness as Ian flung back his chair and said, "Let's get this mess cleared away."

It took some time to clean up after Kelly, and we had barely finished when the doorbell rang, and I went through to the front hall and admitted Briggs.

He tossed his hat on to the table, shrugged out of his coat, and asked, "Where's the houseman?"

"Why, I believe he's off for the evening," I said, feeling very quick-witted.

Briggs grunted and made for the living-room with me in tow, and I decided that he was in a bad humor. I established myself in a comfortable chair with a cigarette and could not, for the life of me, keep my eyes from straying to the set of fire irons.

I saw at once that both pokers were in place—and one was filmed with whitish dust.

CHAPTER SEVENTEEN

"ANYTHING wrong with the fireplace?" Briggs asked politely, and I dropped my eyes with guilty haste.

"I really don't know," I murmured with matching courtesy. "Perhaps if you consulted an architect or an interior decorator—?"

Ian came in, and Briggs turned abruptly and asked him to be seated. He wasted no words but began immediately to lead us through our recent courtship and marriage. The session did not last very long, however. Just as we were getting well into it Briggs messed up the proceedings by asking Ian if it was true that he had married me to prevent my marriage to his uncle.

Ian lost his temper and called Mabel and Briggs all the names he could think of, after which he banged out of the room in a fury.

Briggs eyed me and observed mildly, "He's mad."

I grinned back at him.

"Oh no—not really. He just remembered something he had to do somewhere else."

"Were you thinking of marrying the old man?" Briggs asked.

"No. But I've gathered that the old man and my father were thinking of it—had it practically arranged."

"Hmm. Well—now, about the family here."

I told him what I could, but I didn't actually know very much. The only thing of which I knew that was against them was their extravagance, and Briggs had heard it all before from more source; than one. He was plainly disappointed at my limited knowledge, and I gathered that his question about Ian having marked me to safeguard his uncle had been a deliberate attempt to anger me into spilling the dirt.

He let me go after a while, and I went up to my room, hoping to manage a nap before I had to leave for the hospital. It was not to be. Kelly stepped out of the clothes closet and asked in a hollow whisper, "Are you alone?"

I flopped on to the bed and groaned, " I thought I was."

"Never mind that," said Kelly severely. "I want you to get out of this room. Go out with that drip, or something)."

"You stop calling him a drip!" I shrilled angrily—and somewhat to my own surprise.

"Thanks," said Ian from the bathroom door, and I felt my face blush a deep red.

"What I call him or don't call him doesn't change what he is," Kelly said darkly while I suffered acute embarrassment. "In any case, you'll have to get out of this room."

Ian had emerged from the bathroom and was leaning against the doorjamb. "Come into mine," he suggested companionably. "I doubt if you've ever been in my room."

I looked Kelly up and down. "You can close the closet door; your vigil is over. The poker is with the rest of the fire-irons in the living-room. Briggs has been standing right beside it, but I don't think he's noticed it yet."

Kelly had left the room before I could finish speaking, and Ian, grinning faintly, wandered over and sat down on the foot of my bed.

"There's no use in your talking pretty," I said defensively. "You'll only think of something to raise your suspicions of me in half an hour or so."

He laughed and pulled himself off the bed again.

"Even drips crawl through and get to see the light eventually. The suspicions are dead."

"Splendid," I said, settling my head comfortably into my pillow. "And now if you'll take yourself off, I'll try to get some sleep."

"Certainly. I shall be in my room if you want anything. And don't forget to ask me, if you do."

He departed, and I found myself wishing fiercely that he would show up as a complete hero or an utter villain, because the indecision was killing me.

I had, perhaps, two minutes of peace and quiet before Kelly walked in, wearing a bowler hat and carrying a coat over his arm.

"You got me into a fine mess, you silly mush head. Why in hell didn't you let me know you'd told that mutt Briggs that I was off for the night? It was only by quick thinking that I got myself out of it. I had to answer a lot of his ruddy questions and then find a hat and coat so as to pretend I really was going."

"Seems to me it would have been more simple to tell him I'd made a mistake," I said yawning.

"Certainly not. I want him to think I've gone so that he won't be calling me every few minutes to bring him coffee and doughnuts."

He flung himself into a chair, the coat on to the floor, and fished a cigar from his vest pocket. He had puffed a misty blue fog around himself when Ian materialized once again at the bathroom door.

"If it's all the same to you, Kelly, I'd like my wife to get some sleep.

She has a hard night in front of her."

Kelly glared at him and then looked at me and said, "Go ahead, Miriel, have your nap."

"How in hell do you expect her to sleep with you burning bits of old rope under her nose?" Ian demanded.

"The smoke is soothing to her," Kelly said. "She can't smoke while she's sleeping, and she must miss it."

I broke it up. "What about that poker?" I asked.

Kelly nodded. "Briggs has it now—I gave it to him. But I examined it carefully first, and it's the one that was used, all right. Bloodstained and then dropped into the sand. It's been hidden somewhere where neither the police nor I could find it. I *could* have found it, of course, if I'd had time, but I didn't. Anyway, it was later replaced with the other irons—without being washed or cleaned, mind you."

"Well, why would it be cleaned?" Ian said. "Why would anyone go to a sink or washbasin with the thing, when he might so easily be seen? What would he accomplish by cleaning it, anyway?"

Kelly changed the cigar from one side of his mouth to the other while he thought up an answer to that one. "Nothing, of course," he admitted finally. "But the poker was removed from the scene of the crime, and that must have been done for a purpose."

"Purpose of putting it in my room," I suggested.

"Well, yes—probably. In which case it would be important *not* to wash it. However, since it was returned to its place by the fire I am surprised that it was not washed. That would be the usual procedure."

"The guy had to leave it somewhere," Ian said. "While he was waiting for a chance to sneak into Miriel's room with it, I mean. Before he could get back to it, some perfectly innocent person ran across it and naturally put it back where it belonged. Whoever it was didn't notice the bloodstains because they were coated with sand."

"You know," Kelly conceded, "the drip has something there."

Ian was so pleased with himself that he didn't bother about the "drip" part of it. He went on importantly, "So all we have to do is to find the innocent person who replaced the thing and ask where it was found."

"And then what have you?" asked Kelly, beginning to sneer again. "Simply a hiding place for a poker—unless you think the fellow left his monogram in the dust. Now, what I want to work on is just why that girl was killed. With everyone suddenly in possession of bags of money, it would seem senseless for anyone to kill Leslie in order to get a bit more. Especially since Richard Lang's death apparently passed as natural." He chewed the cigar around a bit and went on thoughtfully, "She left the hospital in the middle of her duties on what was to her a very important mission—and was promptly murdered. You see, she must have known something, and it came to her suddenly there in the hospital."

"But she didn't know about the feathers," I said doubtfully.

Kelly, busy studying the ceiling, said, "No."

Ian stirred and asked with mild curiosity. "Why have you brought Briggs' coat and hat up here?"

Kelly plunged to his feet with the sweat starting out on his brow. "What do you mean? I took them off that God-awful hatrack that Mabel hasn't shifted out of the front hall yet."

"It would seem a natural place for Briggs to hang his things," Ian said, enjoying a little sneer on his own account. "But perhaps you, being a detective, have inside information that he stows them under the dining-room table."

"Funny, aren't you?" Kelly muttered, mopping his brow. "Take them down for me, will you? And put them on the hat-rack again. Hurry!"

"You want me to get arrested?"

"Better you than me," Kelly said grandly. "You must see that."

Ian scooped up the hat and coat. "If questioned," he warned, "I'm going to say I wrested them from you after a terrific struggle."

He left the room, and Kelly got down to business again immediately.

"I must go up to the third floor and go through that girl's things. I know Briggs has been through everything, but he'd miss the significant items as a matter of course. I figure that there should be something in her room to explain this business. Now, I avant you to stand at the head of the stairs and give me the high sign if anyone comes—and let's go now, before that drip gets back. He'll only be underfoot."

I tried to protest, but Kelly was already pulling me off the bed. He hung on to my hand, and after a careful look up and down the hall he led me across and up the stairs to the third floor. It was pitch-dark there, and Kelly fumbled in his pocket and brought out a small flashlight.

"Why don't we just turn on the light?" I asked.

He grunted impatiently and explained, "We don't want anyone to know we're here. That's why I want you stationed at the head of the stairs. Now, if anyone starts up, you're to tiptoe to Leslie's room and whisper to me and then duck into that storage attic and hide yourself before they get to the light."

"All right," I agreed reluctantly, "but see that you hurry. It's a dull assignment."

He went on into Leslie's room, and I retreated to the head of the stairs, where I stood first on one foot and then on the other. In the end I sat down on the top step and leaned my head against the railing.

It was shortly after I had made myself comparatively comfortable that someone opened the door at the foot of the stairs and switched the light on before I could so much as move a hand.

I continued to sit there, blinking down at Ian.

"So that's what he has you doing," he said angrily. "The silly ape!"

"I'm supposed to be a lookout," I explained, "but guess I don't qualify."

Ian shook his head. "Almost any house has a light switch at the bottom of the stairs, but the jughead wouldn't think of that."

He had come up the stairs and he walked to the light and gave the bulb a few turns, which plunged us into darkness again. He asked, still with anger in his voice, "Where is he now? In Leslie's room?" and stalked off.

I heard a jumble of wrathful whispers and then nothing but the sound of drawers being opened and closed. I eased my body to a more comfortable position and then sprang to my feet with my heart thumping as I heard two heavy sets of footsteps approaching. It sounded like Briggs and a henchman, and as I flew along to Leslie's room I heard them try the switch and then start up the stairs.

I hissed a warning and crept to the unfinished attic, where I dropped down behind a trunk. I was annoyed when I realized that Ian and Kelly must have hidden somewhere else; at any rate, they had not followed me.

I was scared and cold and creepy, and I was mentally composing a sweeping repudiation of both Ian and Kelly when, quite clearly, I heard someone moaning.

CHAPTER EIGHTEEN

THE MOANS were low—almost guttural—and although they were not very loud they seemed to me to be somewhere close by. I hesitated, sweating, even though I was chilled through, and then decided that I had better call someone, whether it meant revealing myself to Briggs or not. But before I could move from my cramped position the moans stopped.

It was quiet after that—too quiet—and at last I walked over and opened the door into the hall. I was not going to stay alone in that creepy attic for another minute—no matter who saw me.

Briggs and another man were on the way downstairs, and I waited until they had gone before I advanced into the hall. Ian and Kelly emerged from an adjoining room at the same time, and Kelly seemed puzzled and uneasy.

"What did he want, anyway? Comes up here and gets something, and then goes down again. He can't have seen something here that I've missed?"

"Kelly, shut up and listen to me," I said urgently. "Come into the attic; someone's moaning there."

They both looked at me rather blankly for a moment, and then Ian took my cold hands and tried to rub some warmth into them, stopping once to feel my forehead anxiously. Kelly scowled and went into the attic, and Ian, allowing curiosity to overcome his solicitude, dropped my hands and followed him. I went to the door and watched, while Kelly threw the beam from the flashlight around.

They did not find anything, and after a minute or two I switched on the light, but the place seemed quite blank. Kelly took a quick look around and then switched the light off again.

"I see what it is, though," he said quietly. "The hot-air register over there. It isn't usual to have an outlet in the attic, and I don't know why it was put there. Still, there it is."

"Well," Ian said, rumpling his hair, "in some of these big houses they have things very complete."

"Yes, to be sure," Kelly snarled. "I wouldn't know—I'm only a slum boy. Why do you bother sticking pins into me? You have the girl."

"That's what you think," Ian said gloomily.

94

"What do you mean about the register?" I asked hastily.

"Those moans you heard were probably coming from downstairs somewhere," Kelly explained. "The sound carries through the pipes— sometimes very clearly. We'll go down and investigate."

I made off toward the stairs and said, "Then let's hurry. They sounded awful."

The two of them followed me, but I felt pretty sure that they considered the moans to be merely a symptom of my fevered condition.

I had figured that Sara's and John's room would be beneath the register, and I went straight along there and knocked. I heard a vexed exclamation from Kelly and turned around defensively, but he slid out of sight inside Uncle Richard's room. Ian, after a moment's indecision, went in after him.

There was a short delay before Sara opened her door. She wore a trailing quilted velvet robe of a dark wine color and lined with ice-blue satin, and she had been crying.

"Can I do anything for you, Sara?" I asked, feeling a bit silly, but she answered easily, "Oh no—I'm all right. Come on in and have a cigarette."

I went in and sat down while she returned to one of the beds which was disarranged and from which, apparently, she had got up to answer my knock. She threw the velvet wrap over a chair before getting into bed and then resumed a cigarette which had been smoking in a delicate little china ashtray on the bedside table.

I lighted a cigarette and eyed her, and she said without self-consciousness, "I've been having a weep. John had to go out to a patient a few minutes ago, and I've been indulging. Leslie and I didn't have much in common, God knows, but we've lived together for the last five years, and I was fond of her."

I nodded sympathetically and said, "I thought I heard you moaning." It sounded a bit awkward, and I wondered fleetingly how Kelly would have brought it in.

Sara raised her eyebrows and repeated, "Moaning? Oh no—nothing like that. Just a silent weep."

"Maybe it was Mabel in the next room?"

Sara dropped her head into the pillow and said indifferently, "Perhaps, but I haven't heard her."

I wondered whether the hot-air register in the attic could possibly be as far over as Mabel's room and decided that it could not.

"Five years!" I murmured, trying to make conversation. "I should think you'd have liked your own establishment."

Sara shook her head. "Can't stand housekeeping. Mabel loves it and runs round attending to everything—so as long as we live with her I don't have to so much as think of it."

"Well—but you can't be free to do as you like, really. I mean, I suppose if you want to entertain or anything you have to ask first."

"I do exactly as I like," Sara assured me. "Always have. I know how to handle Mabel."

"Doesn't John want a house of his own?"

"He's mentioned it once or twice," she admitted. "But so far he hasn't started strong-arming. Hope he never does."

"I think you must be unique," I said, shaking my head. "Most girls would blow up in two days if they tried to live with their in-laws."

Sara shrugged it away and asked, "Has that Briggs found out anything about poor Leslie yet?"

"I don't believe so. At least I haven't heard anything."

"But why would anyone kill her? It must have been a thug."

I thought of the poker and said in a low voice, "They've found the weapon, you know. One of the pokers from the living room."

She stared at me, and I went on, "So you see, the thug would have to be in the house."

"Well, he could have been. I don't see why not."

"He wouldn't have carried her out to the pool, though. She must have gone out there herself. No thug would follow her out to the yard just to kill her. It doesn't make sense."

Sara mopped at her eyes with a fragile handkerchief and said in a muffled voice, "What reason in the wide world was there for her to have gone out to that lily pond in the middle of the night!"

"She must have had some reason. She came rushing home, took off her coat, put on a sweater, and went on out there. It was something that seemed very important to her, I suppose."

"I guess so," Sara said doubtfully. "Of course Leslie was very fond of that lily pond. When she was little she used to walk all the way over here from her own house just to play there. She told me long ago that the stone lion was cracked, and she was afraid it might topple over at any time. She'd spoken to Uncle Richard about it, as a matter of fact, but he wouldn't do anything. Said if it looked dangerous it might keep the neighbors away from his sand pile."

"Do you know why he bought the sand?" I asked curiously. "No one seems to be able to explain it."

Sara made a scornful little face. "I haven't an idea. He was always crying out against waste, and yet he bought that sand—had a fit if the neighbors' children went near it—and then never used it."

"I'll ask Aunt Violet," I decided. "She'll probably know."

"I expect she knows," Sara said, "but I don't think she ever tells anything."

I put out my cigarette, dropped the conversation down to the weather, and finally eased out. Ian and Kelly promptly stepped out from behind Uncle Richard's door and gave me a couple of inquiring looks.

I shook my head. "I don't think she was moaning. She says not, and although she's been crying I don't think it was anything more than that."

Kelly nodded and whispered, "Try Mabel."

I went along and knocked at Mabel's door, but Dr. Benson came and said that he had given Mrs. Lang a sedative and she was sleeping. He thanked me for my solicitude and closed the door quietly after I had turned away.

Kelly gnawed his lip for a moment and said, "All right, now see what you can get out of the old lady."

Ian came with me to Aunt Violet's room, and she welcomed us in and carefully locked the door behind us.

"I keep it looked against them all the time," she explained, her pale, anxious eyes traveling from Ian's face to mine.

Ian said, "But, Aunt Violet, if you know anything about them—about any of them—you should tell the police. Poor Leslie has been murdered, and you must realize that that may not be the end."

Aunt Violet's hands began to tear agitatedly at her handkerchief, and her eyes filled up, but all she said was, "She was a sweet little girl. I used to send Annie out to her with cookies."

I asked her about the sand pile, but she looked vague and said she didn't know.

"He never used it," Ian reminded her. "That pile out in the back—he ordered it and then let it lie there."

"I don't know why he got it," she said, shaking her head. "The children played in it, you know—such a nuisance." She pressed her hand against her forehead for a moment and added, "I'm a little tired now; I believe I'd like to rest."

Ian and I stood up immediately, and as we went to the door I asked, "Were you moaning a little while ago?"

"Moaning?" she said, looking surprised. "Why, no, child. What do you mean?"

"I thought I heard someone moaning," I explained awkwardly. "I thought perhaps you were ill."

"No, no—I'm feeling well enough. It's just that I'm tired."

She unlocked the door, ushered us out, and locked up firmly behind us.

Kelly was waiting for us in the hall, and after we had reported to him he gloomed for a bit and then gave it as his opinion that progress was at a standstill. We were still thinking it over when Dr. Benson suddenly opened his door and caught Kelly fairly and squarely. He ordered coffee and toast for one, to be brought up very quietly so that Mrs. Lang would not be disturbed.

We accompanied Kelly downstairs, and Ian laughed quietly all the way. Kelly muttered curses and when we reached the kitchen flung himself into a chair and said, "Miriel, you know I can't make coffee—or toast, either. Besides, I'm doing the brainwork on this thing, and I shouldn't have to work with my hands as well."

I picked up the coffeepot, but Ian took it away from me. "Oh no," he said, giving Kelly an evil look. "The gent must learn how to make coffee—and toast. You can't always be around to smooth his way, and we don't want him to get fired, do we?"

I said no, we didn't, and eased myself into a chair. I added, as an afterthought, that as long as Kelly was making coffee I'd have a cup too. Kelly said we were taking a mean advantage of him, but after a few futile protests he began to blunder around under Ian's supervision. We sent him upstairs with the tray when everything was ready, and Ian and I settled down comfortably to our coffee.

I glanced at my watch after a while and began to hurry, and Ian said crossly, "I don't see why they can't get someone else. You ought to rest after all that's happened here or you'll be ill."

"I'm never ill," I said sadly. "I'm always waiting for a chance to climb into bed and have people wait on me hand and foot, but it never comes."

"I hope not," he said soberly. "How long is this damned appendix going to lie on his fat back while you smooth his pillow?"

"I don't know. He has plenty of money and he may want me until he goes home."

We left the dishes for Kelly to wash, and Ian drove me to the hospital in the car. He promised to pick me up in the morning, and I went on in, wishing wearily that the morning had already arrived.

They were still shorthanded on the floor and were doing some intensive phoning, but I was too tired to be interested and went on into Benjamin's room.

He looked up from his book, which I judged to be a present from Mrs. Oppenheimer, because it was one of those staid prosy travelogues and hardly the sort of thing, I thought, to take Daisy's eye.

"Ah yes. Miss—er—" he said, removing his spectacles. "I'm quite all right now—able to help myself a bit, you know. I'll have to get along without you extra nurses. Too expensive. The cost of these operations is appalling. Appalling. You run along home now and get your beauty sleep."

"I can't run home," I said meekly; "it's too far. So I'm afraid I'll have to charge you for carfare, Mr. Oppenheimer. If you had let me know in time, you see—And then, this way I've missed a night's work too. So—"

"Yes, yes, of course—carfare—certainly," he said hastily before I could start charging him for the night's work that I'd lost.

He hauled a checkbook out of the drawer of his bedside table and dashed off a cheque for what he owed me, plus twenty cents.

I glanced at it and shook my head. "I'm so sorry, Mr. Oppenheimer, I should have explained. I come and go by taxi. Forty-five cents each way, including tips. Comes to ninety cents."

He began to fume a bit. He said, "But that's absurd. Ridiculous. Girl like you riding to work in a taxi."

"The trolley makes me seasick. Taxis are expensive, of course, and what with a whole night's work shot—"

He made out another cheque and handed it over, but he did not open his mouth again, even to bid me good-night.

The floor was in a bit of an uproar, so I stayed and helped out for almost two hours until an aide appeared. She had her cap jammed down over a bun of vigorous black hair and the gleam of duty in her eye, and she listened to the supervisor's instructions with the patience of one who has heard it all before but wishes to be tolerant. When the supervisor had hurried on her starchy way I swallowed a couple of yawns and told the aide that I'd be getting along. She said good-night in the voice of one who is relieved to get the riffraff from underfoot, and I called back a warning not to fuss too much over Mr. Oppenheimer, because he was used to roughing it. After which I took myself downstairs and grandly hailed a taxi.

I had to ring the bell at the house because I still had no key, and after a while Kelly opened up for me.

"Fired for impertinence?" he asked mildly.

I explained, and he nodded without interest and then told me that he was working on the cellar, after having been through most of the house.

"Find anything?" I asked.

"Nope. But once I get this done, the rest will be easy."

He went off to the cellar again, and I climbed the stairs slowly, wondering what he meant. The second floor was so dark that I could not see and had to start groping. But I had not made three steps when I was frozen into my tracks by a succession of fearful screams.

CHAPTER NINETEEN

I FUMBLED frantically until I found the light switch and turned it on. Aunt Violet was standing at the door of her room, and she stopped screaming abruptly as soon as the light came on. She looked at me with eyes like bits of dull, blank glass and then quietly fainted.

I got her back into her room and was loosening the high old-fashioned collar when Dr. Benson, John, Sara, Ian, and even Mabel poured in behind me.

John carried Aunt Violet to the bed and then turned on the others and peremptorily ordered them out

"You know she doesn't like any of us to come in here, and you line up so that the first thing she'll open her eyes on will be a row of your faces."

They went, looking more or less offended, with the single exception of Ian, who said quietly, "She doesn't mind me."

Aunt Violet's first words were, "I thought I was followed," and her first action to reach up and straighten her wig, which was not even slightly disarranged.

She was in shock, and John sent me off to prepare a hypodermic while Ian watched in silence. When John left at last, Ian stirred and approached the bed. "Did your patient die? The appendix, I mean."

I shook my head. "He's fine—well enough to start economizing. So he began with me."

"I'm glad," Ian said simply. "You need a rest." He glanced down at Aunt Violet and added, "I wonder what she meant by that 'I thought I was followed'?"

I shrugged. "We'll find out when she's feeling better."

He looked up at me and asked, "You don't have to stay here all night, do you?"

"No, we can leave her now. She'll sleep for some time."

We went out quietly and across the hall to my room, where we found Kelly making himself comfortable in the armchair. He wanted the whole story down to the smallest details, which was impossible, because neither of us had noticed any details.

"Why didn't you show up yourself?" Ian asked. "Details are more in your line."

"How could I show up?" Kelly snapped irritably. "Mabel would have had me running for coffee and cookies to soothe their blasted nerves, and I haven't time for things like that. I was right on the stairs there, trying to keep out of sight. You say she didn't start screaming until you had reached the landing?"

"No, she didn't," I told him. "I remember it quite clearly."

Kelly went into a brown study, and Ian suggested that he go somewhere else to do his thinking. Kelly ignored him, and Ian made the suggestion again in a louder voice. Kelly continued to play dead, and at last Ian ostentatiously looked at his wristwatch. "It's over the time you gave yourself to solve this thing," he remarked, "so I'd better go and tell the police about those feathers."

Kelly flew out of his chair in a fury. "You'll do nothing of the kind," he whispered, purple in the face. "Unless you want to land Miriel in jail. If that's your object, of course, go ahead—"

"All right, all right. I just wanted to get you out of here so she could have a chance to sleep."

"But I don't want to sleep," I protested. "I'm much too restless. I don't want to lie and think about all the horrible things that have been happening. I—I want some coffee and cookies, or something."

"Then let's go down to the kitchen," Ian said agreeably, and Kelly nodded. They escorted me down the stairs, and in the kitchen Ian and I started to make the coffee, while Kelly sank into a chair and went on with his thinking

Ian glanced at him once or twice and finally asked, "Are you getting anywhere with this business yet, fella?"

Kelly looked fit to be tied and broke into speech as soon as his emotion would let him. "Maybe you'd like to hear a few things about your relatives—things you don't know. Perhaps it's news to you that your uncle Benson and your aunt Violet were a couple of rakes in their youth."

"Ooh, Kelly!" I laughed. "What you said!"

"You can laugh," Kelly said, still seething, "but listen to this. Richard was quiet, steady, stingy, and a poke. Blanche—Ian's mother—was on the staid side, too, but she married one of these poor-but-honest combinations, and Richard never forgave her. He withdrew his moral support, which was no doubt deplorable, and refused all financial aid, which was downright stinking. Benson was Richard's favorite, and for that reason he got away with more murder than any of them. He was given plenty of money while he was studying medicine, and everything was rosy until finally he went too far. He got drunk and married a burlesque queen while he was still under the influence. Richard threw him out into the snow but got over his mad after a while and started pushing patients that way, which was all he could do and still save his face. Benson set up an establishment right here in town and began to make money, and in the end he did very well."

"When did he make his second marriage?" I asked interestedly. "To Mabel, I mean."

"There was no second marriage," said Kelly. "Mabel was the burlesque queen. She and Benson settled down after the marriage and got on very well. One of those rare cases, you see, where both parties had sowed their wild oats and were willing to call it a day. Mabel bought a book on etiquette, invented relatives and ancestors who were the cream of society, and made an outstanding success of the well-to-do suburban wife."

Kelly paused, with a faraway look on his face, while Ian and I quietly placed toast and coffee in front of him and waited for him to go on.

"We come to Violet next," he said presently. "The town's glamour girl, in those days—what they called a wild one. She fell in love with an actor after a while, and her friends dared her to go and see him, so she did. They were friends for some time and then he went to London, and Violet developed typhoid. She was also going to have a child."

I gasped, and Ian asked sharply, "Can you back up that statement?"

Kelly looked at him with infinite contempt. "Listen, soldier, I'm not trying to prove it. It's one of the things I discovered because I am an investigator, and I'm trying to get all these people into proper perspective. Usually the rest is easy after that. When people have lived in a house for a number of years they're apt to leave their biographies lying around in it—if you're smart enough to read them. I can even give you a thumbnail sketch of the absent Annie.

"She was an Irish girl who spent her off hours hitting it up in the tavern of a friend of hers. Liked her beer. She came in handy, though, because she was the eldest of a swarming family and she had an early grounding in obstetrics. She helped to avoid a scandal by delivering Violet's baby—all on the quiet—and whether it was Annie or the typhoid, I don't know, but the baby died.

"Richard managed to convince Violet that her life from then on should be one of penitence. She took to it with her usual enthusiasm and became a hermit—saw no one except Richard and Annie. She kept up with her relatives and friends by mail—wanted to know all their doings and that sort of stuff—but apparently never mentioned the baby."

"Are you making it up as you go along?" Ian interrupted coldly.

"Your uncle Richard, " said Kelly slowly and distinctly, "has written every word of it into the family Bible."

"You mean it's lying around in a Bible where anyone can read it?" I asked, astounded.

"Of course not—don't be a little idiot. The old boy had hidden it, with a great deal of care, in his mattress. First place I looked, as a matter of fact. People act like a lot of silly sheep when it comes to hiding things."

"Where is it now? Have the police found it?"

Kelly shook his head. "It's in my room in the servants' wing lying carelessly on the table as though it belonged to me. They won't give it a second glance."

"Don't be so sure," Ian said. "Some of those cops have been through grade school."

"Ahh, that was only pull," Kelly yawned.

"Do you know what scared Aunt Violet so tonight?" I asked after a moment.

"Probably just hysterical. Swarms of people pouring into her house, and all that's happened—it's no wonder."

I shook my head. "She had a shock of some sort."

"She'll tell us about it when she wakes up." Ian suggested

But I was very doubtful of that and said so. "Somehow, I don't believe she'll talk about it at all."

"I heard her say she'd been followed," Kelly mused. "I figured she'd been around the house somewhere. She takes little tours of inspection at night to see what those people have done to the place, and she probably was returning from one when she saw you on the landing and thought you were a ghost. "

"No," I said, dissatisfied, "it was something more than that. I tell you, she's had a shock—a bad one."

Ian considered it for a while and reluctantly sided with Kelly. "She's none too strong in the head, Miriel—you know that. It was dark and quiet, and she saw you moving and went off the deep end."

I gave it up and decided to try to get some sleep. I went upstairs and into my room, and those two men followed me like a pair of watchdogs.

"Don't mind me," Kelly said airily. "Just want to look the room over for a few minutes."

"For Pete's sake!" I groaned. "You've seen it a hundred times. What are you looking for now?"

"Probably not important," Kelly murmured, "but I don't like to leave any stones unturned. I'm looking for the grave."

CHAPTER TWENTY

I COLLAPSED on to the end of the bed, and I'm sure my eyes were protruding, while Ian exploded, "For God's sake, man, what do you mean?"

"Surely you've been able to follow it," Kelly said. "I've told you all I know."

"Don't brag," I begged through chattering teeth. "Just unfold your brilliant mind and tell us."

Kelly shook his head and said to the bureau "I don't understand it."

"Do you want more flattery?" Ian asked, and I added, "Oh stop showing off, Kelly, and tell us."

"Keep your shirts on," Kelly said mildly. "It's the baby. The whole thing seems to have been kept an absolute secret, so that they were obliged to give it what Richard called 'a decent burial in the house.' "

"That's horrible," Ian muttered. "It means that Aunt Violet and Uncle Richard were criminals." He added belligerently, "I'd like to read that Bible for myself."

"You know where it is," Kelly said indifferently. "Go and look it over."

"But didn't the doctor who attended her for typhoid know that she was having a child?" I asked.

Kelly shrugged. "An old family fusspot, probably. Didn't like to ask any indelicate questions. And it was early days."

I was silent, thinking about it all, and Ian said presently, "I'm going down to look at the Bible. It's always possible, you know, that Uncle Richard had a vivid imagination and fancied himself as a secret novelist."

He left the room, and Kelly really outdid himself in the execution of a sneering laugh. "Some mind the poor drip has. Dear old Uncle Richard has a sneaking talent for writing, so he uses the family Bible for a scratch-pad."

"Oh, shut up!" I said wearily. "Why are you searching for that—that grave, anyway? And why in here?"

He shuffled a bit and finally admitted, "I like to prove things—no matter how sure I may be that I'm right about them. If I find that little skeleton in the house somewhere, then I'll know that I'm right about all this. I'm going through every room in the house."

"What about the attic and cellar?"

"All in good time," said Kelly, and started to lope around my room with an absorbed expression on his face.

I watched him until I found myself shuddering for the third time, when I shook myself and said firmly, "If you want to do Aunt Violet's room, now would be the time. She'll be out cold for a while."

He straightened up, dusted off his hands, and said, "Good. You come along, and then if anyone walks in on us you can be ordering me to get some more ruddy coffee. "

I pulled myself off the bed and creaked after him to the door. "That's all very well, but why would you be in her room? There's no bell pull, and I can't see you coming up to inquire how she does."

"Oh, dammit," said Kelly, "stop splitting hairs. You wanted a little fresh air for your patient and couldn't open the window, so you roused me—I had to dress, because I don't own a bathrobe, being only an impecunious houseman—and came upstairs to open it for you."

Aunt Violet was sleeping quietly. I switched on a small shaded lamp some distance from the bed, and Kelly went to work. He examined the walls and floor and the closet and then began to go through the drawers.

He was kneeling by the bottom drawer of one of the bureaus, when I heard him make a low sound of satisfaction. I hurried over and saw that he had put aside some rather fine old linens that smelled of lavender and exposed some tiny sheer dresses, delicately embroidered and obviously unused, although they had yellowed a little.

Kelly replaced the linens and closed the drawer without comment, and I glanced at Aunt Violet and was surprised to find that there were tears in my eyes.

We left shortly after that, and Kelly made for the front stairs. "You see?" he whispered. "I must find the child's body tonight."

"Aren't the little dresses proof enough?"

"Well—I have an idea that there might be something with the body."

My teeth had begun to chatter again, and I said crossly, "The house is getting cold."

"I'll get the lieutenant to go down and look at the furnace," Kelly said. "He might as well do something useful."

He had reached the living-room, and when he switched on the light I gave a little gasp.

John was stretched out on one of the sofas, fully dressed. He blinked sleepily in the light and then sat up.

" 'Sa time?"

"About four-thirty," I told him, "but I left my watch upstairs. I've been trying to open a window and couldn't budge it, so I got Kelly up," I turned around and added, "Now that you're up, Kelly, would you mind making some coffee?"

"Yes, madam," said Kelly, putting on a dead pan. "And you, sir?"

John nodded and Kelly departed with a swagger, evidently figuring that he could get Ian to attend to the coffee making.

"Strictly speaking," said John, running a hand over his tumbled hair, "I should be upstairs and in bed. But what's the use? I no sooner bed down in comfortable and correct—always correct—gent's nightwear, than the phone rings and I have to go out in the cold to calm the fears of some fool with a bellyache. Tonight I decided to stay dressed so that I might fly on the wings of Mercury as soon as the calls came in. "

I laughed and tried not to laugh too heartily, because it seemed pretty obvious that he and Sara had had a row, and probably she had locked him out.

John had been looking at me and he said slowly, "It seems to me that you were on one of my cases. Yes, by God! What about Mr. Oppenheimer?"

"He fired me. His expenses are bothering him. And as far as that goes, he has some that you and even Mrs. Oppenheimer—don't know about."

John said, "My God!" rubbed his forehead, and gave his head a violent shake. "Who's on the floor?"

I told him that the supervisor was flitting hither and you, but an aide with a tightly skewered bun of hair had the situation well in hand— particularly in regard to Mr. Oppenheimer. It was probable, I added, that even now she had a foot planted firmly on Mr. Oppenheimer's chest.

John said, "My God!" again, and gloomed at the floor.

"Most important patient I ever had," he muttered presently.

"Oh, nuts!" I said impatiently. "If he doesn't want to be specialed at night, that's up to him. And if he develops complications of gout or leprosy and dies, it's all gravy for his relatives. Only Daisy would be peeved."

"Who's Daisy?" asked John.

"Daisy is neither here nor there. The point is, Benjamin K. is going to pare your fee down to the lower-middle-class bone—and you might as well face it."

John stretched out on the couch again and closed his eyes, but he was grinning faintly. "You are quite right, " he said simply. "I am making about half the money that Sara spends, which is quite a healthy sum. And so to hell with Benjamin K. If he lives through the night I shall snap my fingers in his face tomorrow morning."

I laughed until I realized that it was too loud and too long, when I stopped abruptly with a violent hiccup.

John did not even open his eyes. "Hold it," he said mildly.

Ian came in, followed by Kelly who bore a loaded tray. Kelly, however, did not look happy, and I was sure that something had happened to anger him. He lowered the tray on to a coffee table beside John and said fiercely, "Your coffee, sir."

John opened his eyes, and they fell on Ian. "Name of God!" he exclaimed in astonishment. "What gives? No telephone calls to stop you people from sleeping all night long, so you sit around at five in the morning having a coffee party."

Kelly, after nearly making the mistake of sitting down with us, caught himself in time and stalked out of the room. I drew a chair up to the table and said chattily, "This is about my third coffee party tonight."

"My wife seems to be extremely restless, " Ian observed rather formally. "She's presumably looking after Aunt Violet, who apparently doesn't need her, but she should be getting some sleep."

"It is not Aunt Violet who is on her mind," John said, gazing into his coffee. "If I were you I'd keep a sharp eye on Kelly, who cheerfully forsakes his couch in the small hours to open a window. I think she has a crush on Kelly, and you're butting in." He finished with an almost raucous laugh, and I realized for the first time that he was very drunk.

Ian saw it, too, and said, "Drink your coffee, John, and get the hell to bed."

I watched John drain his cup and thought, "He holds his liquor too well—one of those. Very hard to tell when he's under the influence."

He put down his cup with a faint crash and looked very earnestly at Ian.

"You have a telephone in your room, Lieutenant, have you not? Be a great help to me—very valuable. As things are, I am obliged to swear my way out into the hall every time the damned thing rings. Suppose we change around? You and Miriel take our room, and we'll move into your suite. Be a help to poor little Sara too—I can get out without disturbing her. She needs her sleep these days, you know—hospital work and bridge on her free days. Her bridge has fallen off lately, I'm afraid, and we feel the curtailment of revenue."

"All right," Ian said hastily. "Better not air the details—you don't know us very well. We'll change rooms tomorrow; I shall see to it personally."

John finished off his second cup of coffee. "Good!" he murmured. "You explain to Sara, will you? Make a diplomatic approach because she might refuse if—"

"If what?" I asked when he stopped.

"Just if. I have finished my coffee, and I want to get back to sleep—so you two bung off."

Ian gathered the tray together and started for the kitchen, and I tagged along.

"What makes you so tidy?" I asked idly.

"My mother's training. She always said that you could never tell when it might come in handy, and you see, it has. Our private investigator would have been fired out of here on his—er—long ago if I hadn't been here to do the ghost work."

"You'd better think of some reason to go back on that promise you made John about changing rooms."

He said, "No. We move into that room tomorrow, and your only alternative is to go running home to Father. I may be a drip, since Kelly seems so sure of it, but I am not a weak drip—I am a big, loud, strong drip."

I laughed and murmured, "Oh well—tomorrow is another day. But I want to find out what Kelly is up to."

Ian put the tray on to one of the hall tables and took me firmly by the shoulders. "You're going to bed. Kelly can do his work quite well by himself, and you need rest and sleep—and, incidentally, I'd like to get a little myself."

He ran me up the stairs and into my room. "Now, I'll give you five minutes to get undressed and into bed—and I mean it. "

He walked through the bathroom to his room, and I looked down at the bed and lost all interest in Kelly's doings in a sudden desire for sleep. I shed my clothes, crawled in between the sheets, and was vaguely conscious that Ian had stuck his head into the room and then withdrawn before I went out.

I was awakened slowly and painfully by a nagging, persistent ringing at the front-door bell. I lay for some time listening to it, until it was borne in upon me that no one else had any intention of answering it and that the person who was ringing wasn't going to give up either.

I dragged on my ruined negligee and crept down the stairs. It was cold and gloomy, and halfway down I almost turned around and went back, but another strident peal of the bell sang through my ears, and I went on and opened the door.

An elderly woman, badly dressed and with a battered suitcase, stood on the mat. She slipped through the partially opened door and said timidly, "I'm Annie Finnergan."

CHAPTER TWENTY-ONE

I STEPPED BACK and said uncertainly, "Oh—well, I m sure Miss Lang will be glad to see you back."

She gripped the battered suitcase firmly and said, "I'll be getting along to my room—I'll want to settle in—and then I can see Miss Violet later."

"There's a houseman and another maid," I explained, walking toward the kitchen with her. "One of them may have your room, and if so, I expect you'd better go up to the third floor."

"No, I'll not. I want me own room. We won't be needin' those others now I'm back—they can take themselves off."

I raised my eyebrows and followed her through the kitchen to the servants' wing, where she opened one of the doors.

Kelly, fully clothed, lay snoring on the bed.

Annie dropped her bag on to the floor, but it landed on a rug, and Kelly snored on. I mentally sneered at an investigator who could sleep through two alien presences in his room and then sneered again because he had given up his search just to catch a little sleep. Unless he had found the grave.

I turned away quickly and went back to the kitchen, and Annie followed close at my heels. She had removed her hat and coat and was tying an apron around her waist.

"Would you like a nice cuppertea?" she asked amiably

"God, no!" I groaned. "I'm awash as it is."

I decided that she and Kelly could fight it out and left her to it. As I went through the front hall the telephone shrilled out at me, so I snatched it up, and an agitated lady informed me that she wanted Dr. John Lang immediately. She would not wait while I wrote down the name and address, so I repeated it over to myself all the way to the living-room, where I found John still sleeping on his couch.

I finally aroused him by shouting the name and address three times into his ear, and he came to the surface with a dark scowl. He gave me a look that placed me as a nurse instead of a cousin-in-law and asked crossly, "Couldn't you get more information?"

"You're lucky to have that much."

"All right," he said curtly. "Thank you."

"Not at all—my thought was entirely for the patient. Annie's out in the kitchen, by the way—she'll give you a nice cuppertea."

"Annie!" he repeated sharply. "Who told her she could walk herself in here again? Mother has filled her place, and it's my guess that she'll bundle her out within a hour."

"What do you mean?" I asked, matching his tone. "Annie has been the only companion Aunt Violet has had for many years. It would be mean and cruel to try to separate them now."

"Remind me," said John, narrowing his eyes a little, "to hand my conscience over to you." He yawned, rumpled his hair, and stood up. "Maybe the old fool will dish me up some breakfast."

He walked rather unsteadily toward the kitchen, and I went on upstairs, thinking that Sara could have him and welcome—even though he was good-looking and successful. I wondered if she minded his tempers and decided that she did not. She had a happy faculty for getting along with people and for letting troublesome things roll easily off her back.

I went back to bed, determined to sleep through everything as Kelly seemed to be doing. At that I slept until ten o'clock, when Mabel came in and woke me.

Her eyes were red, and her face had sagged into tired lines. "I'm sorry, Miriel, but I'm afraid you'll *have* to get up. The police are here and they want to talk to you, and I'm simply at my wit's end. Sara's sick, and John and Benson are at the hospital, and that nice cook I took so much trouble to get has left. Annie and Kelly are having a fight in the kitchen, and I simply have not the strength to go and interfere. I'm not well—not well at all. Ian brought me some breakfast, but now the police have him, asking questions. That terrible Briggs says he'll question me next, but I want someone with me."

She dropped into a chair and dissolved into tears, but I could not convince myself that her trouble was not more remorse than grief, as far as Leslie was concerned.

I rolled out of bed and got a washcloth soaked in cold water from the bathroom. I patted it gently over Mabel's face and then told her that Leslie would have expected her to be brave and that she'd better go and make up her face because she looked a sight.

She mopped up her eyes, sighed, and said she supposed I was right—after which she trotted off quite briskly. I echoed her sigh, loudly, and began to dress in a hurry. I wanted to see Kelly and to find out if he had discovered anything, but I reminded myself to look in on Aunt Violet first.

She was still in bed, but awake, staring at the ceiling and occasionally mumbling to herself. I approached her rather anxiously, but she turned her head and spoke quite rationally to me. "Come in, dear, and sit down. I'm feeling much better because Annie's back, you know. She cooked me such a nice breakfast—just the way I like it. I haven't eaten so well for a long time."

She looked better certainly, even though her wig was a trifle crooked, and I sat down feeling somewhat relieved about her. "What frightened you last night?" I asked curiously. "You were in a bad way."

She gave a faint, silvery little laugh. "I must be getting old and foolish, my dear, but I keep fearing that Richard will come back to reproach me with not having visited him at the hospital when he was ill. I was out there in the hall and I thought I saw a ghost at the head of the stairs, but this morning Ian told me it was only you and that I must not be nervous and silly."

"I'll have to be more careful about how I creep around in the dark," I said smiling at her. "I'll hang some bells around my neck, and then you'll know I'm coming. But why were you out in the hall? You have your own bathroom in here. "

She dropped her eyes, and her hands moved restlessly on the sheet. Her face colored faintly before she said, "I had not eaten my dinner, and I thought I'd better get a glass of milk for myself. They haven't been giving me the things I like to eat, you see, and I ought to try to keep my strength up. I was just starting out when I saw this white shape in the hall—"

She gave a little shiver, and I said hastily, "But you said something about being followed. 'I thought I was followed.' "

She gave me a blank look and shook her head. "I'm afraid I don't understand."

I left her looking quite comfortable and peaceful, but I felt oddly dissatisfied and generally out of sorts.

Mabel was in the hall, and she looked renewed and fortified. She had given herself a thorough overhaul, and I looked at the result with admiration. Ex-burlesque queen she might be, but her face, hair, clothes, and accent were a credit to the blue-blooded ancestors she had created for herself.

She laid a well-kept hand on her bosom and said, "I shall try to keep going—I feel that I must. I should be on my back this minute, but Sara always manages to retire to her bed first, and we can't all give up, for somebody must manage when the household is as large as this."

She had plenty of assurance too, I thought, still lost in admiration. And probably the aristocratic forebears were vastly more real to her than the old burlesque days.

"Sara is absolutely no use, anyway," she went on, letting off steam. "She never was. But of course it complicates things and makes more work when she invariably gets sick as soon as there is something extra to be done. But no one shows any particular consideration—things left lying around all over the place. It would cut the work in half if people would put things away as soon as they have finished with them."

I was tempted to ask her if the poker was one of the things she had found lying around—and where—but I was afraid it might start her tears rolling again, so I refrained.

We went downstairs together, and the doorbell rang three times before we made the lower hall. Neither Annie nor Kelly appeared, so I went and opened the door myself, although I heard Mabel say "Tch" behind me.

Father stood on the mat with a brown paper parcel which I recognized as my laundry. I very nearly forgot myself and said, "Tradesmen's entrance in the rear," but managed to swallow it. Father stepped in and kissed me tenderly because he knew Mabel was looking. "A little present I picked up for you, honey. Don't open it now—take it upstairs." I tucked it under my arm and reflected that he never gave us credit for having any brains. "I just can't imagine what it is," I said, squeezing it experimentally. "I can hardly wait."

But Father was already greeting Mabel with the right blend of restrained sympathy and admiration for her fortitude. Mabel sucked it in like a sponge and invited him into the music room, and he followed her with head slightly bowed and sympathetic understanding dripping out of his ears. I knew they'd prefer to drool on without me, so I murmured to Father that I'd be along to see him in a day or so and then went out to the kitchen.

Annie was washing dishes at the sink and gave me a look of mild astonishment over her shoulder as I slumped into a chair.

"I'd like some coffee and toast," I said wearily.

She shook water and soapsuds from her hands and dried them on her apron. "You'd better to be having a nice cuppertea," she suggested, eying the kettle.

"No, no coffee, please."

She shook her head at my perverted taste but got out the coffee percolator and then spread a clean napkin over the end of the table in front of me.

"How did you find Miss Violet?" I asked idly.

"Well—"

She frowned at the toaster, and I said in some surprise, "I know she's very thankful to have you back. Aren't you glad to be here?"

"Ah, sure I'm glad to be here. It ain't that." She hesitated, turned the toast over, and added, "But it looks to me like the poor old soul ain't long for this world."

"Who's her regular doctor?" I asked after a moment's silence.

She put my breakfast in front of me and went to lean comfortably against the sink.

"That's just it, Mrs. Miriel—she ain't got a regular doctor. Haven't I talked to her till me tongue's dry and Mr. Richard, too—and we might as well have argued with the sofa. No matter how sick she got it was the same thing: 'Sure, Annie, you can take care of me, and I'll get well if I'm just careful.'

"Now, here about two years back, she's standin' at the window, when, glory be to God, she falls flat on the floor. Mr. Richard was home and yells at me to get a doctor, so I run across the street for that young fella with a brand-new shingle—off to the war he is, now—and he come along and says she has the high blood pressure and she has to be careful. She wouldn't have him again and kept sayin' she felt fine, but she couldn't get around the way she used to. She'd try doin' the dustin' like before, and I'd have to go around after her and do it properly."

She looked off over my head, and a gleam appeared in her eye. "Maybe I can get this Kelly trained so things'll be easier."

"That's what you think," I mumbled into my coffee, and added more clearly, "Where is Kelly?"

"Down in the cellar. He'd be snoring yet if I hadn't woke him at nine."

Kelly opened the cellar door as she finished speaking and said, "Annie, go upstairs and see whether your mistress needs anything."

Annie said, "Yes," almost added "sir," and flew to do his bidding.

He gave a quick glance around the kitchen and then walked over and spoke against my ear.

"Not only was I doped last night, but that Bible was stolen from my room."

CHAPTER TWENTY-TWO

"DOPED!" I exclaimed. "So that's why you were sleeping like a pig!"

He made an impatient movement with his arm. "Never mind the doping. But that Bible must be found, and the sooner the better. You'll have to help me, because we must get it before Briggs stumbles over it. I've searched the cellar, and I'm going to start on this floor now, although it means playing hide-and-seek with Mabel while I do it. Now, you go on up to the second floor and be sure you make a thorough job of it—don't just wander around looking under beds and behind doors. It's easy enough to spot a great big black Bible."

"Well, all right. But I don't like that business of your being doped. I don't understand—"

"Oh, damn your one-track mind!" Kelly exploded. "I wish I'd never mentioned it—except that I knew you'd be snooping into why I slept so deeply and so late. If you must know, I took the blasted pill by mistake. I meant to take an aspirin and I swallowed one of my own knockout pills instead. I always have them with me when I'm working on a case to use on other people if it becomes necessary. I only wish I could ram one of them down Mabel's throat. Now get along upstairs, will you? And don't mention this pill business again, because it embarrasses me."

I went off like a lamb and took the back stairs to avoid Briggs, but I ran into Annie, who was somewhat indignant.

"Sure, Miss Violet didn't need me at all—peaceful as a baby, the poor old soul. But I'm thinkin' that Kelly one is cracked, Mrs. Miriel. Orderin' me to go flyin' around the place—and he don't do a hand's turn himself."

"He used to be a butler with a large staff under him," I explained, feeling clever, "and naturally it's hard for him to adjust himself."

She clicked her tongue and looked impressed, and I passed her by hastily and went on up to my room. I made a quick, thorough search and then went through and did Ian's room, but I did not find the Bible. Sara and Aunt Violet were in their rooms so that I could not do them, but I flew around Mabel's room, stopping only to wipe the moisture from my brow and wondering what on earth I could say if she caught me.

I had left Uncle Richard's room to the last because I disliked going

114

in there, but I forced myself to slip inside and closed the door quietly behind me. It was neat and orderly, and his various personal posses- sions had not been put away. I went over and lifted a corner of the bedspread and found that it had been draped over the bare mattress. There was a long gash in the centre of the mattress and a hollowed place beneath where Kelly had found the Bible. It had not been re- placed, however, so I draped the spread smoothly again and began a thorough search of the room.

I did not find the Bible, but far back in the closet I came upon two bags of cement—one opened and partially emptied.

I sat down and, resting my elbows on my knees and my chin on my hands, I frowned at the carpet and tried to think it out.

Sand in the yard and cement in the closet. Richard had been mix- ing concrete—a secret repair job of some sort. The baby's grave.

I shivered and glanced nervously around the room. It must be the grave—probably it had cracked—and it must be on the second or third floor, or he'd have put the cement in the cellar. Probably Aunt Violet knew nothing about it, since she had not known why he'd ordered the sand. But somebody, I thought feverishly, was still working on the thing, because that shovel had been thrown from the third floor—a shovel for the sand—and someone had been pouring water up there above my bedroom—water and sand and cement for a concrete mix.

I left the room, determined to go over every inch of the attic, but Mabel bore down on me in the hall and declared querulously that she had been looking everywhere for me.

"Your father wants to speak to you, and that man Briggs also. They're talking together now—your father seems to know him."

"Oh well, naturally. Father knows everyone."

Her forehead creased into a perplexed frown, and she said, "Yes, I know—you told me. But I asked the Bartons and the Harpers, and they don't know your father at all."

"He's not very familiar with the middle classes," I admitted going off downstairs. "He considers them dull."

Mabel stuck her head over the banister and called after me, "I don't understand you, Miriel. The Bartons and the Harpers are not middle class."

Ian was in the lower hall, and as soon as he saw me he said immedi- ately, "Miriel, I don't like this damned setup. I think we're skating on thin ice, and we ought to tell Briggs about those feathers at once."

I sent a quick glance around and whispered urgently, "Just wait a little, won't you? Until this afternoon. I—I think we're getting some- where."

"That's just what I'm afraid of," he said grimly. "I think you're getting straight into trouble. I wish you'd leave the investigating to the
police. Kelly promised to make good by 3 A.M., and he's still skulking
around with a magnifying glass and a toupee."

"Yes, I know, but he—er—got tangled up in the tools of his trade.
But listen, I promise faithfully to tell Briggs everything if you'll just wait
a few more hours."

"I won't wait many more," he declared ominously. "It's stupid and
dangerous."

"Perhaps it is. But I still don't like the idea of being dragged off to
jail."

I could hear hearty masculine laughter from the direction of the
living-room, so I left Ian and went in to find Father and Briggs telling
each other dirty jokes. They shut up at once as soon as they saw me and
gave me a couple of silent stares.

"What did you want to see me about, Father?" I asked impatiently.

"Oh yes, yes, yes," he said, and cleared his throat. "I understand
that Miss Lang was moving to my home. I hardly expected her yesterday, of course, after the grievous tragedy, but I should like to know if I
may welcome her soon. I am holding her accommodations."

"I'll find out and phone you," I said uncertainly. "Unless you want
me to go up and ask her now?"

"Go up now," said Father, giving me a fishy eye. "I'll wait."

"I'll go with you," Briggs announced, settling his cuffs. "I've been
wanting to talk to Miss Lang."

I hesitated and said doubtfully, "She isn't very well, you know, and
she's abnormally shy of strangers. Couldn't you postpone it?"

Briggs took my arm and said, "Come on—you can ease her along,
and I'll drift around on the outskirts and insinuate a question or two
when she isn't looking."

We went out of the room, and Father followed more slowly. I heard
him slap Ian on the back and ask how the blushing bridegroom felt,
but Briggs' heavy footsteps prevented me from hearing Ian's reply. At
Aunt Violet's door I knocked and tried to enter, but she had locked
herself in again. She opened up for me and then tried to shut the door
again as soon as she saw Briggs. He put his foot into it, however, and
said pleasantly, "Just a few questions, please, Miss Lang, and then I shan't
have to bother you again."

She backed away with a look of fear, and I brushed past Briggs and
put my arm around her shoulders.

"Don't worry about him," I said soothingly. "He looks savage, but
he doesn't actually bite."

Briggs looked hurt, and Aunt Violet stammered, "But I—I don't know him, my dear. Who is he?"

"Nobody in particular." I urged her into a chair and sat down close beside her, which left a low petit-point stool handy for Briggs.

I touched it with my toe and said, "You'd better sit down, Mr. Briggs."

He hesitated, but he seemed slightly in awe of Miss Violet even though she was behaving like a scared rabbit, and at last he lowered his weight on to the stool and sat there, balancing awkwardly.

"Miss Lang," he began gravely, "where were you the night before last?"

She looked at him vaguely and then turned her head and spoke directly to me. "I went out yesterday—we had Richard's funeral, you know—so many flowers; the perfume made me quite faint. And then I went out again—I took a taxicab. I don't go out very much usually, but just lately—"

"Yes, yes," Briggs said, being patient until it hurt, "but I mean the night before last. What did you do then?"

She was still looking at me so I explained gently, "Not last night, Aunt Violet, but the night before. Did you go out?"

"Oh no, my dear—that was the night I took the pill. I remember it quite well. I haven't been sleeping very well, what with Annie sulking and all those people in my house, so I took a pill to make me sleep. I was nervous, you see, and I felt it my duty to go to the funeral, but I know I would not sleep all night long if I did not take a pill."

Briggs looked a bit blank, so I explained, "Miss Lang took something to make her sleep that night, because she was nervous about having to go to the funeral the following day."

Briggs cleared his throat. "And how was the funeral, Miss Lang? Did all those people bother you too much?"

"Well, I—I kept my veil on—my long black veil—and I did not answer anyone who spoke to me."

"I see." Briggs unobtrusively shifted his position on the stool and made a faint, involuntary face of pain.

"Now, to get back to the night before last. Did you sleep right through, or were you disturbed at any time?"

Aunt Violet, so nervous that she couldn't seem to listen to anything Briggs said, turned her faded old eyes to me for enlightenment.

"That night you took the pill," I said. "Did you sleep all right?"

"Oh yes, indeed. I always sleep when I take one of those pills."

Briggs wanted to see the pills, so she brought a small green circular bottle from the bathroom and shook some into her palm.

"Where did you get them, Aunt Violet?" I asked.

She spilled some on to the carpet, and while Briggs and I were picking them up she explained faintly that the doctor had given them to Richard last summer. He had broken his wrist, and for a while the pain kept him awake at night.

When the pills were restored to their bottle Briggs settled back for further questioning, but Aunt Violet gave up any attempt to answer him at that point. She sat and twisted her hands together in an agonized fashion, and at last the tears began to slip over her cheeks. Briggs took himself off then in a bit of a hurry.

I soothed her until she stopped crying and then asked about Father's rooms.

"Oh no, child, not now. I shall let him know later. All these dreadful things—I shall have to wait until I am more settled."

"Look here," I said firmly, "I think you ought to go back to bed. "

"Oh no—no, no. I am going to read my book. I'm all right if people will only leave me alone."

Well, there seemed to be some truth to that, so I presently took myself off. I heard her lock the door after me, and I went on down and told Father to forget about the rooms until she got in touch with him. However, he brushed me aside with a wave of his hand. He was telling Mabel about Queen Victoria's funeral—the inside story—and she was popeyed.

Ian was not around to bother me about the feathers, so I went upstairs again and on to the attic. I had forgotten about the Bible for which I was supposed to be searching. I was looking, now, for some evidence of cement mixing.

I went to the unfinished attic and to the spot which I judged to be directly over my bedroom. I glanced around, and almost immediately I spotted a battered-looking bucket standing behind an old cedar chest. It had been used for mixing cement, all right—the inside was caked with it. I looked around frowning. Trunks, old magazines, old bits of furniture, and several dusty cedar chests. I opened the lid of the one that had half concealed the bucket, and my heart seemed to turn over.

I had found the little grave.

CHAPTER TWENTY-THREE

MY FIRST IMPULSE was to bang the lid down and run away, but I suppose it was morbid curiosity rather than courage that kept me there.

The chest was filled with cement which had been smoothed off flush near the top, and I recognized it as an amateur job because I had seen Father's cement work around our own house. This had cracked right across the top and neatly halved the word "Eliza" which Richard had evidently printed all those years ago. I could imagine him solemnly making those marks in the wet cement after he had finished the gruesome business, grimly giving the dead baby a plain old name in stern defiance of her disgraceful birth.

I closed the lid and turned away. Out in the hall I lighted a cigarette and sat down in a chair to recover myself, while a host of confused thoughts banged at my brain. Richard had ordered a large pile of sand and two bags of cement to repair a crack in that tiny grave? And then he had broken his wrist and couldn't do it—and finally never did it at all. But there must have been an interval after the wrist healed and before he contracted pneumonia, so why didn't he do it then? And why order too much sand and too much cement, when he never wasted a penny on anything else? He must have had another repair job to do, and somebody was doing it for him. But Annie had returned only this morning, and he was unlikely to have confided in the Langs. Aunt Violet did not seem to know anything about it, and if Annie's report on her health was true, she certainly was not physically capable of mixing cement.

I flicked ashes on to the floor, automatically spraying them around as I did at the hospital.

The cement, I reflected, was being mixed at night and in secret, and I supposed it was possible that Richard had confided in Benson and told him to take care of the job without letting anyone know. Perhaps Benson had botched the first mix as Father often did—and thrown it away. Only where had he thrown it? A bucketful of wet cement is not so easily disposed of.

I gave up the problem, put out my cigarette, and went back into the attic. I searched it thoroughly, but I did not find the Bible, nor was there a discarded cement mix or any evidence of a cement-repair job. But the bucket was there, and I felt morally certain that I had heard

119

cement being mixed in it a few nights before. I frowned at the thing and realized that it was not big enough for a job like filling up the entire cedar chest, and yet no attempt had been made just to fill in the crack.

I took a long breath, gave my head a violent shake, and went out into the hall, where I bumped into Kelly.

"Lunch impends, " he said with a certain amount of manner. "You'd better go down—I'll finish here."

"But don't you have to hand the food around in a white coat? Or is Mabel slipping?"

"The food is handed around on plates," said Kelly, getting funny. "And if Mabel ever slips it will be because she has stepped on a banana peel. It is a buffet lunch because the household is still disorganized— and Annie doesn't like me to work in the kitchen with her, because she says it makes her self-conscious. So I told her I'd see to the cleaning."

"I hate that even more than messing in the kitchen," I said sourly.

Kelly looked a bit blank, so I led him into the attic and showed him the bucket and the cedar chest. I told him of my rather complicated thoughts on the matter, and he assumed a faint, patronizing smile.

"Suppose you allow me to do the thinking, little girl—that's what you're paying me for."

"You can write it," I said coldly, "either on the ice or your cuff."

"You go on down to lunch," Kelly said. "The Bible is up here or it's in the room of one of those dames who won't come out."

"I've done this attic," I told him. "You can do the other rooms up here, and I'll see to Sara's and Aunt Violet's."

I went downstairs and caught a glimpse, in the dining-room, of Sara being seated by Ian, so I raced up again and searched her room— but the Bible was not there.

As I emerged into the hall I ran into Ian, who said crossly "Where on earth have you been? I've looked everywhere. Lunch is half over." He took my arm and more or less dragged me downstairs. "Not that it matters if it gets cold—it's lousy, anyway. Seems Uncle Richard always said Annie couldn't cook."

"I believe she makes a nice cuppertea," I said meekly.

Father was still with us, and he and Mabel were still absorbed in conversation. I wondered fleetingly if Dr. Benson would begin to show pique—and then discovered that he and John were not there. Sara was pale and looked worried. She gave me a watery little smile as I sat down and then went on pushing her food around the plate and not eating it.

I ate heartily. The food was plain, but it seemed palatable enough to me.

"What do you get in the Army," I asked Ian, "that you sneer at this?"

He shrugged. "When I'm in the Army I forget all about food—I'm too busy."

Father turned and gave us his attention.

"My boy, you may think the life is hard in this Army, but you should have been in the *last* war. We—"

"They had to get up earlier in the morning," I said. "They wore putters, and it took time to wind them on."

"A colonel did not wear putters, " said Father, silently daring me to remind him that he had been a private. He added scathingly, "Middle-aged reminiscences are boring to youth, no doubt, so suppose you amuse us with a lively account of how you cut Mr. Benjamin Oppenheimer's toenails."

"I'll do just that," I said ominously, "if you don't shut up."

Mabel clicked her tongue and murmured, "Miriel, my dear!"

Father turned to her, opened his big mouth, and put his foot right in it. "You know how it is with grown daughters today, Mrs. Lang."

Mabel, of course, was instantly reminded of Leslie and was so overcome that she had to leave the table with her handkerchief before her face.

Father looked a bit crestfallen, but, as usual, something happened almost immediately to restore his self-confidence.

Sara asked him to go shopping with her during the afternoon.

"Mrs. Lang wants to go into mourning, and I shall need some dark things myself. I promised her to do it today, and I don't want to go alone."

Father was delighted, of course, and I wondered how Sara had known he would be—except that men were an all-important subject to her, and she probably knew it backward. I thought it would have seemed more natural for her to have asked me to go with her, but Sara was nearly always accompanied by a man wherever she went, and although Father seemed merely an old goat to me, I supposed he looked like an escort to Sara in these trying times when males were so scarce.

As it happened, Briggs caught Sara before she could get out the front door and gathered her in for questioning. Father had to wait in the hall, and I tried to sneak up the stairs behind him, but he caught me and stuck me for three dollars, which was what I had been afraid of. Immediately afterward he stuck Ian for five.

"You shouldn't be such a sucker," I said to Father disgustedly. "She'll use you a few times until the boys come back and then you'll simply be personnel of the chorus."

Father merely looked bored. He said, "Run along, Miriel. I learned not to put all my eggs in one basket before you were born."

I went up the stairs, and Ian followed close behind me. When we reached the top he said, "Now, where's Kelly? I don't want any more fooling with this thing—it's too dangerous."

I led the way to the third floor, but my heart sank when I saw Kelly. He was sitting on the same chair in which I had meditated after finding the grave. My mind had gone around in circles, and it seemed pretty obvious to me that Kelly's mind was going around in circles too.

He glanced up as we approached and simply went on with the conversation that had been interrupted when I went down to lunch.

"You see, what I can't figure is why the poker was used. Someone was preparing to do a small cement mix in the bucket and so had the shovel out there at the sand pile. Leslie learns something, or thinks of something, and comes boiling home from the hospital. The routine was to be: sand from the pile in the yard, then up to Richard's closet for the cement, and finally on to the third-floor bathroom for a pitcher of water—there is a pitcher there; I looked—mix the stuff, and then— blank."

"Yes, but—"

"But," said Kelly, "on this particular night Leslie comes flying out to the sand pile and confronts the guy, so she's hit over the head with the shovel to shut her up. Except that it turns out to be a poker, instead."

He sighed and slumped down in the chair, and I said, " You're dumb, Kelly. If you were picking one of those fireirons from the rack in a hurry it would be quite possible to get the poker instead of the shovel. The tops are all alike."

Kelly leaped up and said intensely, "That's it—that must be it. I'll go on that assumption."

"Wait a minute," Ian broke in. "You're both way ahead of me. What are you talking about?"

Kelly was impatient, but I explained the latest developments, and Ian said thoughtfully, "Leslie didn't know about the feathers, though, so what was she confronting your cement mixer with?"

"I know, I know," Kelly muttered. "It was something else—something wrong or out of line. As a matter of fact, perhaps it *was* a feather."

"Maybe," I agreed. "After all, there were plenty of them in the hall— she had only to take one."

"We're getting off the track," Kelly declared. "Too much speculating. Now, what was the last thing Leslie said to you that night? Or you to her?"

"I don't know," I said feebly. "I remember I told her I'd seen a man's moustache fall off into his soup."

"It did not fall into my soup, "said Kelly, offended. "You're getting to be just like your father—the old liar!"

"Keep a civil tongue in your head," said Ian. "Did you find that Bible?"

"No," Kelly grunted. "I've been all through here."

"Then it must be in Aunt Violet's room."

"I'll eat my hat if it's there," Kelly said, rubbing a fist across his forehead. "I don't suppose she knew Richard kept it, and she certainly wouldn't know that I had it. She doesn't leave her room now the way she used to—stays locked inside and eats whatever food is brought to her."

Ian nodded and said in a troubled voice, "I went in to see her this morning, and she told me that she didn't think she had many hours to live—because she knew now what Leslie had known."

CHAPTER TWENTY-FOUR

THERE was a brief silence, and then Kelly said with elaborate sarcasm, "I suppose it didn't occur to you to ask her what she knows?"

"Don't be an ass," Ian begged. "If I asked her once I asked her a dozen times. I pleaded and I threatened, but she wouldn't budge. She kept saying I'd be in danger, too, if I knew what she did. I tried to point out that I could take the information to the police and make us both safe, but she wouldn't listen."

Kelly groaned. "No finesse. That's the trouble with you amateurs—no finesse at all. Miriel, you'll have to dig it out of her. Wear her down—but get it, and get it as soon as you can. Stay with her all night if you have to, but don't come away without it."

"All right," I sighed, "but remember to knock a bit off the fee for this."

Kelly said, "What difference does it make what I put on or take off the bill? To be sure. I'll send one, but I never heard of your family paying any bill that wasn't presented by the sheriff. And the sheriff and I are not speaking."

"Now, look here, Kelly " Ian began sharply, and was interrupted by the opening of the door at the foot of the stairs.

Mabel called, "Kelly!" and then looked up and saw me preparing to descend. "Oh, Miriel. Have you seen Kelly? Is he up there? All the work to be done, and Annie refuses to leave the kitchen."

"Why, yes, he's here," I said, glancing over my shoulder. "I came here to get something, and it was so dirty that I got him up to clean it out a bit."

Mabel settled her bosom and said, "I'm sure that isn't necessary right now. Suppose you leave the housekeeping details to me—I'm quite capable of managing them as I have for the past thirty years. It won't do for both of us to be running things."

"Yes, of course," I murmured. "I quite see your point. It's just that I'm used to Father's immaculate house, and it never occurred to me that you wouldn't want this cleaned up immediately."

Ian stirred and said, "Kelly, Mrs. Lang wants you downstairs."

Mabel was still talking to me. "I'm sure I've always kept a perfectly clean house—often having to do things myself—"

Kelly brushed past me and started down the stairs. "Yes ma'am—what'll you have now?"

"That will do," said Mabel austerely. "I will not tolerate impertinence. Now, come down at once. Why, the beds haven't even been made yet. Really, I don't know what I'm going to do."

"I beg your pardon, madam," said Kelly, raising his height by an inch. "I do not make beds."

"Yes, yes, I know," Mabel said impatiently. "Though I cannot see why you men always refuse to make beds—it's perfectly simple. However, if you won't, I shall have to do them myself. But the floors and the dusting must be done at once."

"I'll make the beds," I offered, feeling a little sorry for her, since she took her housekeeping so hard.

"Oh, my dear, if you would. Such a load off my mind. Now, I like mine tucked in securely, but the doctor won't have his tucked in at all, so that you have to—"

"Leave it to me. I know what you mean."

We went downstairs in a body, and Mabel took Kelly on down to the first floor. Ian touched my arm and said, "Go and do Mabel's room, and then see what you can get out of Aunt Violet. I'll make the other beds. I want to get this thing cleared up because it isn't healthy."

I nodded and then turned around as John came up the stairs from below.

He said, "Hello. Where's Sara?"

"She's gone out shopping."

"Good," said John, and extracted a silver cigarette case from an inner pocket.

I left the two of them in the hall and went into Mabel's room. I made the beds and resisted the temptation to make an apple-pie one for Mabel. I made an extra search for the Bible while I was there, and though I did not find it I did turn up an old scrapbook that gave the highlights of Mabel's theatrical career.

If Richard had called her a burlesque queen in his Bible he had been untruthful and malicious. She seemed to have been a straight dramatic actress. And there had been no comedy—let alone anything musical. She had had small parts in a number of plays, more or less highbrow stuff, according to the reviews. There was no record of her having had any leading parts, and I supposed her career had been cut off by her marriage. But I had never heard her refer to her dramatic days, and apparently she preferred to present herself as a person of good family, without the benefit of her own talent.

I put the scrapbook away where I had found it and went across to

Aunt Violet's room. I knocked several times without getting any answer, and just before I turned away I tried the door. To my surprise, it
was open.

Aunt Violet was not in her bedroom, nor was she in the bathroom.
I was a little uneasy, and yet it seemed absurd to worry about her in
broad daylight and in a house full of people. I glanced out of the window and saw that it was snowing, and the snow had collected in little
mounds on the shoulders and cap of a policeman who stood on the
sidewalk in front of the house.

I sighed and turned back to the room. It was a golden opportunity
to search for the Bible, and I knew that I must not miss it. It turned out
to be a difficult job, for the room was crowded with Aunt Violet's pos-
sessions—the accumulation of half a lifetime. There was a bookcase so
crammed that some of the books were wedged in double, and I had to
take the front ones out to see what was behind. They were mostly popular novels, dating from the early nineteen hundreds up to the present
time, and there were several French novels.

The Bible was not in the bookcase, and I tackled the rest of the
room. There were tins of cookies in odd corners, and the bureau drawers were crammed with ribbons, bits of lace, and artificial flowers. The
closet was packed with old-fashioned clothes, hats, and even a few para-
sols, and there were the plain, modern dresses which she wore about
the house. In a dark corner of the room I found several bottles of wine
and one of Scotch, but it did not surprise me, because I had come to a
previous conclusion that she drank a bit.

However, there was no Bible—not even one for herself. There was
a rosary hanging on the inside of the closet door, and I supposed that it
was either a memento—and she had plenty of those—or else she had
Catholic leanings.

When I had finished my search I sat down and lighted a cigarette,
using a fancy sea shell as being the nearest thing to an ash tray. I smoked
the cigarette through, but still Aunt Violet had not appeared, and I
began to feel uneasy. She could hardly be in the attic, since we had
come down from there, and I had gone straight to her room. I went out
into the hall, wondering if she could be down in the kitchen with Annie, but John diverted me by emerging from my room with most of my
clothes bundled over his arm.

I fixed him with a cold eye and asked, "What gives?"

John grinned. "You can't have forgotten that you agreed to change
rooms today?"

"I know Ian agreed," I said, frowning. "But I don't believe I told
you to go ahead."

John walked on to his room and called back, "That's all right, then, because the man should be the head of the house."

I went to my own room and found Ian gathering the rest of my things together. He glanced up at my face and said immediately, "Don't blow your cork, because it won't do any good. You can live with me or you can go home to your father, but this halfway stuff is going to stop."

I started to speak, but he dropped my brush and the two halves of my comb, walked over, and put his hand on my mouth

"I've decided that you and I can stick together. I'll admit I was prejudiced—and suspicious—but that's all gone. Either you're my wife or you're not, and if you're not you can pack up and fare forth into the blizzard. But remember this—everyone in town will know that you deserted your soldier husband on his short and precious leave and left him to face the rigors of war without a wife's loving regard. In other words, you will be known far and wide as a rat."

His hand slipped a little, and I hissed, "If I am a rat, then I prefer to be known as one. I don't—"

I caught sight of John grinning in the doorway, and I fell silent as Ian's hand dropped from my mouth.

"Having wife trouble, Ian?" John asked, apparently enjoying himself.

"No," I said nastily, "but I suppose you are."

A faint dark color showed in his face, but he said easily, "We've been married longer than you have, honey. And I really mean it when I say that I don't want to disturb Sara at night when I have to go out. She's not very strong."

"Oh, nuts!" I said rudely. "She's thin, but she's wiry. And she works like a slavey at the hospital."

John shrugged and passed over my bad temper. "I believe we have it all done now, but you'll want to arrange your own things."

I walked out of the room and straight downstairs and felt like a fool all the way.

I went to the kitchen, where Annie was washing dishes, and sat down. She looked over her shoulder and raised her eyebrows inquiringly.

"Where's Miss Violet?" I asked.

I thought I caught a flash of fear before she turned her face back to the sink, but she answered casually enough, "I dunno, Mrs. Miriel. Ain't she in her room?"

"No," I said, "she ain't. Have you seen her in the last hour or so?"

"Well, to be sure, she come down here for her lunch. Walked herself in here when I had the tray all ready and says she'll eat right at the table there. 'Annie,' she says, 'I'm tired of stickin' in my room.' "

"She doesn't have to stick in her room," I said impatiently. "There's no earthly sense to it."

"Oh yes, there is," Annie said too quickly, and stopped.

I stared at the back of her head and asked, "What do you mean?"

She made a great clatter with the dishes and a vigorous splashing of water and did not answer.

I stood up and moved over to the sink. "Come on, Annie—tell me. Why does she have to stay in her room?"

"Well"—she eyed a plate carefully before putting it on the drainboard—"she has that there now high blood pressure."

"Never mind the high blood pressure," I said sharply. "Let's have the real reason."

"Why, you know good and well, Mrs. Miriel, that she don't like to meet people."

"That's not what you meant, though. Let's have it, Annie, or I'll get Briggs out here to work on you."

She hung her head over the hot, steamy water and said in a frightened whisper. "It's the brother—that Benson one. He always was mean to her."

"What did he do?" I prodded.

She raised her head and looked full at me. "Mrs. Miriel, he says she's to stay in her room, and if she don't he'll have her put away in a madhouse."

CHAPTER TWENTY-FIVE

I LOOKED at Annie's hands, red and sodden, moving nervously in the soapy water, and thought about Dr. Benson. He was very quiet and respectable these days—impeccably dressed and gravely ethical at all times. I could not imagine him as the black sheep described in Richard's Bible. But of course boys often cut up in college and then calmed down later. Certainly Benson was a model member of the community now—never a breath of scandal, not even the few mild flirtations that most of them went in for. If he had threatened Aunt Violet with the loony bin, then it seemed to me that he had a good reason.

The whole thing suddenly struck me as being very funny, but I was afraid to laugh for fear I shouldn't be able to stop. Instead, I said to Annie, "You know where Miss Violet is now, don't you? You'd better tell me."

She turned around, raising her hands to the heavens and spraying me lightly with suds. "I do not, Mrs. Miriel, and that's a fact. When she left here she was off to her room, and if she ain't there now, then I don't know where she's got to."

"Did she go up the back stairs?"

Annie nodded. "She uses them back stairs always so she don't run into people."

Well, that was understandable, of course, but I was uneasy. I supposed she could have gone up the back stairs as I came down the front, but that meant that she had spent a lot of time in the kitchen. Chatting to Annie, probably, because Annie was only now doing the luncheon dishes, which seemed a bit late, to say the least.

I decided to go up and see if she had returned to her room, but as I was passing through the front hall Kelly pounced on me and drew me into the living-room.

"For God's sake," he whispered, "come and help me out. The cook used to do all this sort of thing for me, and I gave her all the amateur help I could. But that Gawdhelpus, Annie, won't leave the kitchen, and I don't know one end of these housecleaning tools from another. Mabel says she's coming after me to inspect my work, and if it isn't done properly I'll have to do it all over again. The thing will result in a vicious circle if you don't help me out. Matter of fact, I could have cleared your problem up a couple of days ago, except for the housework. It's slavery, and it's out of all proportion to what it produces."

I worked with him, demonstrating and instructing for three quarters of an hour, before we felt that the result might pass Mabel's inspection.

"Now, " said Kelly, "leave that infernal machine—that vacuum cleaner—running, so that she'll think I'm still working here, and we'll get on up to the third floor again. You go on out into the hall first and see if the coast is clear."

I went out and waved him on, and he came bounding up the stairs while the vacuum cleaner wailed by itself in the living room. On the second floor I noticed that the door to Aunt Violet's room was closed, and I knew that I had left it ajar. I started to make for it, but Kelly's hand closed on my arm.

"Not now—I need you upstairs."

"But, Kelly, wait. I ought to go and see—"

He dragged me to the attic stairs, opened the door, and pushed me through.

I started resignedly up the stairs, but I explained, "Aunt Violet's been missing for a while this afternoon, and I wanted to go in and make sure she's back. I haven't had a chance to ask her what it is she knows yet, and I must ask her about Dr. Benson's threat."

I told Kelly about Dr. Benson and the madhouse and also about Aunt Violet's visit to the kitchen. He nodded with a faint impatience and said, "All right—she'll keep. You can see her later. Now, I'm convinced that the answer to this business is up here. That little grave—it's odd. I examined the bucket, and I'm sure the cement was mixed fairly recently, but where is it? Nowhere. I've been all over the blasted house."

We went to the attic and over to the cedar chest, and Kelly raised the lid while I stood there and shivered.

We were silent for a moment, and then Kelly dropped the lid and sighed.

"You see, there's been no repair work on that crack. The mix must have been thrown into the garbage can and carted off—that's all."

"What about the lily pond and the lion?" I asked.

Kelly shook his head. "I've been over all that. It was all old stuff—hadn't been repaired for years."

"Then I think it's up here," I said decidedly. "I heard it being mixed here, and it's so heavy, I doubt if it was carried far."

We started to look around among the trunks and old furniture, but we did not find any new concrete. There was nothing but the cedar chest with its pathetic little name and the stained and battered bucket.

We looked around in the other three rooms—the large one at the back which had been Leslie's and the two small rooms at the front which were stored with furniture. Leslie's room was furnished with old-fashioned mahogany which I supposed had been taken from the storerooms, and there was a worn Chinese oriental rug on the floor.

I was idly studying the rug when a clear thought emerged from the muddle in my brain.

"Hey!" I said to Kelly. "How was it you didn't find that grave when you were hunting for Leslie?"

"I was wondering when you'd think of that one," Kelly replied, drawing his dignity about him. "In fact, it took you too long to think of it. I'll never offer you a job as assistant."

"I wouldn't take it if you did. But don't try to change the subject. I want to know why—"

"All right, all right. I looked in the ruddy chest, but there were blankets at the top—old and yellowed. I patted them and assumed that the thing was filled with blankets. I was in a hurry, you'll remember, and certainly I was right in deciding that Leslie was not there."

I said, "Hmm. Who took the blankets off?"

"I don't know."

"Well, where are they now?"

"On a trunk near by," said Kelly, thoughtfully studying the Chinese rug.

"Do you think Briggs or one of his men took them off?"

"No," said Kelly, "I do not. I've no doubt that Briggs' man did exactly as I did—opened the lid, patted the blankets, and closed it again. If Briggs and gang had discovered that grave they'd have had a pickax up there in no time and ripped the thing apart. I used to be one of them, and I know their methods. "

"Before they slung you out on your ear."

"They did not sling me out," said Kelly hotly. "I resigned. But anyway, as I was saying, someone removed those blankets and didn't replace them. I assume it was a member of the family, but I don't understand why it was done."

"Well, perhaps whoever it was did not know that it was a grave—didn't know what it was."

"Wrong again," said Kelly patiently. "In that case it would certainly have been mentioned downstairs, and it hasn't been. I think perhaps it was left uncovered so that one of Briggs' men would find it—only they don't know Briggs' men. Once the ground has been covered, their method is to forget about it."

"And what's yours?" I asked.

"I cover the ground periodically because I know it's apt to change color."

"Marvelous! " I said. "And now will you get to work and stop wasting time telling me how smart you are? I'm going to look at those blankets."

I went back to the attic and opened the cedar chest, and after a moment I called softly, "Kelly!"

He appeared at the attic door and asked sulkily, "What is it?"

"The ground has changed color again. The blankets have been replaced."

He came quickly to my side and stared down at the neatly folded old blankets. After a moment he lifted them and looked at the concrete beneath and then slowly replaced them.

"All the time you were busy running the police down in there," I said accusingly, "someone came up and put those blankets back. Too bad you don't have eyes in the back of your head. You certainly need them when the front ones don't work."

Kelly was embarrassed, but he pretended to ignore me and started thinking out loud.

"Benson," he murmured. "Probably looking for it all along. Suspected something of the sort and then got such a shock when he found it that he forgot the blankets and ran off. Remembered about it later, so back he comes and replaces them."

"So?"

"So I don't need to see people doing things—I can follow their movements in my mind."

"Then who took the Bible, and where is it now?"

"Simple," said Kelly airily. "The Bible is a heap of ashes in the furnace, and Benson took it because Benson was looking for it. He took it when I was lying in a drugged sleep in Annie's room. He'd found the slit in Richard's mattress and figured that I might have taken the Bible."

"Why was he looking for it at all?"

"Richard must have mentioned it at some time and hinted at the biographies that were written in it. When he died Benson was scared that it would be found, and the dirt spilled far and wide. He realized that those little biographies must be burned, come hell or high water. He takes his respectability seriously these days, does Benson."

"Richard was well off the track about Mabel, " I said thoughtfully. "She was no burlesque queen:"

Kelly nodded. "I found that too. Nice middle-class girl who went to a nice dramatic school and had a few nice, small, no account parts until Benson married her, and she quit. So Richard writes it down for posterity that she was a burlesque queen. If Benson read it he must have been frothing at the mouth. If you ask me, I think Richard was jealous because Brother Benson had all the fun."

"Kelly!" I exclaimed suddenly. "The vacuum cleaner! It must have bitten a hole in the carpet by now."

Kelly leapt for the door with a look of anguish on his face and muttered, "The woman will have me arrested."

On the second floor he told me to go in and get the information from Miss Violet, and then he raced on downstairs with his coattails flying.

I went to Miss Violet's door, but there was no answer to my knock, so I pushed and found that it was not locked. I opened the door slowly and peered around its edge.

Miss Violet was lying full length on the floor.

CHAPTER TWENTY-SIX

DEATH was in my mind as I stumbled across to her, but I found to my intense relief that she seemed only to have fainted. As I bent over her she moved and opened her eyes, and after staring at me in a dazed sort of way she said quite clearly, "I can't stand this."

I got her to the bed, and she lay quietly on her back, staring at the ceiling. After I had made her comfortable I started out of the room to get Dr. Benson or John, but she called in a frightened, feeble voice, "Don't go."

"I'm coming right back," I assured her, but she started to move her head from side to side in an agitated way.

"No. No. You're going for my brother—or my nephew—and I don't want them. I don't want either of them. I'm all right dear—please believe me. I was just a little faint, I won't do it again. But please don't bring any doctor in. Please."

I came slowly back into the room. I did not want to excite her too much and decided to let her have her way for the moment and tell Dr. Benson about her later.

I stood looking down at her, and she said at last, "Please be seated, my dear."

I pulled a chair over to the bed and sat down. "What's troubling you, Aunt Violet?" I asked. "If you'd only tell me I might be able to help you, but you bottle it all up and so of course it backfires on you."

She looked distressed and said after a moment, "One cannot go against one's own family. I don't like them, but still—I cannot."

"You don't need to tell anyone else, and I'm family now too. I shan't tell Briggs or any of his men unless you say I may, but I'm almost sure that I could help you. For instance, what made you faint just now?"

It was a long time before she answered, and then she said in a troubled voice. "I—don't know exactly. I was thinking of all these dreadful things, and they worried me so."

"Were you worrying about Dr. Benson having threatened you?"

Her startled blue eyes rolled around and fastened on my face. "But—but how did you know about that?"

"Annie told me," I explained gently. "Only I can't believe he threatened you like that. Wasn't Annie making it up?"

She shook her head slowly, and her voice was hardly more than a whisper. "No, child. Annie talks too much, but she didn't make that up—it's true. Last night I thought I'd go down to the kitchen for something to eat."

"Last night?" I interrupted.

"Yes—it was last night. I had just wakened, and my head was not clear—dizzy and—and confused."

Well, she'd had an opiate, I thought; it was natural enough that she should feel muzzy.

"I went into the hall," she continued, "I believe it was near morning, but I don't know. And then Benson ran into me there in the dark. I said I was sorry and I started back to my room again. He called after me. He said, 'Violet, you stay in your room or I'll have you put away, and I mean it.'"

Tears welled in her eyes and dripped from the corners. I got some tissue and dried them off, and presently she went on, "To think that my own brother—and I'm quite sane; he knows I am. He wants my money; that's what it is—the tiny little bit that Richard left me. And it's so little; it comes to barely a hundred a month. I am supposed to live on that. You see, my dear, your father's nice place would be too expensive for me."

"Who told you it was only a hundred a month?"

She seemed a little disconcerted but finally admitted reluctantly that Annie had done some eavesdropping at the breakfast table when Dr. Benson was talking about it to John.

"Well, anyway," I said cheerfully, "you can have a cheaper room at Father's. I'm sure you'll be able to swing it somehow., You won't need to have Annie with you; she can have her pick of jobs right now."

Aunt Violet sighed and regarded the ceiling in mournful silence.

I let a moment or two pass and then said cautiously, "I wish you'd give me the information that Leslie had and that you have now."

"Oh, but it won't make any difference—not now. And if you knew, it might be dangerous. "

"I'll keep it under my hat," I said, trying not to be too eager. "I won't even tell Ian, so how could anybody know that you've told me? And I might be able to help you. It's too much of a strain for you to carry it by yourself. Your blood pressure—"

She got quite annoyed and actually snapped at me.

"My blood pressure is not high at all—nothing of the sort. I suppose that stupid Annie told you that nonsense. It is my heart—not my blood pressure—my heart."

"All right," I said amiably. "It's your heart. And I still think it will relieve you to give me the information."

She said, "Well," sighed, twisted her hands together, and took the plunge.

"Richard was always getting annoyed with Benson. They'd meet once a week, you see, for lunch, and quite often Richard would come home in a rage and immediately make a new will. He always told me about it so that I should be able to produce it in case he died. He'd always get over it in a day or so and destroy the new will, and all the time the original will was in the possession of his lawyer, Mr. Graves. He never consulted Mr. Graves when he drew these new wills—it was always some new man. So childish, I always thought. Well, when he died there was one of these silly wills—he'd drawn it up about two weeks before—leaving everything to Leslie except for my little bit. I did not say anything about it because it was not a fair or just arrangement, and Richard had done it in anger.

"It was hidden behind the lion in the drawing-room, and although I said nothing to Leslie, she must have heard something and thought the hiding place was that old lion out by the lily pond."

I felt a rising excitement, but I tried to keep my voice quiet.

"Did anyone know of the new will besides yourself and Uncle Richard?"

"I don't know, child. I know nothing more than that."

"The lawyer who drew it up knew all about it."

"Yes—yes, I suppose so. My dear, I'd like to try to sleep a little. Will you send Annie up with some hot milk?"

"Yes, of course." I stood up and added thoughtfully. "Does Annie know?"

"I am sure I don't know," said Aunt Violet, and closed her eyes.

I flew down to the kitchen, told Annie about the milk, and then asked her if she knew anything about Mr. Lang's latest will.

She gaped at me and declared that she didn't know nothing about no wills, and I felt satisfied, somehow, that she was telling the truth.

I sped off in search of Kelly, following the moan of the vacuum cleaner, which led me to the dining-room. Kelly was sitting on the window seat smoking a cigar and dropping ashes into a flowerpot, while the vacuum cleaner lay on the floor, sobbing to itself.

I turned it off and glared over at the window seat. "Do you want to be fired, you darned fool? How could you hear anyone coming through all that noise?"

"So long as it works its little heart out," said Kelly imperturbably, "Mabel keeps herself to herself. But when I turned it off in the living-room she materialized at once. Said I'd done a good job, but I was frightfully slow, and shifted me in here. Maybe you'd better clean this up too."

"I'll do nothing of the kind, because on second thought I don't believe she'd fire you, anyway. You'd look too pretty handing tea around to the Ladies' Auxiliary."

He slitted his eyes at me, but I jumped in ahead of him.

"Listen, Kelly, I've picked up something really important."

I told him all about it, and after he had thought it over for a while he asked which room was the drawing-room.

"It's the living-room," I said, "and don't try to pretend that you're younger than you are. You know perfectly well that in your young days the living-room was known as the drawing-room."

"Not to me, it wasn't," said Kelly stubbornly. "We called it the parlor."

"I see. Well, then, you must have been middle class."

This delayed us ten minutes while I was forced to listen to a history of the aristocratic and blue-blooded Kellys. Kelly, himself, seemed to be the only member of the family who didn't have a title of some sort.

"All right, Your Grace," I said finally. "My mistake. Let's go to the parlor and look for a lion."

There were two lions heading a pair of columns that flanked the fireplace, and Kelly whipped out his penknife and fell upon the nearest one. It didn't take him two minutes to break off the head, but there was only splintered wood, and he hastily jammed it back again, muttering that he'd take some glue to it later on.

He began to pry at the other one, and almost immediately the head flew back on tiny hinges and exposed a small hollowed space. Kelly grunted and fished around eagerly, and the first thing he brought out was the will. It was almost as Aunt Violet had said, except that Ian was left the same amount as in the original.

Kelly put it tenderly into his pocket and brought out the remaining papers, which were all letters. We gave them a hasty going over, and they appeared to be love letters to Richard from some girl. Kelly stuffed them into another pocket and said, "We'll have to read them—there might be something. We'll go over them when we have more time."

He stood in meditation for a while and then slowly withdrew the will from his pocket and replaced it.

"Why?" I asked, astonished.

"It's hot stuff, and I have to be fair to Briggs and his yokels. Not that the dolts will ever find it."

We heard Mabel's voice and fled back to the dining-room like a pair of guilty children. Kelly turned on the vacuum cleaner, and I smoothed my hair and dress and walked sedately into the hall.

   Mabel was not there, but as I hesitated at the foot of the stairs Annie appeared suddenly at the top. She began to run down in a queer,
jerking fashion, and before she had reached the bottom she was screaming wildly.

CHAPTER TWENTY-SEVEN

WHEN she reached the bottom of the stairs she started for the front door with blind, frantic haste, but I caught her and swung her around. I shook her and slapped her face, and after a moment she sank down on to the couch and began to cry.

Mabel and Ian hurried into the hall, with Kelly peering eagerly over their shoulders, and Mabel cried shrilly, "What is it? What has happened now? It's this terrible house!"

"It's haunted," Annie moaned. I'm leaving right away—right now."

Ian, seating his weight against the edge of a small table, folded his arms and shook his head a little. "Briggs might not allow it."

"He can't stop me—nobody can," Annie whispered. "I'm going now."

She blew her nose, tucked her handkerchief into her bosom, and stood up.

"But what did you *see?*" Mabel asked, exasperated. "What scared you?"

Annie shook her head and marched toward the kitchen, and we all trailed after her. I glimpsed Aunt Violet's scared face at the head of the stairs, but she backed away and disappeared as soon as she caught my eye.

Annie went straight to her bedroom and started to pack, and the four of us stood about watching her helplessly. We prodded, threatened, and pleaded in an effort to find out what had frightened her, but she merely folded her lips into a thin line and hurried her preparations for leaving.

In the end she walked grandly out the front door while Mabel turned acid and pointed out that she should be exiting by way of the rear. Annie opened her mouth then and informed whoever might be interested that she had always used people's front entrances and expected to do so until she died, and further, that she had no doubt her coffin would be carried out the front door too. Which seemed to settle that.

She ran into some men on the driveway whom Kelly identified as reporters, but she made her way through and beyond them without speaking again.

Ian, turning back into the house with a shrug, said, "I suppose we shouldn't have let her go. Ought to have worked on her and tried to find out what put her into such a dither."

Kelly shimmered up to Mabel and suggested respectfully, "Suppose I go upstairs, madam, and see if anything is amiss?"

"Yes, Kelly, go up at once, and make a thorough search. And then report back to me immediately."

Kelly started up the stairs; Ian went with him, and I trailed along behind, murmuring something about looking in on Aunt Violet. Ian decided to come with me, and we had to knock because the door was locked again. She admitted us, but she was in a bad state of nerves, and I got her to lie down on the bed and covered her with a quilt.

"What happened to Annie?" Ian asked her

Aunt Violet, with her voice shaking, said that she did not know. "She brought me some hot milk a little while ago and talked to me, and then she went away. I thought she had gone to the kitchen, but then after a while I heard her running down the stairs and screaming. What was it? Where is she?"

"We don't know what it was," I said helplessly. "She wouldn't say a word. But she packed her things and left."

"She left?" Aunt Violet said in astonishment. "I don't understand it—I didn't think she'd leave me now. She promised she wouldn't."

We told her not to worry and assured her we'd take care of her. When we left a few minutes later, she was still lying on the bed, her hands worrying absently at the quilt.

Out in the hall Ian said explosively, "God! I'm sick of this whole business! We ought to get out and go to a hotel."

"Bit late for that," I replied thinly.

"I suppose so, but at least we have our own room now. I've been fixing it up for you—pink roses and blue bows."

"Kelly must be up on the third floor," I said hastily. "Let's see if he's found anything."

We mounted in silence and found Kelly in the hall. His face was flushed and his eyes glittered, and as soon as he saw us he began to swear vigorously. When he had more or less exhausted his repertoire he said, "There must have been *something* to scare that haddock-faced clod into hysterics. But I can't find anything—not one blasted thing."

We made a desultory search, but everything seemed to be the same as when we had last seen it.

I glanced at Kelly and asked, "What about the second floor?"

"Nothing and nobody," he said gloomily. "I looked there first."

"Probably it's just as she said," Ian muttered indifferently. "The house is haunted, and she saw a ghost."

Kelly frowned irritably. "She never once mentioned a ghost. She merely said that the house was haunted."

"You're splitting hairs."

"I'm doing nothing of the kind," said Kelly. "If you had a trained mind you'd have noticed particularly that she made no mention of a ghost. When she says only that the house is haunted it leaves the thing open to a great many possibilities."

"Why did you let her go?" I asked crossly. "How can we find out anything about it now?"

"Briggs will keep an eye on her," Kelly explained. "I saw one of the boys fall in behind when she left."

"Will they bring her back, do you think?"

Kelly shrugged. "They won't let her leave town—that's a cert. Anyway, as soon as she settles somewhere I'll get at her."

"What *can* be scaring those two old women out of their wits?" I wondered. "I'm getting frightened myself."

"You have something to be frightened about," Kelly said significantly. "Someone knows about those feathers."

"Yes." I thought about it for a moment and added, "Only that someone can't mention it, or we'll know him for who he is."

"I'm a plain man," said Kelly, "and I wish you'd stop talking around in circles."

Ian asked, "What did you do with the feathers?"

"Why, I left them in the top bureau drawer."

"That's a really outstanding piece of idiocy," Kelly observed bitterly. "John helped to move your belongings, didn't he? But perhaps he won't think a thing about it. Probably he'll just suppose that you've started a collection for a feather bed."

"You go on about your detecting, " Ian said, "and stop wasting time thinking up snappy sarcasms."

Kelly sighed and began to move toward the stairs. "Dinner is the next item on the program, and now that that woman has walked her body out of here, I'm supposed to attend to it. We open with a bowl of soup and close with something called cabinet pudding." He sighed again—louder, and with a quick look at me. "There are two things of that entire dinner that I can handle—and two only. I can place the maraschino cherries on the cabinet puddings and the knockout pill in Mabel's coffee."

"All right," I groaned, "I'll come down with you—but I wish I were dead."

"You may get your wish if you're not careful," Kelly said grimly.

Ian told him to shut up, with more vigor than courtesy, and Kelly remarked that he sounded more like a sergeant than a lieutenant. He added that he had been a sergeant, himself, during the last war, and that he and his brethren had never known a looey who wasn't a weak-kneed mamma's boy.

Ian, restored to good humor, said he'd go one better and admit frankly that the looeys even washed behind their ears.

On the second floor Kelly told me to find the feathers and bring them to him in the kitchen.

He went on down and could be heard talking to Mabel in the front hall, and Ian said, "I believe I told John to move the contents of that top drawer. You go and see if the feathers are still in the drawer, and I'll go to our room and find out if they were moved with the other things."

I nodded and went to my old room, where I pushed open the door and made for the bureau. When I was halfway across the floor Sara's voice spoke from the semidarkness.

"Wrong room, dear."

She was lying on the bed, and she stretched an arm and snapped on the light. "I've been resting. Your father was so amusing that my shopping tour lasted overtime." She reached for a cigarette and added, "Mabel told me about the change of rooms when I came in."

I sank down into a chair and said, "I'm sorry, Sara—I'd forgotten. It's a bit embarrassing, anyway—only I had nothing to do with it. The two men thought it up and carried it out."

Sara gave a slightly brittle laugh and sent a spiral of smoke toward the ceiling. "It almost looks as though John were trying to shrug me off. But he hasn't a chance—especially since he came into some money."

I cleared my throat and assumed a rather silly smile, and she said quickly, "Just strike that off the record. I'm tired and upset and I always talk through my hat when I'm that way. Mabel just told me about Annie, and I'd like to do the same thing myself. Run screaming down the stairs and out the front door—and never come back."

I thought fleetingly of Dr. Harris Colton-Smith and wondered why she couldn't be satisfied with John and a few mild flirtations.

Almost as though she had sensed my thought, she said soberly, "I haven't made things right for John, I know, but I'm turning over a new leaf. I intend to get a home of our own—"

But I had stopped listening and was staring at a man's handkerchief spread out on the desk and containing a little heap of feathers.

CHAPTER TWENTY-EIGHT

I FORCED my attention back to Sara and said inanely, "Perhaps you'll even have the patter of little feet," and knew, by the blank stare, that she had changed the subject in the meantime.

I got up, sauntered over to the window, and made some silly remark about the beauty of the snow. Sara agreed indifferently, and I edged around so that I stood with my back to the desk while I gathered the feathers and handkerchief into my hand with one quick scoop behind me.

"It's beautiful, of course," I said brightly, still babbling about the snow, "but such a nuisance."

Sara hid a yawn behind a delicately embroidered little handkerchief and murmured in a bored voice, "Quite so."

I said, "Well—" and made for the door on winged feet. John was entering as I left and I nearly knocked him over, but I fled downstairs, passing Mabel—who seemed to be annoyed about something—in the hall, and pushing into the kitchen, where I pressed the feathers into Kelly's hand. "Burn them immediately, handkerchief and all; he's after me," I whispered incoherently, and left him standing there with his mouth hanging open.

I went back to Mabel, who was starting up the stairs just as John started down.

"What were you saying?" I asked politely.

She turned with her hand on the banister and said in a vexed tone, "My dear, I can't make you out. I told you, a minute ago, and you rudely rushed away—and now you come back and ask me to repeat myself."

John moved in on us and asked me, "What were you in such a hurry about?"

"Well, it's that Kelly, you know," I said confusedly. "He doesn't understand much about cooking, and I wanted to give him some instructions before he put the dinner on."

Mabel gave a little moan and said, "The servants these days—really dreadful!"

John patted her arm. "All right, Mother; I expect we'll pull through it. Now, you go upstairs and try to relax. Take one of your little white pills. You worry too much about your housekeeping. No one expects

143

things to be perfect at a time like this."

Mabel put her handkerchief to her eyes, and I tried to get away, but John caught my arm.

"I must do my work, John," Mabel wept. "It takes my mind off things."

He shrugged and said, "All right, Mother."

She put her handkerchief away and took a long breath. "I'll go up and rest in a minute, dear, but first I want to show you what someone has done to the mantel in here."

She led the way into the living-room, and John followed, still holding firmly to my arm, so that I had to go too.

Mabel waved a dramatic hand at the lion's head which Kelly had broken. Apparently he had not got around to gluing it, because it now lay on the hearth.

"I suppose that Kelly did it," Mabel said tragically. "Broke it off when he was dusting, I've no doubt, and then stuck it on again, as they all do. I simply brushed my hand over it to see if he had dusted properly, and it fell right off."

John looked at it in silence for a long minute and said at last, "Well, don't worry about it, Mother. I'm sure it can be glued on again easily enough; I'll do it myself. I don't know why it troubles you so much, though, since we're not going to stay in the house."

"Oh, but we are. Your father has changed his mind and declares we're staying here—and nothing that I can say will move him."

John looked a bit startled and asked, "But what about Aunt Violet?"

"I don't know," said Mabel, "and frankly, I don't care. She has not been a bit sociable or cooperative."

I made a restless movement, and John glanced at me and said hastily, "You must have a rest before dinner, Mother—I insist."

"Well, all right, dear, but why are you holding Miriel's arm like that?"

John smiled. "I want to talk to her, and when you want to talk to a nurse you have to hang on or she'll flit away."

"I'm sure that's nonsense," said Mabel, and took herself off.

John led me to a couch, and we sat down. I had had time to calm down and think a bit, and I decided simply to deny everything.

"It must be something very solemn and important," I said

"It is." He handed me a cigarette and then settled back. "In fact, it's fantastic."

I waited, and he presently went on, "There was a little heap of feathers in your bureau drawer."

"Really?"

"Do you deny it?"

"No," I said composedly. "If you say there were feathers in my drawer, I'm quite prepared to take your word for it. But what is it supposed to mean to me?"

He looked down at his cigarette and turned it over in his fingers.

"I gathered that pile of feathers into my handkerchief and put it on the desk, and then you went in there and took it. Now what did you do with it?"

I registered surprise and said, "What are you raving about? I didn't take anything from that room—I was talking to Sara."

He sighed. "You *are* going to deny it, then. Well, I don't quite know what to do about it. I suppose I'll have to talk to Ian. "

He looked at me, probably to see if I was frightened, but I had my face set in what I hoped was an expression of puzzled innocence. "I do wish you'd tell me what you mean," I said earnestly.

"Let's not waste time." He stood up and threw his cigarette into the fireplace. "Since you won't explain, I must talk to Ian."

I draped myself in a little chilly dignity and said, "But I don't like the insinuation. I'll go with you when you talk to Ian."

"No. I prefer to see him alone."

He turned toward the door, and I ducked under his arm and went up the stairs ahead of him, keeping myself from running by sheer will power. I burst into our new room and was intensely relieved to find Ian there. He was stretched out on one of the beds, with an arm folded comfortably behind his head, and blowing smoke rings at the ceiling.

He turned his head to look at me, and I hissed, " Just say you don't know anything about those feathers. Give Kelly a few more hours, please!"

He looked astonished, but he had no time to answer before John knocked and then walked in without waiting to be invited.

"Ian, I'd like to talk with you alone, if I may."

Ian, more puzzled than ever, said, "Of course," and I backed out of the door, murmuring, "Forgive my clumsy intrusion."

I nervously hoped that everything would be all right, and after deciding that the door was too solid for even my sharp ears I went on down to the kitchen to steer Kelly through the intricacies of the dinner.

I told him of the latest developments, and he admitted that the whole feather situation perturbed him, to say the least. "That mug of a husband you have will probably spill the beans all over the floor, if I know anything about him."

"Well, but you don't know anything about him," I pointed out.

"Why didn't you get rid of the blasted feathers?" Kelly asked, suddenly irritable. "What were you saving them for—Christmas?"

"You peel those potatoes," I said, "and don't ask me how to do it. Just take a knife and get the skin off by any method that occurs to you."

"Oh, don't be so funny," said Kelly, still cross. "I can peel potatoes— I'm an ex-soldier."

I set to work and tried to keep my mind on the dinner and off the feeling that Briggs's hand was about to fall on my shoulder.

We were silent for some time, and then Kelly glanced at me and said, "Wipe the gloom off your face. If they put you in the clink I'll spring you sooner or later."

"Thanks," I murmured. "Just so you spring me before they sit me in the chair."

"Talk sense," he said peevishly. "Do you think I'm a silly amateur? As a matter of fact, I intend to reveal the truth of this thing tonight. With Mabel out cold until morning, I can guarantee it. "

"Look, Kelly," I said uneasily, "Mabel wouldn't bother you at night, in any case—and remember, there are a couple of doctors in the house. You'd better keep those pills for your own insomnia. "

The front-door bell rang, and Kelly stalked off to answer it while I worked on furiously. He was back again almost immediately and said in a low voice, "Briggs. Looks worried, too. He still hasn't recognized me— called me 'my man' and told me to put his hat and coat away, so I did. Put them under the couch in the hall so I'll know where to get them when he demands them again. He used to hang his things up himself, but I suppose his wife told him that the man without hayseeds in his hair always uses the butler when there is one."

"Very amusing," I said thinly, "but I'd enjoy your conversation a lot more if I could hear that you'd made some progress."

"I've made progress all right," he said, looking offended. "But I can't tell you anything—you spew it all around."

"One excuse is as good as another. For Pete's sake, Kelly, can't you give me any encouragement? What's Briggs here for?"

"Briggs wanted old man Benson, whom I produced in something under three minutes. And as for encouragement, I'll tell you this much. I know where that cement mix must have been used. Thought it out while I was waiting for you to come and start the dinner."

"Oh, what?" I gasped. "Tell me, Kelly. Please don't wait to be pompous."

"Don't get so excited," he said coldly. "I've been all over the house, and the only place for a small cement mix is in that solid brick wall in the attic. One or two of the bricks probably fell out, so someone went up there at night and repaired it."

I had been drying my hands on a fancy linen dish towel, and I believe I dropped it into the wastebasket. I looked up at Kelly and whispered, "What does it mean?"

He shrugged. "I'm not jumping to conclusions—I'm simply telling you. But tonight I'm going to the attic, and I intend to tear that brick wall down."

"You can't do that. I mean, that's where the chimneys are."

"The chimneys are in the center part, " Kelly explained, "but there's a triangular section of brick at each side, and there must be space behind those two pieces. They seem to be mere architectural ornamentation—if there are two such words. But I suppose architects must have their fun like anyone else."

"You expect to find something hidden in there?"

"Might be another one of those wills."

"Maybe," I agreed doubtfully. "There must be *something.*"

"Can't you hurry up with the dinner?" Kelly suggested. "I want to get it over with—and anyway, I'm hungry."

I went back to work and asked presently, "What do you think Briggs wants with Dr. Benson?"

"No doubt he's quizzing him about a little matter that I've known for two days. The story of how Benson lost his shirt—not to mention his vest and shorts—in a stock-market flier."

CHAPTER TWENTY-NINE

I PICTURED our conservative Dr. Benson gambling wildly on the market and shook my head. "Seems to me he must be one of these dual personalities. Is he badly in debt?"

"Up over his ears, and then some," Kelly said briefly. "But don't stop to talk. If we don't get this infernal dinner out of the way soon I won't be able to get the thing solved tonight, and in that case I can't answer for your safety tomorrow."

"What about the money he's due to get now?"

"He'll need it."

"But, Kelly—" I said doubtfully. "I mean, Leslie— She was his own daughter."

Kelly shrugged. "Not only that, but I think he was the only one who gave a damn about her. Not that she was the kind of daughter he'd have ordered—but still, I think he cared more for her than the others did."

"Maybe," I said grimly. "But I'll tell you this—if I get into any trouble over those feathers we're going to produce that latest will at once."

"We're going to produce it anyway. It's perfectly legal, and we've no right to suppress it. In any case, the lawyer who drew it up will probably come forward and say so. I'm just keeping quiet about it for the present."

"Well, I hope you know what you're doing." I went to the sink and washed and dried my hands. "I'm going upstairs for a minute; I want to find out what happened between Ian and John. "

"You don't have to go upstairs for that," Kelly said. "I can tell you. Your poor dolt of a husband spilled the whole thing."

"He did not!" I said furiously. "I particularly asked him not to."

Kelly gave a couple of horselaughs—the second one for emphasis.

I ignored the implication and said, "Now, don't touch anything while I'm gone—not one thing—do you hear? Sit down and think some more—but don't touch."

He sat down at once and put his feet up on another chair, and I went up the back stairs and along the quiet hall to our new room.

Ian had left his comfortable position on the bed and was standing at the window, frowning out at the snow. He turned around as I came in and asked immediately, "How much longer is this thing to go on? I denied knowing anything about those feathers to John, and he went off saying it was all highly suspicious, significant, and a few other things, and he thought he ought to go to Briggs about it."

I shivered and twisted my cold hands together. "It's only for to-night, Ian; Kelly has something up his sleeve. He—he's going to the attic to tear the chimneys apart."

Ian lost his temper and exploded into a shower of colorful profan-ity. "I ought to have my head examined for letting it go on as long as it has," he said when he finally became coherent. "I'm damned if I'm going to let that silly mutt spoil your chance of being properly cleared. We should have gone to the police with the truth at once, and probably the thing would have been wound up by now. Perhaps even poor Le-slie—" Rage overcame him again, and he relieved his feelings by throw-ing my shoe brush violently to the floor.

"Pick it up," I said coldly, "and put it back where you found it. And the sooner you stop losing your temper, the better it will be all around."

By way of an answer he kicked it under the bed. "I'm a spoiled boy," he said, "and don't think you can reform me, because I don't reform that easily. When I want to get mad I'll get mad—and I'm mad now."

I turned toward the door. "Then stay that way for a while, it will give me an excuse to avoid you."

He reached the door ahead of me, put an arm around me, and kissed me rather roughly. "At least we have our own room now, and you can't tell me to go because you're tired and want to rest."

"No, but I can do my resting in one of the servants' rooms near Kelly." I jerked myself free of his arm, slipped out of the door, and hurried down to the kitchen by way of the back stairs.

Kelly was sitting where I had left him, and when I appeared he courteously removed his feet from the other chair and lowered them to the floor. "Something," he said mildly, "seems to be burning."

"O God!" I had forgotten to turn the gas low under the oven, where the chicken was roasting. I peered in at it, and it was sizzling furiously, as though it felt somewhat the same way as Ian.

"Well, anyway," I said wearily, "I don't think Mabel will fire you even if the wretched chicken goes to the table in cinders. "

"Never mind Mabel," he said peevishly; "what about me? I've been looking forward to that bird, and now you've ruined it."

I said, "Shut up!" and turned to find that Briggs had quietly insinu-ated himself into the kitchen.

My face relaxed into a silly smile, and I murmured feebly, "I've been giving the man a bit of a hand—he doesn't understand very much about cooking."

Kelly muttered, "Neither do you," but I don't know whether Briggs heard it or not. I thought he had a look of secret satisfaction about him, and it made me uneasy.

He nodded at me and then said abruptly, "Kelly, did you break that lion's head in the living-room?"

"Yes sir," Kelly replied promptly. "I done some cleaning there today, and that there head come smack off in my hand. I pushed it on again and hoped the madam wouldn't notice."

Briggs kept his eyes steadily on Kelly's face and asked, "What about the other head? Anything happen there?"

"Oh no, sir—I was more careful with that one on account of what happened the first time. Don't tell me it's broke too, sir?"

I had an uneasy feeling that Kelly's grammar did not ring true, and I was afraid to look at Briggs's face. I heard him say, "Were you, by any chance, searching for something when you broke that head?"

Kelly tried to look puzzled by twisting his forehead into a mass of wrinkles. "No sir, I ain't lost a thing—not recent, that is."

Briggs regarded him in silence for another moment and then turned to me.

"Mrs. Ross, I believe Kelly was employed by your father before he worked here?"

"Why—er—I've seen him around the house. But Father supervises the domestic staff. I'm away so much, you know. I—"

"Yes, I see," Briggs interrupted. "Do you know why Kelly left your father's employ to come here?"

"I couldn't say."

Briggs said, "Hmm," and added, "Well, I got in touch with your father, and he's on his way over here now—I think things should be cleared up shortly. Kelly! I'll want to question you further after dinner, so don't leave the house."

"No sir," said Kelly, and was quiet until Briggs had left the kitchen, when he gave a short laugh.

"*Still* doesn't know me. What a memory for faces!"

"He's on your tail about something, though. I suppose he found the will."

"Yeah," said Kelly. "His biggest find since 1888—when he walked out of the house and found a lot of snow. You can see by the happy glow on his face that he has it all figured out now. Somebody hired me to come here, find the will, and throw it away—on account of they're society people in this house and can't be bothered finding things for themselves."

"They can't be bothered setting the table, either," I said, "so you'd better go and do it. And don't stumble over your own humor. Father will dine with us, no doubt, so put out a few extra tools for him. I suppose he's rushing across the town this minute, which reminds me that I'd better meet him at the front door and tell him what to say."

Kelly stepped into his room and came out pulling on an overcoat. "Your father won't dine here because he isn't going to get into the house at all. I'll waylay him outside. It so happens that I don't want him to confer with Briggs." He turned the collar of the coat up around his neck and asked, "Have you any money? There's a burlesque show in town, and I'll send him there."

I sighed and reached for my bag. "I knew you'd find some way of getting out of the little work you're able to do."

Kelly took the money, gave me a look of reproach, and slid out the back door as Ian entered by the one from the hall.

"I knew I'd find you here. It's ridiculous for you to be doing all his work for him. Why don't you just let him use the cookbook?"

"He can't read," I said, "and we have to eat."

The doorbell rang, and I realized with a feeling of panic that Kelly could not have got around to the front of the house yet. I flew to the hall and opened the door, and as I had feared, Father stood on the mat.

"Don't come in," I whispered frantically. "Kelly doesn't want Briggs to talk to you."

Father said, "Nonsense!" and Ian, directly behind me, exclaimed, "What are you talking about, Miriel! Come in, sir."

Father was already in, and he shut the door firmly behind him. "Kelly can go to hell," he said simply. "I want to talk to Briggs. I want to find out exactly what is going on here."

I opened the door again and slipped outside. I wanted to get hold of Kelly, but instead I ran into one of Briggs's men who eyed me with mild suspicion and asked if he could help me in any way.

I backed up, explained that I just wanted a breath of fresh air, and then found, to my confusion, that I was locked out.

I rang, and Briggs himself opened the door. He looked me up and down with a certain amount of surprise and said, "I thought it might be your father. I'm waiting for him. Did you get shut out?"

I nodded and explained rather feebly, "I was waiting for Father too."

I hesitated in the hall, trying to make up my mind which way Father would have gone and at last headed for the dining room in the hope that Ian had steered him there for drinks.

I drew a sharp breath of relief when I found them at the sideboard among the bottles, and I urged in a low voice, "Come on into the kitchen and get some ice—and you can keep me company."

They were deep in a discussion of whiskey, and they followed me without particularly noticing what they were doing.

The dinner was ready to serve, and since Kelly had not appeared I began to set the table with feverish haste, running in and out of the dining-room and occasionally peering into the hall, where Briggs was still waiting with obviously growing impatience. He looked to me as though he wouldn't last much longer, and finally, in desperation, I went out to him.

"Mr. Briggs, if you want to go off and have dinner I'll see that Father waits for you."

To my surprise and relief, he brightened up and agreed. "I'll be back in an hour. But I must see your father tonight."

"I'll keep him for you," I promised.

I hurried back to the kitchen, breathing freely again, and found Kelly busily engaged in trying to persuade Father to go to the burlesque.

Father—perhaps under the influence of the house of Lang—had his nose in the air. "I like a good show as well as the next man, but those things! When they don't disgust me, they bore me."

"Don't hand me that stuff," Kelly snarled. "Was it disgust or boredom that night we went to the show and you asked the striptease artist—"

"Let him alone," I interrupted sharply. "We're safe for an hour, anyway. Briggs has gone off for dinner, and we can chase Father as soon as we've fed him. How do we get the family down to the dining-room?"

Kelly shrugged. "There's a gong in the hall. It usually brings them."

"Smooth your hair, then, and stand by. I'm going to ring it." I went along to the hall and found the gong, and I had my arm raised to strike it before I saw Aunt Violet.

She was sitting on the couch at the end near the front door, and her face was well painted and powdered.

CHAPTER THIRTY

I LEFT the gong and walked over to Aunt Violet, who gave me a faintly defiant look. I sat down beside her and said pleasantly, "It's nice to see you downstairs. Are you going to have dinner with us?"

"No. No, no—I'm just sitting here for a change. I don't see why they think they can keep me in my room that way."

"Certainly not," I said heartily, thinking of Dr. Benson, "but I wish you'd join us for dinner. It's just ready to be served."

"No, no, child, I can't do that. But you might bring my dinner to me here."

"Here?" I murmured.

"Yes. I'll just have a tray right here on this couch. That will be a nice change for me. But I don't want to sit with them; I couldn't touch a mouthful if they were all around me."

"All right," I agreed, "if that's the way you want it—"

I stood up, but as I turned away she gave a pull at my skirt.

"Miriel, I put a little powder on, and some lipstick. Does it look all right?"

I regarded her critically. "Take some of the lipstick off," I decided. "The powder's all right."

She nodded, produced a lavender-scented handkerchief, and mopped up a little.

"All right now," I approved, and went off to ring the gong. That done, I waited quietly at the foot of the stairs, because I wanted to hear what Dr. Benson would say when he caught Aunt Violet out of her room.

Sara and John came down first. They seemed to be having a spirited argument, but as soon as they came within hearing distance they saw me and stopped talking abruptly. They did not notice Aunt Violet until they reached the foot of the stairs, and then they stopped dead and gaped.

John recovered first and said, "Well, well. How are you, Aunt Violet?"

The old lady stared fixedly at an oil painting on the opposite wall and ostentatiously ignored him.

Sara touched John's arm and said quietly, "Come on—don't tease her."

They went on to the dining-room, and almost immediately Mabel appeared and came down with one plump ringed hand trailing the banister. On the bottom stair she halted suddenly and exclaimed, "Well!" in a loud voice.

Aunt Violet quivered but continued to look the oil painting in the eye.

Mabel took a long breath. "I must say, Violet, I think you've behaved very badly, making such a point of avoiding us all. I think it's most inconsiderate of you—and very embarrassing for us."

There was no sound or movement from Aunt Violet, and Mabel hesitated and then moved on. "I hope you've made up your mind to be more agreeable in the future," she observed by way of a parting fling.

"Where's Dr. Lang?" I called after her.

"Just coming," she said over her shoulder and disappeared into the dining-room.

I waited for him, but the thing turned out to be a disappointment. He came down the stairs, stood at the bottom for a moment, staring at Aunt Violet, then nodded to me and made for the dining-room. Aunt Violet had not moved, but she relaxed quite visibly as he passed on.

Ian met me at the door of the dining-room, and I turned back with him because he wanted to see Aunt Violet for himself. He took a long look at her from behind the newel post, shook his head, and said in a low, serious voice, "She's cracked from ear to ear. Must be."

I began to laugh hysterically and had to muffle it in my handkerchief as we returned to the dining-room.

Kelly was dishing up the dinner under a barrage of criticism from Mabel—with Father backing her up. When I was able to get his harassed attention I told him to arrange a tray and take it out to the hall—and he very nearly forgot himself. He asked me in an aside, and out of the corner of his mouth, if he should eat it when he got it there or leave it for Briggs.

"Just do what I tell you. When you get the tray out there, even you'll know what to do with it."

Father monopolized the conversation at the meal, as usual, but nobody seemed to mind. They ate in gloomy silence until he choked over a piece of potato, when Mabel took the opportunity to say, "You know, I'm beginning to think she's a bit crazy."

"Oh, I don't know, Mother," John demurred. "She's always been odd."

I turned my attention to the dinner after that and was somewhat mortified to discover that the chicken—so far from being burned—was a trifle underdone; there was no salt in the vegetable, and I had forgotten to make any gravy at all. To Ian, who sat at my left, I apologized in an undertone.

"I can cook a little better than this when my mind's on it," I whispered.

He grinned and muttered, "It's all right, baby. I've weighed the problem carefully in my mind for the last ten minutes and I've decided not to divorce you."

Father's eloquence stretched the meal so that Briggs's hour was up as we rose from the table. I caught Ian's arm and whispered urgently, "Get him out of the house before Briggs catches him."

"Why are you trying to keep them apart?" Ian asked impatiently. "Why shouldn't he talk to Briggs?"

"Because he'll certainly be put in jail for perjury if he does," I snapped. "Please, Ian!"

He hunched his shoulders and turned away, and I saw him run Father out into the hall, get him into his coat, and hand him his hat. Father tried to pay his respects to Aunt Violet, but Ian pushed him out the door without ceremony. "I wouldn't do this, pal," he explained, "but your daughter is a most unreasonable woman. I'll walk down the street with you until you get a cab."

Father threw me an anguished look, and I knew at once that it was the burlesque show—he didn't want to miss it after having it dangled before his eyes. I called after Ian to please give Father the five dollars I owed him, and Ian nodded. They went down the drive, and I saw a small group of men surround them at the gate before I closed the door.

Mabel had come into the hall behind me, and I turned around to find her heckling Aunt Violet.

"It wouldn't hurt you to be friendly now that you've decided to come out of your room," she suggested querulously.

She was standing between Aunt Violet and the oil painting, but Aunt Violet never shifted the direction of her eyes, so that she now appeared to be concentrating on the second button of Mabel's dress.

I took Mabel by the arm, and she allowed me to lead her away. "I think it would be better to leave her alone," I said. "Let her come out of it her own way."

"Well, it's no pleasure to me, I'm sure. I was merely trying to have harmony in the home, as I always do. Besides, I want to find out what she knows about Leslie."

Her tears spilled over, and I said gently, "Look—why don't you go to bed and take one of your pills? You need rest and sleep."

"I can't stand it, she sobbed. "My poor baby! And nobody cares— it's dreadful! She had no friends—none to speak of, that is—and it just doesn't matter to anybody. Even my own family—they won't discuss the funeral with me."

I went into the living-room with her, and we sat down together.

"I'll talk it over with you. Probably they're too upset and don't want to think about it, and so, as usual, all the work is left to you. You've spoiled them, you know. You've always kept things running smoothly, and they simply don't realize how much work goes into it."

She blossomed like a flower and dried her eyes almost at once. It was soon obvious to me that she did not want help or advice about the funeral: she simply wanted to talk about it, and since it seemed to relieve her feelings, I let her ramble on.

"You see, after Richard's funeral I was so distracted about Leslie being missing that I could not allow anyone to come to the house, but some of the relatives must come this time, and of course they'll expect refreshments. But I simply cannot trust Kelly to see to it; he is utterly incompetent. Look at the dinner tonight! Badly cooked—badly served— if only that Annie would come back. I tried to get a cook today, but they would not promise anything. I need rest, too, or I shall break completely."

I thought, myself, that she looked fit for a break if she couldn't relax, and I knew that she'd never relax until the foolish, unimportant details of a funeral were properly in order.

"Now, listen," I said firmly. "I'll get you a cook. Perhaps I'll get Annie back—I believe she's right in town. Will you promise me to go to bed if I get Annie here tonight?"

"Oh, could you?" she cried eagerly.

"I think so. In any case, I'll get you some competent help, and you can rely on it."

She leaned back and closed her eyes, murmuring that she felt better already, that I was a dear and worth two of Sara.

But I had an ear stretched toward the hall, where I heard Kelly admitting Briggs.

I got up quietly and went to the portieres that hung in the archway, and I saw that Briggs had seized the golden opportunity and was questioning Aunt Violet. She gave him a yes or a no occasionally, but that was about all, and he began to exhibit a faint impatience.

"But I don't understand, Miss Lang, why your brother left all his money to your niece, since he never saw her. How do you know that he never saw her, by the way?"

"I don't know," said Aunt Violet without interest. "He just said he didn't."

"Did she ever come here to visit? Lunch? Dinner?"

"No. None of them did. I didn't want to see any of them."

"Why didn't you want to see them?"

"I did not like them," said Aunt Violet simply.

"But you liked your brother Richard?"

There was a brief silence after that one, and then Aunt Violet said, "Yes."

"Are you sure?" Briggs asked, trying to hold her eye.

She made no reply, and after a moment he started again.

"You like your nephew, Ian, don't you?"

"Yes."

"But you don't like your sister-in-law, Mrs. Mabel Lang?"

"No," said Aunt Violet, beginning to give off sparks. "I have already said so, have I not?"

"And you particularly disliked your niece, Leslie?"

"On the contrary," said Aunt Violet acidly, "I liked her better than the others. I used to send Annie out with cookies for her."

"Out where?" asked Briggs, trying not to look confused.

"Out in the back yard when she came over to play at the pond."

"Didn't you ever ask her to come in?"

"No, I didn't," said Aunt Violet, "and I'm tired of talking. I wish you'd go away."

Briggs sighed, straightened up, and headed for the living room. I had just time to resume my seat before he appeared.

Mabel opened her eyes, started to say something to me, and caught sight of Briggs.

He was giving her a cold eye, and before she could speak he said impersonally, "Mrs. Lang, do you know that yours are the only finger-prints on that poker that killed your daughter?"

CHAPTER THIRTY-ONE

MABEL'S BOSOM heaved, and her diamond pin glittered expensively. She said with magnificent hauteur, "You will find my fingerprints on a good many articles in this house, Mr. Briggs. I may have handled the poker when it was in its rack here beside the fireplace—naturally. But how dare you insinuate—"

But she looked guilty—you couldn't miss it—and I knew Briggs was pleased. He broke in sternly, "I am making no insinuations, madam; I have simply stated that only your fingerprints were on that poker. Further, you must know that your husband's financial situation is serious and that if your daughter had inherited the money she would almost undoubtedly have used it to finance a photographic expedition to South America."

I shook my head and declared, "That's silly. Leslie couldn't have used all the money on an expedition; she would certainly have kept her parents out of debtors' jail with some of it. And anyway, it seems to me that only an innocent person would have left a set of fingerprints on the poker." I turned to Mabel. "You found it around the house somewhere, didn't you? And automatically put it in its place before you knew why it had been taken."

She dropped her eyes to her lap in confusion, and I noticed that Briggs's face had darkened to an angry red.

"Speak up, Mabel," I said urgently. "Where did you find the thing?"

She began to pleat her skirt in an agitated fashion and said faintly, "You shouldn't call me Mabel—you don't know me well enough."

"Tell Briggs the truth and let him get on with the investigation, then. You've nothing to be afraid of. It was perfectly natural for you to have picked the thing up and put it where it belonged."

"Young lady," said Briggs with long-suffering patience, "suppose you allow me to handle this. Now, Mrs. Lang, perhaps you will explain just how your fingerprints came to be on that poker."

Mabel drew a couple of nervous breaths and backed down.

"It is as she says. I found it lying around and returned it to its proper place. Later, when I learned its—its significance, I was afraid to mention it for fear you would involve me. Although how you—or anyone— could think that I would harm my own child—"

158

She began to cry hysterically, and Briggs backed up a little with a defeated look on his face.

"Mrs. Lang, you should go to bed and get some sleep," I said soothingly. "If you'll just tell us first where you found the poker?"

She composed herself after a while and said reluctantly that she had found it lying on the kitchen floor. I did not believe her, but Briggs released her without further comment, and she made her way upstairs, still mopping at her red eyes.

Briggs turned on me and said briskly, "Now, where's your father?"

"Why, Father was here for some time," I replied vaguely, "but he had to go to a show and he couldn't wait. But you'll be able to get him in the morning—I'm sure of that."

I went off before he actually bit me in the arm, which seemed imminent, and found Kelly surrounded by a debris of dirty dishes in the kitchen. He was gloomily picking his teeth.

"*Must* you do that?" I asked coldly.

"It's never been a habit of mine, but when I found a packet of these things in the drawer I figured it must be all right if wealthy people like the Langs used them."

He glared at me defiantly, and I glared back. "Don't show your ignorance. Mabel must have brought them here, and she uses them for sticking into little sausages and things. They serve them with cocktails."

"They're more useful this way," said Kelly sulkily. "What about all this mess?"

"Let's get it cleaned up," I groaned. "I'll help you with it, but I won't do it alone."

He started in with a great clatter, and we worked together for a while before I asked, "Did you hear about Mabel's fingerprints?"

He nodded, "I was listening—got back to the kitchen here just before you did. But why didn't you let Mabel speak for herself instead of putting words into her mouth?"

I was leaning over the dishpan, and I brushed a strand of hair out of my eyes with the back of my bent wrist before I explained slowly, "I didn't want to waste time. We're sure that's what happened, and I knew she was just scared because she had touched the thing at all. But she never found it in the kitchen. I'm convinced she was lying about that."

Kelly turned to look at me, knocking a plate, two knives, and half a lemon on to the floor as he did so.

"Are you sure about that? That's the worst of eavesdropping—you can't get the expressions." He regarded the plate, which had broken into four pieces, with an absent expression. "Interesting—very."

"Well, that was my impression," I said definitely.

We reduced the kitchen, finally, to a state of immaculate cleanliness, and Kelly heaved a long sigh.

"I have a night's work in front of me now and I suppose you'll be tagging along, but I'm warning you, now, that if you want coffee every half-hour like you did last night I'll throw you to Briggs, and he can jail you, for all I care."

"What are you going to do first?" I asked mildly.

"Those bricks in the attic. Someone mixing cement at night means something secret, and it must be behind that brickwork. I'll have to tear them down, and it will take me some time—even if I'm left in peace."

"I'll join you after a while," I decided. "First I'm going to work on getting Annie back—or someone to do the cooking here. It's to relieve Mabel's mind—and my back."

Kelly said, "Good! Get Annie if you can. I've an idea I'd like to see her again."

"Briggs!" I murmured suddenly. "He'll know where she is. I hope he hasn't gone."

I found him pacing up and down the hall with his hands jammed into his trouser pockets. He flung an occasional glance at Aunt Violet but apparently had not attempted to question her again.

I felt a spasm of pity for the poor old thing and delayed my errand long enough to try to urge her to go to bed, but she shook her head stubbornly. She liked sitting there, she told me. She felt fine and intended to stay there until she was tired.

I gave it up and approached Briggs. When I asked for Annie's address he blandly demanded to know what I was talking about.

"Oh, come on," I said impatiently. "We're in desperate need of a cook, and all I want is to get her back into the house. I'm quite certain you know where she is."

He looked me over in silence for a moment while he stroked his chin, which needed a shave. "You're a bit too smart altogether," he said finally. "I have an idea that you know a good deal more than you're telling."

"All I know," I said innocently, "is that I have to get a cook into this house tonight. I've given my solemn promise."

"Well"—he raised his shoulders and let them drop again—"I'd just as soon she came back, anyway. She's at that little hotel by the station. Registered as Mary Perkins."

"Why the change of name?" I asked in some surprise.

"Oh—scared of something, I guess. We couldn't get anything out of her. All she's interested in is when she'll be allowed to go home to her sister."

"The one who lives in Maine?"

Briggs said, "Yeah. Respectable widow with two grown children—name of Emily Reilly."

It crossed my mind that he was showing off, but I merely said politely, "I see. Well, I'd better get along and start working on Annie. I want her here tonight at all costs."

John was coming down the stairs, and as I turned to go he stopped me with a gleam in his eye.

"Patient at the hospital," he said, falsely casual. "I'd like you to special him until eleven. It's only two hours. You'll do that for me, won't you?"

Ian had banged in at the front door and apparently heard the last of this, for he came over and said, "Look here, John, she's on her honeymoon, and I'm on the tag end of a leave—for God's sake, go away and leave us alone."

John had an air of reasonable patience. "It's only until eleven, and I need her badly. I promise not to ask her again if she'll just do these two hours—to oblige me. By way of return I could forget a few feathers you left around my wife's room—when you really should have had it quite clean and tidy for her."

Ian took a sharp breath, and I laughed. "All right," I said airly. "Seeing it's blackmail, I'll go."

John relaxed into a satisfied smile and said he'd drive me over at once, and Ian told him to go and boil his head. "I'll drive her over myself and I'll wait for her and drive her back again. And if she isn't out on the stroke of eleven I'll go in and raise hell."

"All right," John agreed mildly. "Take it easy. I've said she'll be finished at eleven, haven't I?" He turned to me with an outline of the patient and a few hasty instructions.

I whistled. "Even richer than Benjamin K., is he?"

"Yes, he is," said John with a faint grin. "And although he shows temper now and then, he pays his bills promptly and without argument. He just fired his nurse for spilling orange juice on his pajamas, and he's yapping for another to take her place."

I went upstairs and changed into my uniform, feeling that I was more or less in the right mood to cope with a rich and bad-tempered old man.

It was snowing again, lightly, when I ran down the steps and got into the car. Ian tucked a small rug over my lap and around my legs and then swung the car down the drive and out into the street.

"We shouldn't have let John see that the feathers mattered to us at all," he said presently in a worried voice.

"It wasn't John or his feathers," I protested. "I knew I'd have to go, anyway. But what took you so long about seeing Father off? Trying to get out off the dishes?"

"The dishes at least wouldn't have cost anything. The old man said I was a fine son-in-law, so he invited me into a bar for a few drinks. That set me back four-sixty, and what with the five you told me to give him, I am now flat broke."

"Well, don't look to me for sympathy," I said. "We both found out that marriage means in-laws as well."

"It seems to me," Ian observed as he drew up at the hospital, "that I've pulled the in-laws without the marriage. I'll wait for you here."

I said, "Thanks," and hurried up the steps.

My patient was asleep, and I was conscious of a faint annoyance. I'd have enjoyed a fight with someone with whom I need not make up later on. I got him some fresh water, and when I brought it back the tinkle of ice against glass woke him up.

He opened a pair of choleric blue eyes and bellowed, "Who are you?"

I set the water down, smoothed his pillow, and said, "There! Are we more comfortable now? I'm your new nursie."

"Oh, for God's sake! Leave my pillow alone, will you? What's new Nursie's name?"

"Pansy," I said modestly.

He laughed heartily and told me he'd once had a cow named Pansy.

I gave him a look of reproach and suggested that it wasn't very nice to be compared with a cow.

"All right, sweetie, I'm sorry. Come on over here and let's make up."

I sighed. It was obvious that he wasn't going to fight—he merely wanted to play. It was a disappointment, but I played with him until his night special turned up, when I crept out, hoping that the emergency shortage on the floor had been relieved and that my conscience needn't nag me into staying and helping out.

I need not have worried. The aide with the bun was on duty, and she gave me a kindly smile and wished me Godspeed with every indication that the floor was in excellent shape and would remain that way as long as the specials went about their business without trying to interfere.

Ian was waiting and gave me an enthusiastic greeting.

"You never go into that dump but what I have a feeling that I might never see you again."

"The hospital has been a bit shorthanded and upset," I said vaguely, "but they're all right now. There's an aide with a bun in charge. Look, Ian, I want you to drive me to that hotel at the station. Annie's staying there, and I want to try to get her back."

He protested a bit, said he wanted to go straight home, and even offered to do the cooking himself, but at last he gave in with a couple of swear words and drove along to the shabby little hotel.

A pimpled clerk located Mary Perkins in room 304 and asked if we were expected. I said, "Definitely," over my shoulder and made for the stairs, while Ian followed in silence. We mounted two long dusty flights and found 304 at the end of a dim narrow corridor. Ian knocked and then knocked again, but there was no answer, and I noticed, with a sudden bouncing of my heart, that the door was slightly ajar.

I pushed it open, and we saw Annie in the glare from an overhead light. She was huddled, awkward and quite still, in a faded old armchair.

CHAPTER THIRTY-TWO

IAN pushed me back out of the room, but not before I had seen the head—beaten and smashed, as Leslie's had been.

I leaned against the wall in the hall outside, with my hands clenched against the shaking chill in my body, and presently Ian came out and closed the door.

"I'd better stay up here," he said quietly. "Go down and telephone the police. This is going to be bad, I'm afraid."

I went down, wondering rather wildly if my knees would last the distance. The clerk with the pimples watched me all the way across the lobby, and when I said huskily, "You'd better phone the police—the woman upstairs has been killed," he jumped as though he had been shot. He began to run toward the stairs, but I caught him and held on.

"Phone, first. You must get the police."

"Maybe it was just an accident," he said hysterically. "Maybe she's not dead—just hurt. I don't want the police in here if I can help it."

"You can't help it," I told him grimly. "She's dead all right—some-one smashed her head in."

He gave up then and went to the telephone with drops of perspiration standing out on his forehead. I told him to make sure that Briggs was notified and when he replaced the phone asked him if Mary Perkins had had any visitors.

"Yes, yes—there was a woman," he said impatiently, trying to make for the stairs again.

I kept hold of his coat. "What kind of a woman? What did she look like?"

"Somewhat shabby—same type as the one up there—and she stayed half an hour or more. Let me go, will you? I must get up there."

I dropped his coat and he sped away, while I found a fairly comfort-able chair in the lobby and collapsed into it. But it was not long before Briggs appeared with a formidable retinue. He was in a bad temper and started by trying to take it out on me, but I merely told him to be quiet or he wouldn't be able to hear what I was saying. I did not mention the woman visitor, as I supposed he'd get that for himself, but I told him the rest and ended by asking if I could go home.

He didn't bother to answer, but Ian came down just then and told him the same story as the one I had just finished. "Let us know if we can give you any help on this. We're going home now, because my wife has had about all she can stand."

He took my arm, and we sailed out into the street. I raised my hot face gratefully into the light snowfall and drew a long, quivering sigh of relief. "I thought he was going to keep us there all night."

Ian snuggled my arm against his coat and said, "Oh no, he couldn't do that."

"Well, he didn't, anyway," I murmured.

The house seemed to be in darkness when we drove up. Ian opened the door with his key, and we found only a dim light burning in the hall. Aunt Violet had apparently tired of her seat on the couch at last and was no longer there. We went upstairs and saw cracks of light showing under Sara's door and John's. Aunt Violet's room and the one occupied by Mabel and Dr. Benson were dark.

"We must tell Aunt Violet," I said uneasily. "I want to get it over with."

"Let me tell her," Ian suggested, but I shook my head.

"You come with me, but I want to be there. She might get hysterical, or have a heart attack, or something—she's been under quite a strain."

We knocked and then tried the door, but it was locked. After the fourth knock we heard her moving, and presently she asked who was there in a rather quavering voice. We identified ourselves, and she let us in. She was wearing a wrapper over her nightgown and had washed the powder and lipstick from her face. She tightened the wrapper around her body and said in an aggrieved voice, "I was asleep."

Ian put her gently into a chair and then told her that Annie was dead—that there had been an accident. She became hysterical, and I had quite a time with her. She kept asking what had happened, and in the end we told her. Oddly enough, she took that more quietly and said merely, "They'll get me too. They did not like Annie—she was too nosy. I knew she was nosy, but she was a good girl."

She began to cry quietly, and I tried to put her to bed, but she whispered, "No—oh no. I must lock the door. You go now. I'm all right, but I must lock the door after you, you see."

We had to agree to that in the end, but I gave her one of her sleeping pills first. She locked the door after us, and I waited until I heard her patter back to bed.

The doorbell rang, and Ian swore softly. "Must be Briggs. I'll have to let him in."

I nodded. "You go on down, and I'll wait here. I don't want to see him unless I have to."

Ian started down the stairs, and I turned and raced up to the attic. I found Kelly working on the brick wall, and it seemed to me that he hadn't even made a dent in it.

"You'd better go down the back stairs to your room," I puffed, trying to get my breath, "and pretend you're asleep."

He was on his feet in an instant and asked, "What's happened?"

I told him everything as quickly as I could and ended by saying that Briggs was coming in the front door at the very moment.

He let out a few curses and ran for the stairs without a backward glance. He took whatever tool he had been using with him, and I looked at his work with a sinking heart. He had started right over at one side, under the eaves, but beyond chiseling out a little of the mortar, he seemed to have done nothing. I inspected the brickwork more closely and began to realize that he knew what he was doing, after all, for the mortar was slightly different in color at that end.

Something was hidden there, then—something secret that had been walled in quietly during the night. I had not quite believed it before, and I wondered with rising excitement if it would clear up the whole dreadful business. I switched off the light and crept down to the second floor where I met Ian looking tired and grim.

"You'll have to go downstairs. Briggs is holding a reception. I've been sent to rouse the others."

I went on to the first floor, and Briggs caught up on all the questions he had forgotten to ask me at the hotel. There were two men with him who remained silent throughout. They were busy, however—one writing notes in a pad and the other chewing hard on a toothpick.

Briggs's face was a dark red, and he put a positive snarl on it as one of his men marched in with Kelly in tow.

I looked at Kelly in awe and admiration. He was completely undressed; his hair was rumpled around the toupee, and he had pulled a dressing gown untidily over his striped pajamas. His feet were bare and his eyes looked genuinely sleepy.

"He was asleep in bed," the man said to Briggs.

"Oh, sure," Briggs gave Kelly a hard stare and added, "I could be asleep in bed at a moment's notice too."

Kelly looked offended. "I'm sure I don't know what you mean, sir."

"Why don't you all sit down?" I suggested hospitably. "I'm sure Kelly would be glad to get some coffee for us."

Kelly winced, and the stooges looked hopefully at their boss, but Briggs refused, although I'm sure it cost him a struggle. He sent me out of the room and said, "Wait in the hall with the others. I'll question this man first and then I want to talk to the rest of you together."

The others were coming down the stairs—Sara wearing a breath-taking negligee of palest green satin and smoking a cigarette, and John looking distinctly cross. Dr. Benson was calm and grave, and Mabel voluble.

"It is utterly absurd!" she stormed. "What has it to do with us if Annie has been murdered at a hotel? Why should we be dragged out of our beds? I will not put up with it, Benson—it's too much. I was having my best sleep in some days."

"If we just answer his questions quickly and truthfully," Ian said, trying to be soothing, "we won't be kept up long. It's just a routine matter."

I stopped them at the entrance to the living-room. "It's no use going in now—Briggs will only throw you out again. He's doing Kelly, and when he finishes it will be our turn."

"That man Briggs is impossible," Mabel said shrilly. "Now we are to wait for Kelly, if you please! As though I didn't do that all day long!"

"All right, Aunt Mabel," Ian said "I'm sure he'll be ready for us in a few minutes. No use in antagonizing him or he'll probably keep us here longer than necessary. Sit down and try to relax."

Mabel sat down but didn't waste much effort on relaxing. She asked suddenly, apparently having just thought of it, "Why should Violet be excused, pray? She knew Annie better than any of us, and yet she is allowed to sleep on in peace."

Ian's voice was beginning to take on an edge; but he explained quietly enough, "I told you—we had quite a bad time with her, and she's sleeping under a sedative."

"So was I sleeping under a sedative—" Mabel began, when Briggs appeared and asked us, quite politely, to step into the living-room.

We trailed in and found seats for ourselves. Sara used up a whole couch, putting her feet up and assuming a lying position, which forced Ian and John together on a dainty love seat.

I could see at a glance that Briggs was in a much better humor. He no longer looked baffled; he knew all—or thought he did.

"Why should we be interviewed en masse this way?" Mabel asked, getting her oar in first. "And just why should Miss Violet Lang be allowed to rest on comfortably while we are dragged from our beds?"

Briggs almost beamed on her. "Miss Violet Lang," he said kindly, "is physically incapable of these vicious attacks with a poker—and that's according to the testimony of her doctor."

"She has no doctor," Mabel mentioned, and patted her bosom.

"She had one—about two years ago. He's in the Army now—had to wire him. But his testimony is conclusive."

Mabel sniffed, and Briggs motioned to one of his men who was lurking in the shadows of the dining-room. The policeman stepped out into the light, and we saw that he carried some shabby feminine clothing.

Briggs fingered the things lovingly. "These clothes of Annie's have been out in the elements tonight and almost certainly were on the back of the visitor that Annie had at about the time she was killed. I'd like each one of you to try them on for fit."

CHAPTER THIRTY-THREE

FOR ONCE Mabel was speechless, and Dr. Benson spoke up instead.

"I don't believe you can force us to do that, Briggs."

Briggs said diplomatically, "Don't you see? It gives you the opportunity of completely clearing yourselves. The night clerk at the hotel will be here in a few minutes to try to identify Annie's visitor."

John spoke in a lazy voice with the chill on. "The night clerk could easily make a mistake. I dare say any one of us would give the general outline if we were draped in those things. So I, for one, refuse—unless you have the authority to insist, which I very much doubt. And anyway, aside from the main objection, I dislike having to put on Annie's old clothes."

Mabel and Sara promptly refused as well, and Dr. Benson nodded to indicate that he was aligned with the rebels.

Briggs, with a couple of veins showing on his glistening forehead, nevertheless kept a civil tongue in his head "I suppose you have no objection to the night clerk coming in, anyway, to look you over?"

"None whatever," John said amiably. "If it will give you or him any pleasure."

"When do you expect him?" Mabel asked peevishly. "I cannot sit here all night waiting for him."

Briggs turned on her. "He should be here at any moment now, Mrs. Lang. In the meantime, would you mind telling me what you did this evening after dinner?"

Mabel gave a loud, exasperated sigh, seemed to consider a refusal, and said finally, "As I believe you already know, I took a sedative shortly after dinner and went to bed immediately—at the insistence of my husband and my niece, Miriel."

I swallowed a laugh as I realized that I had been taken into the fold. Now I was Mabel's niece.

Briggs turned to the man who still held Annie's clothes and said irritably, "Take those things into the hall and have the clerk identify them when he comes."

The man departed, and Briggs proceeded to get a statement from each of us as to our activities during the evening.

Nothing could have sounded more innocent. Ian had remained in

169

the car outside the hospital, thinking. He even offered to tell what he had thought about, but Briggs shut him up. Sara and John had read improving books in their rooms, and Dr. Benson had attended a patient until nine-thirty, when he returned, drank a glass of warm milk, and climbed into his little bed.

Briggs took it all without comment and went out into the hall. He returned shortly, guiding the pimpled night clerk, and indicated us with a wave of his hand. "Go ahead—look them all over, and give the men as much attention as the women. You've identified the clothes; now try to imagine each one dressed up in them. And don't pass over the man and girl who came in later and found the body."

We waited with a certain amount of nervousness, but the big moment never came. The clerk looked us over vaguely, scratched his head, and then shook it. "It's no use. She wore that brown veil over her face, and I didn't notice her much, anyway. She just asked me for the room number and said she was expected, and then she went up."

"What time was that?" I asked.

The clerk said, "Around ten-thirty," and Briggs said, "All right, all right—I'll ask the questions."

He ran the clerk out of the room and then came back and asked us all the questions he could think of, to get even with us for spoiling his plan. He left in the end because he got tired himself, but he promised to be back bright and early in the morning. John murmured that it would be hard to wait, but we'd try to be patient.

Unexpectedly Kelly appeared with a large tray of coffee and cookies. He lowered it to the coffee table, said, "Fooled ya!" and departed hastily. Sara dropped her head back on to a satin sofa cushion and laughed helplessly until John went to her and put his hand over her mouth.

Mabel busied herself with the tray and poured the coffee. She remarked that she would not be able to sleep a wink—and repeated it four times, for emphasis.

We all drank it gratefully, though, and presently the Langs drifted upstairs, leaving Ian and me to stare gloomily at the tumbled tray and soiled cups.

Ian heaved a sigh and stood up. "I always thought that when I got to be a lieutenant I'd be through with K.P.," he observed mildly.

"We'd better get them washed," I said, helping him to load the tray. "I know Kelly has gone back to the attic, and taking that wall down looks like an all-night job to me."

We carried the tray to the kitchen, and I filled a dishpan while Ian picked up a towel.

"Silly crackpot," he said gloomily. "Why can't he go to the police if he thinks there's something behind the wall? They'd have it broken down in no time."

"Yes, and then they'd get the credit if there's anything there. It's Kelly's idea, and he wants to work it himself."

"I can't see what could be there that would be important in any way."

"Well, I don't either," I admitted. "But probably Kelly isn't telling all he knows."

"Why not?" Ian asked bitterly. "It wouldn't take five minutes."

When we had put the dishes away and the kitchen was tidy, Ian said, "Now let's go to bed."

I laughed at him. "Don't be silly. You have to get a chisel and help Kelly with that wall."

"I suppose," said Ian, "you mean that you're not going to bed until you find out what's behind the wall."

"Right. At the moment nothing would induce me to go anywhere but to the attic."

He sighed and went to a corner of the kitchen, where he opened a toolbox and selected a chisel. "Come on, you pest," he said, and made for the back stairs. On the second floor we took a cautious look around and discovered that all the Langs except Aunt Violet had their lights on.

"Mabel will have to read until late," I whispered, "after all that coffee, and Benson will have to read along with her—even if he did retire at nine-thirty to catch up on his sleep."

Ian said, "Quiet. You shouldn't pull my relatives to pieces. It's not a good foundation for marriage."

"I think you must be wrong," I replied astounded. "Everybody does it, and despite that there are many happy marriages."

As we passed Mabel's door on our way back to the stairs I noticed that it was slightly ajar. I slowed down, with my ears waving, as her voice drifted out to us.

"I don't think Violet is as weak as they're making out, Benson. It seems to me she must be fairly strong. After all—"

"Please, my dear!" said Dr. Benson. "I've been in touch with that fellow who attended her about two years ago. I felt it my duty, now that Richard is not here, to take care of her. Her heart is in deplorable shape and her blood pressure very high. She is in far too weakened a condition to have dealt out such savage blows."

"Then who did it?" Mabel asked, her voice shrilling up.

"How do I know?" he said shortly.

"What about the money? How long will it be tied up? We need it so desperately."

"I know, I know. It will come eventually. I'll just have to borrow on the expectancy."

Ian touched my arm and whispered, "Come on—that isn't nice."

We went upstairs to the third floor and into the attic. Kelly had had the door closed and the light on and was chiseling away quietly. He looked up as we came in, gave Ian a few terse directions, and went silently back to work.

It seemed incredibly slow to me. I was sure that it would be morning before they got more than a few bricks out, and after a while I said impatiently, "Surely there's a more efficient way to go about that job. It will take you forever."

"There's no other way to do it without making too much noise," Kelly explained austerely. "You go on down and take a nap. This is men's work."

"You won't miss anything," Ian said, wiping gritty dust off his forehead. "When we break through and find dust and a couple of dead mice Kelly will tell us how glad he is to have got that item off his mind. I'm hoping, myself, that Briggs will have solved the thing by that time."

Kelly laid down his chisel. "Listen, soldier. If Briggs solves this puzzle before I do I'll hand you a fifty-dollar wedding present—cash money."

"Good!" said Ian.

I stood up and moved away restlessly. "I believe I shall take a nap if you don't mind. I'll be back later."

Ian wanted to escort me downstairs and, when I would not let him, made me promise not to roam the house and to lock the bedroom door. "You needn't worry about me," I assured him. "After all, there are no pokers on the second floor." I stopped and shuddered. "Was it a—a poker—with Annie?"

Kelly nodded. "It's an old building—that hotel—and there's a fireplace in every room. Most of them have been closed off, but the former occupant of that room was a non-transient and wanted the fireplace kept open. There is a set of fire-irons there and the poker was used."

"How on earth do you find these things out?" I asked admiringly.

Kelly shrugged. "I got it out of Briggs and his boys while they weren't looking."

"Well, I have to hand it to you—I really do."

"Don't hand him anything," said Ian, "until he produces."

"You're talking too loud," Kelly snapped.

"Loudly," said Ian.

I left them to it and went off down the stairs. The darkened second floor brought goose-pimples out on my arms, so I switched on a light and then went into my new room. I knew, though, that I could not sleep; I had to know first what was behind the brick wall. I moved around aimlessly for a while and at last wandered out into the hall, where I switched off the light again, just to see if the Langs had bedded down yet. Sara's room and John's were dark now, and there was no light under Aunt Violet's door. But Mabel's room was still lighted, and she was still talking. I moved up quietly and deliberately listened.

Benson had the floor by that time, and he sounded irritated.

"—and that's all there is to it. You know perfectly well that I haven't played golf for months—haven't had the time or the weather—and I haven't been near my golf bag during that time. As a matter of fact, I didn't even know whether it had been moved here or had gone to storage."

"You must know, Benson, that I wouldn't have dared to put it into storage."

"All right," said Dr. Benson, and the light went out. I could hear the springs of his bed as he lowered his weight on to it, and he went on, "I don't want to hear any more about it. If I'd found a poker in my golf bag I'd have taken it out and put it where it belonged—as you did. So suppose we drop the subject and go to sleep."

Quiet reigned, and I moved away, completely absorbed in this new development. I had got all the way down to the front hall before I stopped to wonder where I was going, and then I went on to the kitchen and had eaten two cookies before I realized that I was not hungry at all. Instead of going back to my own room, curiosity took me into Annie's bedroom, and I looked around idly. There was not much to see—a few practical personal effects in the bureau drawers and perhaps half a dozen shabby dresses and two coats hanging in the closet.

I had started to close the closet door on these limp and rather pathetic garments, when my eyes fastened on them with sudden attention, and I flung the door wide again. I brought one of the dresses out and held it up against me—and realized at once that it would be much too short for Annie.

CHAPTER THIRTY-FOUR

I HUNG the dress back in the closet and pulled out another dress and a coat. They matched the first dress in length, and I let them drop from my hands on to the floor, while I fought down a terrified impulse to run out of the house and go home. Instead, I forced myself back to the closet and took a look at the hats. There was a straw and two dusty felts—a black and a brown. The brown was the one worn by the mysterious visitor, and it had a tacky veil hanging from it. I dropped it on to the bed and stared at nothing for a moment, and then found that I was looking at a religious picture that hung on the wall over the head of the bed.

I turned abruptly, left the room, and went back to the kitchen, where I picked up another cookie and then found that I couldn't eat it. I moved slowly into the front hall, with its dim center light, and looked at the couch and at Mabel's fancy cushions which dribbled feathers. I mounted the stairs, still going slowly, and found the landing in darkness, with no lights slowing under any of the doors except my own.

I went into my room and groped around in the closet until I found my ruined negligee. The damage was mostly at the bottom, where there were a few tears and a lot of mud and dirt, but the sleeves had been ripped at the seams as well.

I threw it over a chair and stretched out on the bed with my brain going furiously. Annie was a Catholic, and the Langs were Presbyterian, but Aunt Violet had a rosary hanging in her closet. And then Annie had often given Leslie cookies when Leslie was a child. And she wore some kind of brace on her teeth.

I shifted my head on the pillow and stared at the ceiling. Just last summer Richard had bought a pile of sand and had hidden cement in his closet. Only he hadn't done anything with it— hadn't got around to it. But somebody else had done it for him—in a hurry and secretly—after he died.

It must have been important, but certainly it was not the hiding of that pathetic little grave. And yet it would be a natural assumption that Uncle Richard's intention had been to hide the little coffin—and perhaps that outspoken Bible as well.

I wondered whether Dr. Benson really considered Aunt Violet in-

174

sane or not. If he actually had ordered her to stay in her room, then he must have changed his mind since, because he had passed her in the front hall almost indifferently. It was possible, I supposed, that Uncle Richard had led him to believe that she was insane, but since he had observed her himself he had changed his mind. Because she was not insane—I was nearly sure of it.

I rolled over on my side, with my head resting on the crook of my elbow, and thought about Leslie. She had spoken to Uncle Richard about the stone lion—told him it was crumbling and might fall—and that must have been fairly recent, because he had said he hoped it would keep the children away from the sand pile which had been in the yard only since the previous summer.

Leslie must have been in the back yard sometime since the summer, then, and did Aunt Violet still send Annie out with cookies? No, that was silly. Leslie had walked around the lily pond—probably intending to take a picture of it. Yes, that was it, because Mabel had declared that none of them, except Benson, had ever been in the house until they moved there. Benson, of course, had lived in the house as a boy and then left to go to college, later married Mabel, and had not been allowed to darken the door again until just recently.

Why did Uncle Richard suddenly allow them all to move in? The impending bankruptcy, probably, and its threat of scandal. Uncle Richard practically worshipped the family honor. He was malicious, too—his description of Mabel's theatrical career proved that—and he might have let them in to get even with Aunt Violet for something. He knew well enough that she'd hate it.

It seemed probable that she was annoyed with him about something because she had never once gone to see him at the hospital, although she had managed it easily enough after he was dead. Her object, then, apparently had been to get his things before Mabel did. She knew the number of his room, since she had telephoned him once or twice, and she must have slipped past the desk downstairs and taken herself up in the self-service elevator. I thought about her refusal to see any of the family except Ian and myself—until tonight, when she issued forth with a lot of powder and too much lipstick on her face. She had never painted up for Ian and me.

I pulled myself off the bed and walked slowly out of the room. I felt queer and light-headed and a little dizzy, and I found myself mounting the stairs to the third floor without having made any decision to go there.

I heard the muffled tapping of the two chisels, and I went quietly into the attic and stood watching the two men as they worked.

They glanced up at me, and Kelly said, "It's not going badly, now—we'll have a whole section out pretty soon."

"In about half an hour," Ian added. "And then we'll be through, for the night."

I nodded vaguely. "Kelly, what was the name of that tavern Annie used to go to?"

"What do you want to know for?"

"Never mind, just tell me. And the name of the proprietor."

Kelly stood up and faced me. "What do you think you're going to do about it when I tell you?"

"For heaven's sake," I said plaintively, "don't be such a lemon. I'm merely curious, that's all. What's the matter with you, anyway?"

Kelly wiped dust from his perspiring face and said shortly, "It's called Smith's Tavern, and the name of the proprietor is Smith—if that helps you any."

I assumed a false interest in their work and saw that they seemed to be planning on getting three bricks out at once.

"It's tough work," Kelly muttered. "The damn things seem to be more cemented than mortared."

"What's the difference?" Ian asked, and Kelly snarled, "I don't know. I never laid bricks or tried to get them apart before. "

I slipped away and went straight down to the telephone in the front hall. I looked up the number of Smith's Tavern, called it and was answered by Smith himself. I asked him one question to which he replied promptly, and then I put down the phone and looked fearfully up the stairs.

I had to go up and get past that second floor somehow; I had to get back to Ian and Kelly—to warn them. I started up slowly shaking with fear and feeling that if I could only pass the second-floor landing in safety I'd be all right.

There was no sound but the absurd chattering of my own teeth, and the landing was quiet and dark. I paused at the head of the stairs and then flew across and up the stairs to the attic.

I was panting when I arrived there, but the two men did not notice me, for they had their three bricks half out.

I whispered, "Oh, don't," but they did not hear me and went on pulling—and presently the bricks came away.

I crept forward in fascinated horror, and Kelly picked up his flashlight and directed the beam into the opening.

It was there, as I knew it must be. The dreadful, bald head of Violet Lang.

CHAPTER THIRTY-FIVE

THERE WAS a camp bed in the narrow, dusty space under the eaves, and the small, pathetic body lay stretched on it, wearing a nightgown and covered with a blanket, the bald head toward us.

"My God!" Ian muttered. "Who is it?"

"I'm afraid it's your Aunt Violet," I said faintly, and peered into the opening again. I knew she was dead, and yet I had to make sure, since I had heard her moaning such a short time ago. I touched the cold forehead and drew back quickly.

Kelly pulled me away. "What did you ask that tavernkeeper Smith?"

"But who is that other—that one downstairs?" Ian asked in a stunned voice.

"Annie—it must be Annie; she's short enough. That's what I asked Smith—if she were tall, medium, or short, and he said short without any hesitation. You see, all her dresses were too short."

Ian looked from one to the other of us and asked, "But what are you talking about? Annie was here."

I shook my head. "That must have been the sister—Emily Reilly."

"Come on," Kelly said grimly, "we'll go down and yank her wig off."

Ian set his jaw and turned away in silence, and the three of us went down to Aunt Violet's room, where Kelly knocked peremptorily.

It was some time before she opened up for us, and then she saw Kelly and tried to close the door again, but they pushed it without ceremony and I followed them, feeling small and miserable.

Ian walked straight up to her and pulled the wig from her head, and we saw that she had iron-gray hair pulled tightly into a small knot. She backed away, her shallow blue eyes round and terrified, and cried, "What is it? My hair—it grew in again—but I always liked the wig better."

"Oh, come off it, Annie," Kelly said irritably. "We've found your mistress up there—and I've seen better acting than you're doing."

She sank into a chair then and began to shed tears, and Kelly regarded her with a coldly critical eye.

"You were always able to cry easily, weren't you? Smith mentioned that—said you were always weeping buckets over nothing."

"And why wouldn't I?" Annie flared. "The kind of life I've had with that one up there—mad as a hatter. Mr. Richard knew she was crazy, but he wouldn't admit it; that's why he never would get a doctor in to her only that once, and he thought she was dying then—he was scared it would be found out, and she'd have to be put away and bring disgrace on the precious family.

"It was all his fault, anyway. When she lost her baby after the typhoid and all, he talked and talked to her and drove her out of her mind. We had to keep her in then, and I talked to her friends over the telephone and made believe I was her—that's how I learned to talk like her.

"She got a bit better after a while, but she didn't want to go out, and although she talked sense most of the time, she was never really right again.

"So then Mr. Richard went to the hospital, and they said he wouldn't get better; it upset her, and the day before they all moved in she had a stroke, or something—anyway, she looked like she was dead. I thought she was. And there I was—with her dead, I'd have to find a new place, and I'm too old—I spent my life here. He wouldn't leave me anything, not him, he was the stingiest man in the world.

"I took her to the attic and put her in that space up there. There was a hole in the bricks large enough for me to get in and get the camp bed in and put her on it. See, the old man meant to put that cedar chest in there—the one with the little baby's grave. He got scared, having it around in the attic, and he bought sand cement, and I was supposed to help him. But it took us so long to get the bricks out, and first he broke his wrist, and then he got pneumonia. They said he couldn't get well, and she was lying dead there—I *did* think she was dead— and I didn't see it would harm anyone if I just took her place. So I put her up there and started to get the bricks back. And then they phoned to say that Mr. Richard was going to be all right, after all.

"What could I do? First I thought to haul her out again and call a doctor, but she being dead all day, as I thought, I was afraid I'd get into trouble because I didn't call one right away. Then I nearly ran away—only where could I go? They'd only find me, and they'd certainly find Miss Violet behind those bricks because Mr. Richard would know.

"Anyway, Dr. Benson phoned the next morning and said they were all moving in. I didn't have time to think or plan—I just decided to be Miss Violet and to hope that Mr. Richard would die after all. I'd been to the hospital a couple of times to bring him things he needed, and it seemed to me he didn't look so good. I even had ideas of going again—as Annie—and helping him on his way.

"I had to fit the bricks back in a hurry, and I figured on cementing them when I got more time. I'd only just finished making myself up like Miss Violet when the whole bunch of Langs came trooping in. I was scared, although I didn't think any of them had ever seen me, only Leslie. She used to play at the lily pond when she was little, and then last summer she came and walked around the yard, smoking cigarettes and taking pictures of the lily pond and the old lion. Once she saw me looking at her out of the kitchen window.

"I wouldn't meet any of them. I left the front door open a little bit and ran back to Miss Violet's room here. They bothered me a lot, but I wouldn't come out, and I told them Annie had left when she heard about the mob of them coming in.

"Ian had phoned me soon after Dr. Benson and told me he was about to marry Mr. Richard's nurse and could they stay here in the house? I told him to come right along, because I thought with the nurse here I could keep track of Mr. Richard. I didn't tell Ian the others were coming for fear he'd change his mind and go to a hotel.

"I let him and his wife into my room when they came—I thought it would give me practice in being Miss Violet—and it went off fine.

"That night I went downstairs to get something to eat and wandered about a bit, and I noticed those cushions in the hall right away. I thought how mad Mr. Richard would be because he was always so careful to keep feathers out of the house—they always gave him awful hay fever. I ripped a corner of one of the cushions and pulled out a handful of feathers. I wasn't sure what I'd do with them, and I wasn't sure what they'd do to Mr. Richard, but it seemed like spasms of sneezing might set him back, at least, and give me more time.

"When I got back upstairs I thought of the nurse's pocket— the little one where they like to keep a fancy handkerchief dangling. I went to her door and I couldn't hear anything—I thought she'd be with her husband, anyway, on her wedding night. I crept in and saw the uniform on a chair, and then I saw her sleeping on the bed. But the uniform was so close, I decided to chance it. The fancy handkerchief was already in the pocket, so I put the feathers in and stuck the handkerchief on top and crept out again. Only she woke up—I heard her—and I got into bed as fast as I could and hoped she didn't know I'd been there or what I'd done.

"I heard later that Mr. Richard had a sneezing spell, but it didn't seem to hurt him as much as I'd hoped. Just the same, I went ahead with the bricks that night. Leslie had a room up there, which fretted me, but I had to go ahead anyway. I used a flashlight and moved a big trunk so I could hide behind it, but I couldn't finish that night. I got too tired and I ran out of cement, so I had to give up and go to bed. I couldn't sleep, though. I got up early and had breakfast downstairs. I thought it was too early to run into anybody, but Ian and the nurse were there.

"That was the day it worked. Mr. Richard sneezed himself to death, and I could hardly believe it. I laughed and laughed. He was a mean, stingy old man, and I knew everybody would be better off without him.

"I was scared again, though. I knew he always carried some snapshots in his wallet, and I was afraid he might have one of Miss Violet. He was forever taking pictures, and he'd taken an indoor one of her last summer.

"It worried me so, I couldn't think, and finally I just up and went to the hospital to get his things. I knew there would be different nurses at night, and the one who had seen me as Annie wouldn't be there. I had to dress in the only outdoor clothes Miss Violet had, and they were terrible.

"I knew Miriel was there, but that didn't matter. I took a cab and just went right up to his room—nobody stopped me. But it was all for nothing, because his things were gone, and I worried and fretted until they sent them up to me next day. I got the picture out of his wallet, then, and all the ones I could find of her in his room and burned them.

"I felt pretty safe after that, and I began to be a lot more careful about everything. I did try to get the feathers out of the uniform, but I couldn't.

"Before I went to the hospital that night I found I'd lost a brooch I'd been wearing, and I was terrified it was lying in the sand pile. It was evening, and that Mabel one was hanging about, but I had to get the brooch, even though I was afraid of being seen out there. I don't think now it was so important as I thought then.

"I got a bit excited and felt I had to have something on me to make me look like somebody else, so I ran into Miriel's room and saw that negligee and picked it up. I put it on as I went down the back stairs, and it was too long and too tight over my heavy dress—it was silly, and I never wore anything but the dark dress the other times I went out, except my gloves, of course.

"I got the brooch all right—it was one Miss Violet always wore because that actor fella gave it to her, the one she was in love with—but I nearly got caught, anyway. I heard someone coming around from the front just as I picked the brooch up, and I got inside just in time. That Mabel was on her way out to the kitchen, too, and I just missed her.

"I finished the brickwork that night, too, after I came back from the hospital, but I was so tired I left the bucket and shovel right there in the attic. I had to run up next morning, and I threw the shovel out the window, where it would be handy when I could get out to it that night. I just pushed the bucket to one side—it looked natural enough among all that junk.

"I was fretting again, though. Leslie had caught glimpses of me several times, and although I didn't think she'd know me with the wig and all—still, I wasn't sure. I kept away from her all I could, but she was at the door with Miriel once when I opened it, and she got a good look at me.

"I went down early that night and got the shovel. I was anxious to put it away, and I felt safe because they all seemed to be out or in their rooms. I went to the sand pile and smoothed over the place where I had been digging. I went back in, bold as brass, and put the shovel where it belonged and got back to my room all right. I thought everything was fine then—I'd just wait until I got my annuity and leave this house forever. That's why I wrote to Miriel's father, but after what had happened about Leslie I had to stay.

"It was sometime after I got back to my room that night that I began to worry—about the sand, I mean. I was afraid I had made it too noticeably smooth and perhaps left the marks of my shovel. I had to go back. I couldn't rest. I waited until it was quite late and took the poker with me. I pushed the sand around a bit as if the kids had been playing in it. Then I heard a sound behind me, and here it was Leslie. She must have been looking for me and seen me from the window, dark and all as it was. She just said, 'Hello, Annie,'—that was all—and I found I'd hit her with the poker, and she was lying on the ground there. I wanted to hide her where she'd never be found, like Miss Violet, but I was in a state and had it all to do myself. I got her into the pond and toppled the lion—it was all crumbling away at the bottom and easy enough to move.

"I ran back in and put the poker in the back closet in a golf bag. I meant to put it where it belonged later—never dreaming anyone would bother their heads about a golf bag in winter. I found Leslie's coat in the hall and put it in Miriel's room, because the feathers had been in her pocket and I'd used her negligee.

"I got back to my room safely and cried for a long time because I hadn't wanted to kill Leslie. Only I had to make plans. I thought of the will—one Mr. Richard threw out last summer, but he'd just crumpled it without tearing it, and I'd got it from the wastebasket, thinking it might come in handy—which it did. I put it in the lion's head in the drawing-room, where Mr. Richard had his silly love letters hidden, and then directed Miriel to it—and it worked beautifully. I made out I was scared I'd be the next to die.

"But the night after Mr. Richard's funeral a dreadful thing happened. With the police all over the house, I began to think that cement bucket would look more at home in the cellar than up in the attic. Not that I didn't feel pretty safe, knowing there was a doctor who could say Miss Violet didn't have the strength to hit Leslie like that. Anyway, it was quite late and the house was dark, except for a light in the downstairs hall. I crept up to the attic and groped my way to the bucket—and then she started groaning! I heard her! And I'd thought she was dead! It gave me a queer turn, and I dropped the bucket and ran—and felt all the time that her spirit was coming after me. When I got down to the second floor I stopped at my door and tried to get my breath—I thought I was going to faint. And then I saw a white figure standing right beside me. I don't remember so much after that, except I think I raised the roof.

"The next day was terrible, because my mind felt cloudy—they'd given me something to put me out. But it didn't keep me under, because I woke up in the early morning and I went stumbling out in a kind of daze. It kept going around in my mind that she was still alive up there—and maybe she would start screaming for help—but I met Dr. Benson in the hall, and he told me to stay in my room or he'd have me put away. Mr. Richard told him, I suppose, that Miss Violet wasn't right.

"The next thing my sister came—Emily. I had sent her a letter saying not to write me any more as I was going away and I'd get in touch with her. I got Miriel to post a letter addressed to me in care of Emily later, but it missed her. She thought something was up because she read in the paper about how Mr. Richard had died, and she came on to nose it out. She knew all about the family—she was always asking me things when I visited. When she got in town late Sunday night she phoned, and one of the doctors told her that Annie had left and was staying with her sister, and Miss Violet could not be disturbed. So she just waited at the station until early morning and then came on and said she was me. She knew I was pretending to be Miss Violet, because I'd often told her I could—before I ever thought of doing it. Told her I'd been Miss Violet on the phone for years—and nobody ever saw Miss Violet, and only the tradesmen ever saw me.

"Emily walked herself up here to my room as soon as ever she could. I told her to get out, but she got nasty and wanted to know what I'd done with Miss Violet. I told her Miss Violet was safe and for her not to worry.

"I left my room after you'd all had lunch and went down the back stairs to the kitchen. I talked to Emily for a long time and thought I'd got her persuaded to go. I went up the back stairs again and heard you all on the landing. I waited until you went down and then went on up to the attic. I told myself I was after the bucket, but I knew all the time I couldn't keep away—I had to know if she was quiet. And she wasn't. I went right up to the wall and listened, and she was breathing loudly, in a queer way.

"I don't remember much about getting back to my room—I know I fainted before I got to the bed. But it was all right. Miriel took care of me, and I persuaded her not to call the doctors.

"Later I heard Emily flying down the attic stairs, and then she started to scream—and I knew she'd heard it. She left at once, but I knew she'd send a letter, or some sort of message, and I dared not chance anyone else getting hold of it. I didn't worry about the telephone—I knew she never used it—she was scared of it.

"So I had to sit at the front door in full view of everybody. I painted my face before I went down, because Miss Violet used paint all her life. I hoped Dr. Benson was out, because I was scared he'd order me up again, but he just passed by and didn't pay any attention.

"I heard the Briggs one telling Miriel where Emily was staying and the name she was using. I waited until everyone had left the hall and then went to my real room near the kitchen. I wanted to warn Emily to keep still about everything, and I knew Miriel had to go to the hospital before seeing her, so that I had time enough. I changed into my own clothes and wore my hat with the veil, and I left the other things and the wig in the closet. I went out the back way and across the neighbors' yards to the next street.

"I saw the poker as soon as I walked into Emily's room, and I couldn't get my mind away from it. Emily talked all the time in a loud voice and kept saying I'd buried Miss Violet alive and that she didn't like any part of what I was doing, and she didn't want to be mixed up in it. I told her to pack and go home, but she said she was staying right there—and she meant it. She was never one to keep her mouth shut, and this time I thought she wasn't even going to try.

"I began to walk around the room while she was still talking, and then I found the poker in my hand—and she had stopped talking."

CHAPTER THIRTY-SIX

ANNIE ended her long recital with a burst of easy tears, and Kelly, who had been posing with folded arms and bent head, stirred and turned to me. "Go and phone for Briggs, Miriel. And when you get him out of a deep sleep and his warm bed, tell him he'll have to come over here right away—and don't forget to mention that the temperature has dropped five degrees and it's still snowing."

I crept down to the telephone through the cold and dark, hating the whole gloomy house and the queer, cold-blooded woman upstairs as well. When I got back Kelly had his toupee off, and Ian was silently pacing the room. Annie sat with her hands quietly folded in her lap, and she had stopped crying.

When Briggs arrived at last it was a blessed relief to hand the whole thing over to him. To Kelly it was more than a relief; it was a rare pleasure. He gave Briggs a short talk on the art of a disguise that would confound even the police and followed up with a few patronizing remarks on "Deductive Reasoning for Beginners."

The family had collected and listened avidly to an outline of the story, but when Kelly began to overdo his triumph they lost interest and drifted downstairs to the living-room. Ian put an arm around me and said, "Let's go down and wait with them. You won't want to see any more of this. Later we'll pack up and go to a hotel."

Mabel was talking in a shrill, excited voice, but she looked more relaxed. "I found that poker in Father's golf bag, and you can imagine how I felt when I discovered that it was the—the weapon—my poor child—"

"When did you find it, Mrs. Lang?" I asked hastily. "It must have been after you came home from the funeral—and yet you went right to bed."

"Yes—well, but I was restless. I woke up and came downstairs and you were all having supper and I couldn't see how you could be eating anything, so I didn't go into the dining room and I saw that closet door slightly open, so I went to shut it, but I looked inside first to see if the closet was in order and I saw that poker in the golf bag right away. I couldn't see why it was there, so I took it out and put it in the drawing room—and—"

Dr. Benson patted her shoulder and said abstractedly, "Poor Violet. She was so short, you know, and that's the only thing I remembered about her—her size. I suppose that's why I didn't suspect anything." He was silent for a moment and then added, "Paralytic suspension—and that woman thought she was dead. As a matter of fact, this whole thing is Richard's fault, really. Violet was never very well balanced, but he tipped her right over, jawing at her when she was so sick. He wrote a lot of nasty stuff about us in a Bible too. I knew about it and I searched the house for it as soon as we got here, but I found that little grave instead. I had always suspected that Violet had had a baby, but it jarred me when I opened the cedar chest and saw the name Eliza. It was our mother's name. I'd been pawing under some blankets, and I piled them on a trunk and forgot to put them back.

"I finally found the Bible in that room Kelly was using—Annie's room—and took it while he was sleeping. I'd come down early and wandered in there while the Reilly woman was getting me some breakfast. I thought she was Annie, of course. Richard's family sketches in the Bible were as malicious as I'd thought they would be, and as soon as I had an opportunity I burned the whole thing in the furnace."

"You remembered those blankets later and put them back in the cedar chest, didn't you?" I asked.

"Yes. I was passing the house on my way to a patient, and I thought of it rather suddenly. I didn't want anyone to drag that secret out at this late date, so I simply slipped into the house, went up and replaced the blankets, and left again. I did not meet anyone at all."

"Emily Reilly seemed quite familiar with the house," I said thoughtfully. "Had she been here before?"

Dr. Benson nodded. "Oh yes, she came down for an occasional visit—but not often. Richard complained about the extra mouth to feed, but he couldn't afford to lose Annie, who was doing the work of an attendant and a servant for only one salary, so he let it go."

"Aunt Violet used to write to Mother," Ian said after a moment, "and she sent the money for my education. Was she really insane?"

"She was rational enough a great deal of the time—quite capable of writing a letter and I believe Annie took care of the details when she sent the money. You know, after I'd seen Annie a couple of times I came to the conclusion that she was quite normal and that Richard had been exaggerating Violet's trouble. So I said nothing when I saw her sitting in the hall."

"What about the will leaving everything to Leslie?" I asked. "Does that stand?"

John shrugged. "According to Annie, he had thrown it away, but since poor Leslie left no will, the money comes to us in any case. I can't understand, though why she decided to confront Annie in the middle of the night like that."

"I suppose," I said, "when I mentioned having seen a man lose his moustache it put the idea of disguise into her mind, and after a while she realized that Annie was disguised as Aunt Violet. So she rushed home, dropped her coat in the hall, and tried to find Annie. She probably saw her from a window, so went out the back way, picking up that old sweater as she went."

Kelly walked in at that point, dressed to leave and hat in hand.

"Good-bye, everybody," he said superciliously. He turned to Mabel. "And good-bye to you, madam. Being a servant in your home shouldn't happen to a dog, but in the life of a great detective you take the rough with the smooth. Concerning the coffee that you probably desire at the present moment, I have no regret in informing you that you must make it yourself." He shifted his overcoat from one arm to the other and added, "If ever you are moved to call in the police, count ten and make it the Kelly Detective Agency instead."

"Beat it, Kelly," I said. "You probably have a lot of drinking to catch up on."

He bowed from the waist and departed, and Mabel hissed, "Impertinence!" But her mind was already on other things, and she mumbled, "I'll have to phone the agency—see what they can do—"

"Mabel," said Dr. Benson, "you need an absolute rest. We're going to a hotel."

Sara glanced from one to the other and said quite gently, "Maybe she'd be better to keep busy. If she wants to continue to run the house, I'll help—I mean, really help. I—I think I'm reforming."

John grinned at her. "Don't. I like you the way you are."

Sara actually blushed and murmured, "Well—it wouldn't be too drastic."

Ian heaved a sigh that nearly snapped his buttons.

"Does anyone mind if I start off on my honeymoon now?"

"Not at all," I said graciously. "I hope you have a good time. Try Niagara Falls."

"And you might take Miriel's father with you," Sara added. "He needs a change."

Ian took my arm. "Come on—we're packing up now. And you're all invited to have breakfast with us at the hotel."

"Oh, delightful!" said Mabel happily. "Especially since there isn't a servant in the house."

"Good idea," Dr. Benson nodded. "Get us out of the house for a while—and we can begin to feel normal again."

John murmured, "Splendid. We accept with thanks."

"Who's going to pay the check?" Sara asked warily. "I don't suppose you're going to that hotel by the station."

"We are not," said Ian. "We're going to the best place in town. And you may all have exactly what you want—no need to scan the price list first."

"Wonderful! " Mabel sighed. "And we'll get Miriel's father—he ought to be with us. After all, it's—it's almost a celebration."

I felt myself grow pale. "Well—er—yes. But you don't know how grand Father can be at a fancy hotel. I doubt if I have that much money with me."

THE END

Other Rue Morgue Press titles

The Black Gloves
by Constance & Gwenyth Little

Welcome to the Vickers estate near East Orange, New Jersey, where the middle class is destroying the neighborhood, erecting their horrid little cottages, playing on the Vickers tennis court, and generally disrupting the comfortable life of Hammond Vickers no end.

It's bad enough that he had to shell out good money to get his daughter Lissa a divorce in Reno only to have her brute of an ex-husband show up on his doorstep. But why does there also have to be a corpse in the cellar? And lights going on and off in the attic?

Lissa, on the other hand, welcomes the newcomers into the neighborhood, having spotted a likely candidate for a summer beau among them. But when she hears coal being shoveled in the cellar and finds a blue dandelion near a corpse, what's a girl gonna do but turn detective, popping into people's cottages and dipping dandelions into their inkwells looking for a color match. And she'd better catch the killer fast, because Detective Sergeant Timothy Frobisher says that only a few nail files are standing between her and jail.

Originally published in 1939, *The Black Gloves* was one of 21 wacky mysteries written by the Little sisters and is a sparkling example of the light-hearted cozy mystery that flourished between the Depression and the Korean War. It won't take you long to understand why these long out-of-print titles have so many ardent fans.

0-915230-20-8   **$14**

Murder is a Collector's Item
by Elizabeth Dean

"Completely enjoyable"—*New York Times.*
"Fast and funny."—*The New Yorker.*

Twenty-six-year-old Emma Marsh isn't much at spelling or geography and perhaps she butchers the odd literary quotation or two, but she's a keen judge of character and more than able to hold her own when it comes to selling antiques or solving murders. When she stumbles upon the body of a rich collector on the floor of the Boston antiques shop where she works, suspicion quickly falls upon her missing boss. Emma knows Jeff Graham is no murderer, but veteran homicide cop Jerry Donovan doesn't share her conviction.

With a little help from Hank Fairbanks, her wealthy boyfriend and would-be criminologist, Emma turns sleuth and cracks the case, but not before a host of cops, reporters and customers drift through the shop on Charles Street, trading insults and sipping scotch as they talk clues, prompting a *New York Times* reviewer to remark that Emma "drinks far more than a nice girl should."

Emma does a lot of things that women didn't do in detective novels of the 1930s. In an age of menopausal spinsters, deadly sirens, admiring wives and air-headed girlfriends, pretty, big-footed Emma Marsh stands out. She's a precursor of the independent women sleuths that finally came into their own in the last two decades of this century.

Originally published in 1939, *Murder is a Collector's Item* was the first of three books featuring Emma. Smoothly written and sparkling with dry, sophisticated humor, it combines an intriguing puzzle with an entertaining portrait of a self-possessed young woman on her own in Boston toward the end of the Great Depression. Author Dean, who worked in a Boston antiques shop, offers up an insider's view of what that easily impressed *Times* reviewer called the "goofy" world of antiques. Lovejoy, the rogue antiques dealer in Jonathan Gash's mysteries, would have loved Emma.

0-915230-19-4 $14

Cook Up a Crime
by Charlotte Murray Russell

Meet Jane Amanda Edwards, a self-styled "full-fashioned" spinster who complains she hasn't looked at herself in a full-length mirror since Helen Hokinson started drawing cartoons for *The New Yorker*. But you can always count on Jane to look into other people's affairs, especially when there's a juicy murder case to investigate. This one starts when Jane's friend, Detective Captain George Hammond, puts the idea of publishing a cookbook in her mind. That leads her to visit Jessie Nye, an irritating woman who unfortunately is the safekeeper of her family's famous recipes. Jesse thinks a cookbook a marvelous idea but immediately announces that she is far better suited to put it together than Jane. So when Jessie turns up dead, Jane decides to look for clues—and recipes—among the murdered woman's effects.

In the meantime, Jane's hapless brother Arthur—a true lily of the field—gets a valentine from a secret admirer and goes courting, only to find himself accused of the murder. Sister Annie warns Jane to stay put and goes off to watch female wrestling on television. Through it all,

Theresa, their long-suffering cook and general housekeeper, keeps one and all well fed with tempting treats from her kitchen (the recipes for these and other dishes are included between chapters).

First published in 1951 and set in a fictionalized version of the author's hometown of Rock Island, Ill., *Cook Up a Crime* is what you might get if Joan Hess or Charlotte MacLeod wrote the culinary mysteries of Diane Mott Davidson.

ISBN 0-915230-18-6   **$13.00**

Murder, Chop Chop
by James Norman
A classic late Golden Age novel of
detection and adventure set in China
in 1938 during the Sino-Japanese War.

> *"The book has the butter-wouldn't-melt-in-his-mouth cool of Rick in* Casablanca.*"—Jane Dickinson, The Rocky Mountain News "Amuses the reader no end."—Mystery News*

Fans of Golden Age mysteries set in exotic lands with eccentric characters will love this long out-of-print masterpiece that many critics said should have been included in the Haycraft-Queen list of cornerstone mysteries, written by a man who fought in the Spanish Civil War and was a victim of the Hollywood Blacklist.

In these pages you will meet Gimiendo Hernandez Quinto, a gigantic Mexican who once rode with Pancho Villa and who now trains *guerrilleros* for the Nationalist Chinese government when he isn't solving murders. At his side is a beautiful Eurasian known as Mountain of Virtue, a woman as dangerous to men as she is irresistible, and a superb card player as well— so long as she's dealing. Then there's Mildred Woodford, a hard-drinking British journalist; John Tate, a portly American calligrapher who wasn't made for adventure; Lt. Chi, a young Hunanese patriot weighted down with the woes of China and the Brooklyn Dodgers; Nevada, a young cowboy who is as deadly with a six-gun as he inept at love; and a host of others, anyone of whom may have killed Abe Harrow, an ambulance driver who appears to have died at three different times.

There's also a cipher or two to crack, a train with a mind of its own, and Chiang Kai-shek's false teeth, which have gone mysteriously missing.

ISBN 0-915230-16-X   **$13.00**

The Man from Tibet
by Clyde B. Clason
The only witnesses to the murder
were the masks of Tibetan gods

Locked inside the Tibetan Room of his Chicago luxury apartment, the rich antiquarian was overheard repeating a forbidden occult chant under the watchful eyes of Buddhist gods. When the doors were opened it appeared that he had succumbed to a heart attack. But the elderly Roman historian and sometimes amateur sleuth Theocritus Lucius Westborough is convinced that Adam Merriweather's death was anything but natural and that the weapon was an eighth century Tibetan manuscript.

If it's murder, who could have done it, and how? Suspects abound. There's Tsongpun Bonbo, the gentle Tibetan lama from whom the manuscript was originally stolen; Chang, Merriweather's scholarly Tibetan secretary who had fled a Himalayan monastery; Merriwether's son Vincent, who disliked his father and stood to inherit a fortune; Dr. Jed Merriweather, the dead man's brother, who came to Chicago to beg for funds to continue his archaeological digs in Asia; Dr. Walters, the dead man's physician, who guarded a secret; and Janice Shelton, his young ward, who found herself being pushed by Merriweather into marrying his son. How the murder was accomplished has earned praise from such impossible crimes connoisseurs as Robert C.S. Adey who cited Clason's "highly original and practical looked-room murder method."

But *The Man from Tibet* is more than a classic fair play detective novel. Clason carefully researched his subject and in between the planting of clues he presents a vivid, in-depth portrait of forbidden Tibet and its religion, one of the earliest examinations to be found in popular fiction. Clason's work was also remarkably free of the xenophobia that marred so many Golden Age mysteries. At a time when anti-Japanese sentiment was at its height, Westborough offers up some deft social commentary and gently rebukes his associates for their racist attitudes.

ISBN 0-915230-17-8   **$14.00**

The Mirror

by Marlys Millhiser

"Completely enjoyable."—*Library Journal.*
"A great deal of fun."—*Publishers Weekly.*

How could you not be intrigued, as one reviewer pointed out, by a novel in which "you find the main character marrying her own grandfather and giving birth to her own mother?" Such is the situation in Marlys Millhiser's classic novel (a Mystery Guild selection originally published by Putnam in 1978) of two women who end up living each other's lives after they look into an antique Chinese mirror.

Twenty-year-old Shay Garrett is not aware that she's pregnant and is having second thoughts about marrying Marek Weir when she's suddenly transported back 78 years in time into the body of Brandy McCabe, her own grandmother, who is unwillingly about to be married off to miner Corbin Strock. Shay's in shock but she still recognizes that the picture of her grandfather that hangs in the family home doesn't resemble her husband-to-be. But marry Corbin she does and off she goes to the high mining town of Nederland, where this thoroughly modern young woman has to learn to cope with such things as wood cooking stoves and—to her—old-fashioned attitudes about sex. Shay's ability to see into the future has her mother-in-law thinking she's a witch and others calling her a psychic, but Shay was an indifferent student at best and not all of her predictions hit the mark: remember that "day of infamy" when the Japanese attacked Pearl Harbor—Dec. *11*, 1941?

In the meantime, Brandy McCabe is finding it even harder to cope with life in the Boulder, Colorado of 1978. After all, her wedding is about to be postponed due to her own death—at least the death of her former body—at the age of 98. And, in spite of the fact she's a virgin, she's about to give birth. And *this* young woman does have some very old-fashioned ideas about sex, which leave her husband-to-be—and father of her child—very puzzled. *The Mirror* is even more of a treat for today's readers, given that it is now a double trip back in time. Not only can readers look back on life at the turn of the century, they can also revisit the days of disco and the sexual revolution of the 1970's.

So how does one categorize *The Mirror*? Is it science fiction? Fantasy? Supernatural? Mystery? Romance? Historical fiction? You'll find elements of each but in the end it's a book driven by that most magical of all literary devices: imagine if . . .

ISBN 0-915230-15-1 $14.95